The Doctor's Devotion

Cheryl Wyatt

D0027696

Love Inspired

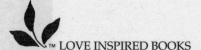

™ LOVE INSPIRED BOOKS

Recycling programs
for this product may
not exist in your area.

ISBN-13: 978-0-373-87754-6

THE DOCTOR'S DEVOTION

"Lauren, listen to me. I need your help," Mitch said.

She shook her head vehemently.

He swiveled his neck to watch the next chopper prepare to land.

No time to argue.

"Nurse Bates, I'm not asking. I'm ordering. Triage chopper number three, then meet me at four."

Desperate hands came up to clutch his. "Mitch, please," she rasped. "I can't. I'm not qualified for trauma. I worked OB."

Compassion vying with impatience, Mitch leaned close to her ear. "Lauren Esther Bates, I'm convinced God put you here for a reason. I don't have enough manpower. I need you. People are dying. They need you. Go." He gave her shoulders a gentle nudge—okay, more like a shove.

Tears streamed from her eyes. She spun and ran to the chopper.

Books by Cheryl Wyatt

Love Inspired

*A Soldier's Promise
*A Soldier's Family
*Ready-Made Family
*A Soldier's Reunion
*Soldier Daddy
*A Soldier's Devotion
*Steadfast Soldier
**The Doctor's Devotion

*Wings of Refuge
**Eagle Point Emergency

CHERYL WYATT

An R.N. turned stay-at-home mom and wife, Cheryl delights in the stolen moments God gives her to write action- and faith-driven romance. She stays active in her church and in her laundry room. She's convinced that having been born on a naval base on Valentine's Day destined her to write military romance. A native of San Diego, California, Cheryl currently resides in beautiful, rustic southern Illinois, but she has also enjoyed living in New Mexico and Oklahoma. Cheryl loves hearing from readers. You are invited to contact her at Cheryl@CherylWyatt.com or P.O. Box 2955, Carbondale, IL 62902-2955. Visit her on the web at www.CherylWyatt.com and sign up for her newsletter if you'd like updates on new releases, events and other fun stuff. Hang out with her in the blogosphere at www.Scrollsquirrel.blogspot.com or on the message boards at www.LoveInspiredBooks.com.

May the Lord turn his face toward you
and give you peace.
—*Numbers* 6:26

This book is dedicated to the memory of my grandmother, Leavada Pauline Elliott, who passed away during the writing of this book. She was a lavish giver and lived a truly sacrificial life. She was all about others.

I am pretty sure God's construction angels had to build an addition onto her house in Heaven in order to contain the rewards she had waiting for her when that sweet chariot came forth to whisk her from this life into eternity. I'm also pretty sure she had a mob of loved ones and friends racing to be first to meet her with a fishing pole. I'll bet Jesus was the point man.

Utmost thanks to God for giving us time with her. Thank you, Jesus, for being Grandma's perfect example of true sacrifice. For coming humbly, then living and dying hard in order to hand us the hope of Heaven. Thank You, Sweet Spirit, for hovering to help us look forward through grief clouds and glimpse assurance of seeing our loved ones again.

Immense thanks to Herrin and Memorial Hospital of Carbondale, Illinois, ICU and IMCU departments in particular. Every doctor, nurse and ancillary staff member who went above and beyond to not only care with deep compassion and dedicated skill for Granny Veda but for providing extraordinary emotional support and comfort care to us. Thanks also to Hospice of Southern Illinois. Denise (our fellow Okie), you are truly gifted and a blessing.

Special thanks to Sally Shupe, whose efficient eagle eyes with proofreading enabled me to spend more precious time with my grandmother. You are a wonderful line editor!

Melissa Endlich, thank you for continuing to believe in me. I have grown as a writer due to your editorial guidance. No doubt God put us together. I am so thankful you know my writing better than I do and that you steered me toward crafting stories about caregivers. Thank you for putting wind to the sail of this series.

To Rachel Kent, much love and thanks for your encouragement and character. You are blessed to be part of a stellar agency iconic in the industry and to be mentored by someone as well respected and forward-thinking as Janet Grant. May God turn His face toward you and give you, Books and Such and your families peace and blessings for your futures.

Chapter One

"Change of plans, carrottop."

Suitcase in tow, Lauren Bates smiled at Grandpa Lem's voice coming through her cell phone. "What, you're picking me up in your tractor?" She exited Refuge Airport. Southern Illinois welcomed her with breezy warmth and a bouquet of bright June colors she wasn't accustomed to in Texas.

Lem chuckled. "Ought to since you haven't come to see me in five years."

Guilt *whooshed* in like planes on runways nearby. "I know, Grandpa. I'm sorry. What's this plan change?"

"Accompany me to the ribbon-cutting of a new trauma center Doc Wellington founded at Eagle Point? Starts in half an hour."

Anxiety knotted her gut. Not only was she weary hearing about Dr. Wellington, a medical facility was the last place she wanted to be. She sighed. "For you, Grandpa, I'll endure it."

"Good. We're in a blue Dodge Ram. See you in a few."

"We?" She maneuvered past people cluttering the sidewalk.

"Yes. Dr. Wellington's helping me pick you up."

"Why would you need help?" Lauren canvassed curbside cars and spotted a spiffy blue truck near the front.

"I don't drive on streets anymore. Only fields."

Alarm slowed her steps. "Why not?"

"In case you forgot, I'm nearing a hundred."

She almost pointed out he was only turning seventy, but swift remembrance of her reason for this spur-of-the-moment trip halted her. Anticipation spiked as Lem exited the truck.

"Look who's here!" Grinning and hunched, he seemed older and slower than she remembered. Lauren rushed him with a hug. His bear strength was gone. Tears welling, she squeezed thin ribs.

She'd come because of his sudden uncharacteristic fear over turning seventy. Terror struck her now, too, but according to that Dr. Wellington he always spoke of, Lem was healthy. Still, she'd had to come see for herself. She should've come sooner.

"I'll take your bags," a deep voice said behind her. Strong hands reached around and deftly lifted Lauren's purse and colossal suitcase from between her and Grandpa.

Lauren turned. Grandpa leaned aside. Up stepped the most gorgeous creature ever.

Lauren gulped then remembered her manners. The tall man looked less like a doctor and more like a landscaper, with his deep tan and fit build. Intense and chiseled, yet polished like an airbrushed movie star. And he was her age. *Not* Grandpa's.

The doctor's easy smile tilted her world. His eyes were a stunning mixture of mostly silver with hints of blue. She gawked like a junior high geek facing the football captain.

"Mitch, this is my granddaughter," Lem said.

"Lauren, pleased to finally meet you."

Ooh, his voice! Pleasant. Deep. And, wow. He knew her name? She blinked. He blinked. Her gaze inched to the hot pink handbag draped over his manly shoulder. She tried not to laugh at the sharp contrast of megamuscles toting a tiny pink purse.

As though the striking doctor with the black hair cut in a military buzz and epic eyes suddenly caught on about the purse—and also diagnosed this weirdness between them as attraction—he lowered her handbag. He offered a sheepish grin and a masculine hand. When she settled hers into the strength of his, the warmth flowing from it enveloped her entire being.

No dead-fish handshake here. His was firm. Confident. Alabaster teeth gleamed from a mouth framed by a strong jaw. His grin gave way to a shy laugh.

She knew the feeling. She'd been bamboozled by attraction, too. "Nice to meet you, Dr. Wellington." She rescued his endangered ego by retrieving her purse from his fingers.

"It's Mitch." He tilted his head, openly assessing her. His hearty smile expanded and he seemed in no hurry to look away.

She cleared her throat and searched for something else exciting to stare at. Unfortunately, sidewalk cracks weren't near as interesting to behold as the dashing doctor.

Observing them, Grandpa chuckled as if having a private party with himself. Mitch moved first. He placed her suitcase behind the seat then assisted her in so she sat in the middle of the truck's seat. His grip was as sturdy, warm and steady as his fond gaze.

Mitch approached Lem. "Up you go, Gramps."

Gramps?

Lauren's irritation overrode Mitch's appeal, as he helped Grandpa in, then approached the driver's side. His shoulders were broad enough to require a rather pleasant pivot to enter the vehicle and, once inside, for her to move closer to Grandpa.

Not that she noticed.

"Where to?" Mitch asked Lem.

"Since Lauren's flight was delayed, she's coming to the ribbon-cutting so you're not late to your own party," Lem said.

Mitch laughed. The sound both grated and soothed. Grated because of the closeness he obviously shared with *her* grandpa, which stirred a surprise pot of jealousy. Soothing because Mitch's Grand Canyon voice could make a typhoon swoon.

At a red light, Mitch caught her stare. The corner of his mouth slid into a colossal smile.

"I expected you to be older," Lauren explained. "Grandpa talks about you nonstop."

"Likewise," Mitch said. "I feel like I know you."

Yikes! What all did he know? The failure she'd been?

"So, Lauren, how long will you be in town?" Mitch asked.

"Three months!" Lem announced. "I couldn't be happier." He beamed. Mitch did, too, which meant he obviously cared about Lem. How close were they? Drizzles of dread seeped into her stomach.

"How'd you manage to get so much time off?" Mitch asked.

"I'm between jobs right now. I'm opening a specialty shop in Houston with a friend this fall. We started the business from scratch in her home a year ago. Our client list and workload grew to the point where we needed more space."

"What's the specialty?" Mitch kept a keen eye on traffic.

"Sewing. We're leasing an historic building in town after receiving permission from local government and the Historical Society to open it. It'll be called Ye Olde Time Seamstress Shoppe. We're restoring the building's nineteenth-century period decor. Took a lot of wrangling and red tape but it's in the renovation stage now, so this was a perfect opportunity to finally visit Grandpa."

"She's getting over a much-needed breakup," Lem inserted.

Lauren smirked. "Grandpa's not letting me live it down."

Lem harrumphed. "Told you from the start he was no good."

Lauren noticed that Mitch navigated the roads with extra care. "You're a very safe driver," she commented. "I like that."

"A welcome change from her ex who regularly drove ninety. I know because she called me, often upset," Lem announced.

"My ex got arrested for speeding past a school bus and almost striking a child. That was my last straw," she explained.

"He was reckless in general. With others' lives and their relationship." Lem relaxed. "I'm glad she refused to marry a man who'll have little regard for his future children's safety."

While Grandpa was right, Lauren felt like sinking into the

seat. She didn't like Mitch knowing about the poor judgments she'd made.

"Do you miss him?" Mitch asked gently.

"No, actually I don't."

He'd not only ignored Lauren's frequent pleas to slow down, he'd ridiculed her for caring. Mitch was obviously the precise opposite kind of person. One who cared deeply about the safety of others. If only that would ease her concern over his closeness with Lem. Maybe in time. Right now, it hurt. Badly. Still…

"It makes me feel better knowing Grandpa has someone like you looking out for him." Lauren meant it. She shouldn't be jealous. The men's friendship should ease her guilt about living in Texas. But being here with Grandpa and the fear that he contended with made her never want to leave him again.

Unfortunately she'd given her word to her best friend, who'd forfeited her career to start the specialty business with Lauren. They'd poured their talents, time and savings into it. The first pangs of doubt about her decision assailed Lauren.

Lauren studied Mitch. Did he know why Grandpa's fear surfaced now? He needed to. Maybe he could help alleviate Grandpa's anxiety. Just because Lem's grandfather and father died in their seventieth year didn't mean Lem would. Right?

For a fleeting moment, she hated that she'd taken out a loan to start her seamstress shop and bound herself to be a business partner with her friend. It hog-tied her to Texas.

"He misses his only granddaughter." Mitch raised his chin in a perceiving manner. "Lem tells me your parents died within hours of one another. I'm deeply sorry. What was it?"

His frankness surprised her. "Carbon monoxide poisoning. Their room sat over the garage of a house we'd moved into that winter. Daddy started the car to warm it up before taking me to school and Mom to work. They lay back down and…never woke up." Lauren blinked swiftly against a wave of emotion.

"Losing her mama and daddy made Lauren want to become

a nurse to help people," Lem inserted. "And educate on safety and accident prevention."

"I hear you," Mitch said soberly. "I believe every accident is one-hundred-percent preventable. My dad perished in a motorcycle wreck."

"Across the road from the trauma center site," Lem added.

Had that inspired Mitch to build it? Lauren studied him.

Mitch turned onto the interstate that led Refuge to Eagle Point. "Dad was critically wounded. He could've been saved by surgery, had a hospital been closer, and if the person who pulled out in front of him had been looking."

Lem clicked his tongue. "He also lost his mama. She died from cancer not caught in time. She didn't have insurance and put off going to the doctor until too late."

"But thanks to Lem inviting me to church chili-suppers and becoming like a second dad, I turned out all right." He grinned.

Lauren's heart arched toward Mitch. "I know what it feels like to lose someone to something preventable."

Lem harrumphed. "Yeah, preventable like me losing you to Texas again when your building renovations are complete. I hope you hired horrible contractors who delay the timeline."

"Grandpaaaa. Don't be cranky. My friend sacrificed a lot to go into business with me. She'd be devastated if I bailed."

"Yes, it's prudent to honor your word, but that doesn't make up for the fact that you made this big decision out of duress."

"I'm glad you're here, Lauren." Mitch's chuckle dissolved the squabble. He sounded like he really meant his words.

She crammed her hands under her knees. "Thanks. The seamstress shop will specialize in costumes and uniforms. A percentage goes toward charities for children who've lost parents." For some reason her formerly noble plans felt barren.

"She makes specialty clothes for free to needy little kids and nursing home patrons, too," Lem added. "Nice, although I hate that she's not using her nursing skills like her sewing gift."

"Grandpa! We don't discuss that," she remarked gently. Futile since she inherited her stubborn streak from Lem.

A determined scowl bore down on Lem's bulbous nose and farm-freckled grin. "She don't like me pestering her about it."

"So I won't tread there, either," Mitch said with another tension-diffusing smile, which thinned into a tenacious line as his gaze gripped Lauren's in the mirror. "Yet."

What did that mean? She eyed Lem, smug now, then Mitch. Neither man's expression offered clues. "This smacks of conspiracy." She folded her arms and refused to look into that mirror, or Mitch's arresting eyes, again.

Her resolve lasted an entire eighth of a mile.

At the next red light, she caught Mitch studying her through the rearview mirror. He said nothing at first, then, "Feels almost like we're having a family spat here."

"Yeah. Hatfield and McCoy caliber," she quipped. Especially if he joined forces with Grandpa and tried to talk her back into nursing. Not happening. Even if Lem put him up to it. And no one softened her like Grandpa could.

He'd essentially raised her every summer since her tenth birthday after her parents died. She spent the rest of the year changing homes with the seasons, depending on which relative had room. Lauren's mom was Lem's only daughter. Grieving over her had bonded the two like suture glue.

Now it seemed as if Mitch's bond with Grandpa was stronger.

She shifted in her seat to put some distance between herself and Mitch. His overwhelming presence in the truck's cab made her feel snuggled next to a nuclear reactor with a compromised cooling system. Lem stretched, scooting her closer to Mitch again. She shot Lem a *that-did-not-help* look.

Which he ignored with fervor.

The whistling old scamp clearly had matchmaking in mind, which meant he was *out* of his mind. Lauren would no more date a doctor than Grandpa would give up his greasy biscuits and gravy.

These last twenty minutes were going to be one long ride.

Despite her pulse pounding, the ribbon-cutting was not something she could bring herself to joyfully anticipate. Hopefully her unruly heart rate had nothing to do with notions of romance.

Mitch never thought this day would come. Or end.

But here he was, standing at the door of a dream. He poised an outrageously large pair of scissors over the ribbon. "They're heavier than my military rifle."

Laughter erupted from the crowd. Bulb lights flashed and popped from every angle. Townspeople and reporters snapped images of Eagle Point Trauma Center's grand opening.

Surgery tech Kate Dalton leaned over the microphone. "You'd think our top trauma surgeon would slice right the first time," she teased in reference to this being Mitch's second attempt.

"Cut me some slack. These are duller than your bedtime stories." Actually Kate's stories coaxed countless soldiers to sleep, though she claimed she bored them into oblivion instead.

"Come on, Mitch! Those scissors can't be older'n me," Lem heckled good-heartedly from the crowd.

Laughing, Mitch sought out his friend in a sea of onlookers but snagged on a stunning redhead instead. Her gaze hit the ground like platelets in a blood storm, and her face turned just as red.

Same attraction that had jolted them earlier. Mitch hadn't counted on this distraction.

Therefore his inner guard better be on its best behavior.

Lauren was profoundly attractive in pictures Lem so proudly displayed, but exponentially more beautiful in person. Her eyes were so unique he could barely look away. Mitch diverted attention to Lem, who watched him studying Lauren with peculiar interest. Lem's grin heated Mitch's neck.

He shifted uncomfortably at the podium, unable to recall the last time he'd blushed.

"*To-day,* Dr. Wellington." Kate gave a dramatic sigh.

Though the sash-cutting delay was staged by request of news camera crews, Mitch's team joined the crowd in genuine laughter.

Getting cues from reporters to continue the stall, Mitch pivoted. "If I had a scalpel rather than these turn-of-the-century scissors, I'd be set."

Kate's eyebrow cocked. Having worked with her in Afghanistan performing combat surgeries, he knew the look.

Mitch turned his palm up. "Scalpel?" He used his official surgeon voice. Kate produced the stainless-steel instrument.

The crowd went wild. Cheers and clapping abounded. Jubilation escalated when Kate raised the blade and saluted the building's flag with it. The curved edge glinted in sunlight.

"Scalpel," she repeated per surgery protocol and gently smacked its handle into Mitch's palm.

How he loved that feeling. Only, this was epic. The moment turned surreal. Mitch hardly believed they were standing at the newly built trauma center, set to open part-time the first of next month. Seventeen days, and his team's battlefield dream would become reality.

Next the mayor started a speech about how the center would bring their town economy-reviving revenue.

Mitch's gaze drifted to the building, an undeniable answer to prayer. Awe for God engulfed him as he studied the magnificent steel-and-glass structure. It took his breath away, because despite titanium faith, he was a frontline fighter who'd wondered if he'd ever live to see this day.

Thank You, God, for bringing us through and to.

His eyes caressed a scripture etched above the Eagle Point Emergency entrance logo. A battlefield promise he'd clung to and prayed over every service member his scalpel came in contact with. His architect cousin had engraved it on the building: "The Lord turn his face toward you and give you peace. Numbers 6:26"

Speech ended, the mayor left the podium.

Ian Shupe, Mitch's best friend and head anesthesiologist on his trauma team, stepped up and pulled the ribbon taut. "Ready?"

Mitch drew an elated breath and inhaled pure joy. "Ready."

"Don't amputate your fingers." Ian slid his hands farther apart and grinned, evoking more crowd laughter. "Or mine."

Mitch chuckled and set scalpel to ribbon, camouflage to celebrate the team's war-veteran status.

He opened his mouth to utter the dedication, but sounds of distantly approaching helicopters ripped wings from his words. Probably news choppers.

Mitch didn't look because he really didn't fancy the notion of slicing or suturing his best friend's finger.

That instant, Ian's hands went lax. The uncut ribbon fluttered like a feather to the ground. Mitch looked up at Ian.

But Ian wasn't looking at the fallen ribbon.

He stared at the sky. And he definitely wasn't smiling.

Mitch turned, saw what Ian saw and straightened. Sheathed the scalpel and handed it to Kate, who said, "Hey, are those…?"

"Trauma choppers," Mitch finished for her.

"What a show!" a crowd member yelled. Mitch and Ian stared at the two incoming helicopters. Medical, not news.

If this was part of the show, Mitch had missed the memo. He faced Ian. "You set this up?"

"No, you?" Ian followed Mitch, who stepped off the stage. They headed toward an adjacent field where the choppers seemed destined to land within minutes.

"What, have mock trauma teams come?" Mitch shook his head, adrenaline surging. "No. This is no drill. This is the real deal."

Chapter Two

Mitch and his sparse trauma crew sprinted toward the field. Reporters and onlookers chased.

"Stay back!" Mitch commanded the engulfing crowd. Lauren skidded in her steps. Did she think he meant her?

He waved her to follow, but she froze in place. Her wind-tousled fiery hair rose up from her face like a crown of silken flames. Remarkable emerald eyes darted awkwardly between him and the landing choppers. Abject terror wrestled other emotions on her face. She was concerned. Conflicted. Stricken.

His heart was full of compassion for her as it had been in the car when she'd mentioned the tragic way her parents had died.

Lem once told him that she'd been traumatized by not knowing how to help her parents she'd found barely breathing. That tragedy birthed her dream to become a nurse who had moonlighted as a CPR coach so other families wouldn't have to live her nightmare.

Mitch didn't make a habit of questioning God, but what a terrible twist of fate it had been for sweet Lauren to lose her first patient off her obstetrics orientation a year ago.

Lem said the subsequent lawsuit also raked Lauren over the coals. Mitch knew because Lem, in his love of telling stories concerning Lauren, had left nothing out.

According to Lem, the ordeal had so devastated her, she

had not only bolted from nursing, she had pulled away from God, faith, friends and family. Then wrapped herself up in her only other skill—sewing. Something Lauren's mom had taught her and was their special mother-daughter connection before her mom died.

Mitch's heart broke for Lauren now, seeing in person the unleashed emotion on her face. The unshackled fight-or-flight reaction in her eyes. He knew it.

That instant a veil lifted, allowing Mitch to see the huge gaping wounds Lauren's own trauma had left her with. Hurts she had yet to be healed from.

The moment suspended Mitch in time and made him wish for words that would heal and not harm.

For Lem, Mitch wanted like crazy to comfort her but he'd have others to focus on soon. He couldn't be everywhere at once.

But Someone could.

Jesus, rescue her. Show her the truth. Draw her back.

No idea what the last phrase encompassed, but that's the prayer that pressed out of him so he let it fly.

He maintained eye contact with Lauren as long as possible to keep stride and still send visual cues that she was not only welcome to help, but worthy and needed.

Apparently misinterpreting his directive gaze, she whirled toward the encroaching crowd. "Cameras off!" Lauren yelled above chopper noise to reporters. "They may have real victims here."

They? By that word, Mitch knew Lauren no longer thought of herself as part of the medical community, which saddened him.

Nevertheless, the authority in her voice impressed him because even the most aggressive reporters complied instantly.

The crowd stopped as one unit and fell back in silence. Concern infiltrated faces. Mass murmurs rose.

Mitch trudged forward. "I hope this is someone's idea of a very bad joke," he told Ian. Ian's jaw clenched as he nodded.

But when a crew medic jumped from the chopper before it fully landed, Mitch knew with sick certainty it wasn't. The strained look on the man's ruddy face confirmed it.

"Incomiiiing!" Ian yelled.

Mitch's team rushed ahead, leaving him to obtain report and issue orders.

As when overseas, they worked like neurons not having to be told their duty.

Ian and Kate met one chopper. Mitch's circulating and triage nurses approached another.

Gratitude for their professionalism filled him.

His pre-op and scrub nurses weren't flying in until next week, and his recovery nurse had pulled out to reenlist. Mitch would need to replace her ASAP.

He grabbed a man with a microphone. "Clear paths. This isn't part of the ceremony. We have injured on the way."

The microphone man complied. Officials looked as baffled as Mitch felt. "But are you set up for that?" one sputtered.

Mitch's risen hands both halted and calmed them.

The mayor jogged to keep up. "Sir, you're not officially open…."

"We are if those choppers have wounded in them."

The mayor's face turned grim. "They radioed they were coming to see the trauma center opening, but not with patients. Dr. Wellington, I fear something terrible has happened."

Mitch's sentiments exactly. "We'll handle it, Mayor. We've handled worse situations before."

Respect gleamed from the mayor's eyes. "I'm sure you have. What can I do?"

"Send any available Eagle Point EMTs and other first responders. And thank God choppers were right there."

"Yes, indeed, but are you sure the center is ready to—?"

"Absolutely." *We'll make it ready.* Mitch turned, ending

the conversation. The crowd parted as he plowed through. He paused to focus on a third approaching chopper.

What had just happened?

If distant smoke billowing above trees lining the interstate was an indication, something massive.

A horrible thought struck. There was one major road in and out. If this was a northbound motor vehicle accident, the victims had most likely been on their way here to the ceremony.

So in building the trauma center, he'd created catastrophe?

No. He refused to believe that or doubt God's goodness.

Until another medical chopper ripped through the clouds. Disbelief coursed through him. How many more casualties would come? No matter. They'd handle it.

Mitch peered into the domed windows of medical choppers to get an idea of how many patients occupied each.

Rushing air and the high-pitched *whup-whup-whups* of whistling rotor blades pushed all other sound away.

Mitch mentally counted his staff. Not nearly enough. More nurses were flying in next week. He needed help now.

Instantly Mitch thought again of Lem's granddaughter.

He turned, scanned the crowd.

Lem had said her biggest regret was that intense college years had prevented her from visiting Lem. Hadn't he mentioned something about her working as a surgery tech while in school?

If so, that meant she had the experience he needed. Mitch hoped like crazy she hadn't let her license or certifications lapse.

He ran toward the throng of people. Found her huddled next to Lem, whose eyes rivaled hers for biggest and roundest of the crowd.

Gauging that his staff was triaging the ground choppers and he still had a minute until the others landed, he sprinted over.

Mitch faced Lauren and placed firm hands on her shoulders. Willed her to look him in the eye. "Lauren, are you current?"

"Wh-what?"

"Your nursing license. Is it current?"

"N-not in this state." She blinked furiously.

"In Texas?"

She nodded slowly, looking confused as to why he'd ask.

"Are all of your emergency certifications up to date?"

"Y-yes, but—"

"That's good enough. You're legal in a mass casualty situation, which is what I fear we have here."

"What? No, you can't possibly ask—"

He could and he would.

"Lauren, listen to me. I need your help."

She shook her head vehemently.

He swiveled his neck to watch the next chopper prepare to land, its flight crew frenziedly working over someone.

No time to argue.

Facing Lauren again, he increased hand pressure, hunkered his shoulders and got nose to nose with Lem's granddaughter. "Nurse Bates, I'm not asking. I'm ordering. Triage chopper number three, then meet me at four."

Desperate hands came up to clutch his. "Mitch, please," she rasped. "I can't. I'm not qualified for trauma. I worked OB."

Compassion vying for impatience, Mitch leaned close to her ear. "Lauren Esther Bates, I'll tell you what a wise man told me when I doubted I had what it took to be a doctor."

He eyed Lem respectively, then Lauren pointedly. "God doesn't call the qualified, He qualifies the called. I'm convinced He put you here for this precise moment. I don't have enough hands. People are dying. We need you. Go." He gave her shoulders a nudge—okay, more like gentle shove.

Rage streamed from her eyes, then tears.

She spun and ran to the chopper. He caught the piercing cry she hurled at him upon turning.

Her scathing reaction promised she'd never forgive him for

this. But practicing triage medicine wasn't a popularity contest. He had a job to do and people to save.

He faced Lem. "Sorry, but—"

Lem shook his head. "Just do your job, son. I'll get a ride home." Lem affectionately clasped his shoulder.

Mitch eyed the last chopper hovering above a windblown field. "I meant sorry for speaking to Lauren in that manner."

"She'll be all right."

Mitch hoped so as he observed her taking a report from the third chopper crew on his way to meet the fourth.

She probably wondered how he knew her middle name. But Mitch knew nearly everything about her because, true to what he'd said in the car, Lem never stopped talking about her.

He'd already known how her parents had died, but had asked out of sensitivity in order to gauge how many details Lauren knew so he wouldn't mistakenly speak of it.

Mitch had heard many times how she was named after the Biblical Esther at Lem's request at her birth.

If Lauren Esther was made of the same moral fiber as her namesake and as her grandpa, she wouldn't bail on him, his skeleton crew…or the people injured in those choppers.

Lord, I hope like the end of hiccups that You bestowed Lem's courage, compassion, intelligence, recall, integrity and unflappable grit upon Lauren.

The next two hours would tell.

Chapter Three

Satisfied Lauren was on board with his plans, Mitch sprinted to the last-landed chopper. Three's crew worked feverishly, but he had peace Lauren could handle it. A medic disembarked and rushed Mitch, who eyed his beeper to be sure he hadn't missed pages about this.

"Status?" Mitch asked the out-of-breath flight medic.

"Three-car accident. High-speed head-on." He hitched a thumb toward the interstate. "Mass casualties…" He indicated the array of life flight choppers. "Obviously."

Blades wind-whipped Mitch's lab coat as they approached the fleet. Gas fumes permeated the air. "What happened?"

The medic's eyes hooded. "Texting teen crossed the center lane. Hit a minivan, which spun into a third car. Perpetrating car ejected unbelted passengers. Twelve victims in all. Van folks in bad shape, but we can make it to St. Louis with them."

"Who're you leaving with us?"

"Both ejected teens. Driver's bad, but not as grave as her passenger. Three more too critical for Refuge, and St. Loo's too far. Place is a godsend." He indicated Mitch's center.

"Who's the imminent death?" Mitch searched chopper windows.

The paramedic pointed to where Ian worked on a critical

patient as Kate hurtled the gurney toward the entrance—which Mitch just now realized was still belted in uncut camo ribbon.

He dashed over, pulled his hook knife and slashed the band machete-style seconds before Ian and Kate torpedoed through.

"Not the way you envisioned the ribbon-cutting, huh?" Lauren, who'd jogged up, asked. "Got an extra stethoscope?"

Mitch draped his over her neck and squeezed her shoulders in respect and gratitude. She nodded, then bolted back to the field. Her previous terror and hostility had vanished. *Thank You, Lord.*

He headed toward operating rooms. Had they even taken the plastic off the equipment yet? If only they had a bigger crew.

But Mitch had wanted to honor the community by saving remaining positions for townspeople needing work.

Ian looked to be thinking similar thoughts. "I got this case. You rally the troops. We need more help. I wish your para-rescue jumper friends were here. We could use the PJs' elite medical skills."

"No doubt." But the special operations paramedics were on a mission. Mitch ran back out. Scanned the crowd.

Lord, come on. You know I can't do this without—

Like exclamation points on the end of his prayer, Mandy Briggs, pediatrician wife of one of the PJs, rushed up. "I'm here to help."

Mitch nodded. "Anyone else medical, we need 'em. Check ID then team up with a nurse named Lauren at chopper three."

"Will do." Mandy instructed medical people to see her immediately. While she vetted, Mitch skimmed accident reports texted from EMTs and police officers on scene.

Amid nurses bearing badges, a uniformed man came forward. "The mayor sent me over, ma'am. I'm an experienced army medic on family medical leave."

"Excellent. See him." Mandy directed him to Mitch.

He approached Mitch, raring to go. "Name's Caleb Landis. What can I do, sir?" He bounced on the balls of his feet and looked unafraid and eager to help. He had the air of a born leader. Good.

Mitch pointed to a chopper. "Triage that one."

"Yes, sir."

The head flight medic faced Mitch. "Those three are red-light critical and one grave. Wanted to give you a status. We didn't have your contact info before because—"

"No one expected this," Mitch finished for him.

The paramedic nodded. "Most docs would take my head off for not calling first. Thanks for letting us drop without notice."

Mitch waved him toward his rig. "I call it teamwork."

"I'd offer my teams to stay and help but we've had two more trauma calls across the river." Apology resided in his eyes.

"We'll take it from here. You're free to fly."

The second the medic settled in his chopper, it lifted.

How was Lauren holding up?

Mitch found her hovering expertly over a patient. She didn't appear frazzled, but focused and quick on her feet. She held a terrified patient's hand and spoke softly while wheeling the gurney. Mandy walked alongside, adjusting IV lines. No one rushed, so the patient must not be as critical. Just scared. The way the trembling woman's eyes fixed to Lauren's convinced Mitch that Lauren knew calmness was contagious, and she deftly infused it.

Despite the carnage outside, Mitch smiled. Lauren was meant to do this. Take care of broken people.

Lem had given Mitch a summer to-do list that included several big repairs prior to them learning Lauren was coming.

Perhaps repair of a different sort was meant to happen this summer. More than what they had anticipated. Mitch could fix Lem's tractor, his deck and his aging kitchen and other projects. But he also determined to get through to Lauren's broken place by summer's end. Repair the rupture that had so wounded her soul, she'd walked away from the career Mitch was confident had comprised her calling. Then Lem would worry less over her.

Mitch got updates on all triaged patients then headed to the next critical. He threw on a surgical cap and mask, scrubbed in and backed through his sterile suite. Thankfully, someone had readied the room. Nurses from somewhere were gowned and counting instruments. *Eagle Point. Welcome home.*

The staff gowned and gloved Mitch, then transferred the patient in. Mitch began exploratory surgery. "Clamp."

Someone pressed it into his hand. "Clamp."

"Scalpel." Mitch grew impressed at the speed and accuracy with which she passed instruments.

Intense part of the surgery over, Mitch tilted to view the assistant and found himself absorbed in Lauren's eyes. Delight rippled through him. He smiled, though she couldn't see through his mask. "Hello, Nurse Bates. Thought you sounded familiar."

She blinked rapidly, which revealed how nervous she was. Her cheek above the mask twitched.

He leaned closer. "You're doing great, Lauren."

"You, too," she whispered back.

"Suture."

She pressed it confidently into his hand. "Suture."

He hadn't even told her what thread size or type. Nice.

Upon closing the wound, Mitch rested his elbow against Lauren's. He liked the feel of her working at his side. "So, Bates, my recovery nurse pulled out at the last minute, which means I'm hiring. You interested?"

She scowled above her mask. "Are you *insane?*"

He laughed. "Guess that's a no."

She shook her head, proving she really thought he was crazy. After the patient was moved to recovery, Lauren stayed while Mitch checked the progress of other patients. Surgeons and staff had come from nearby Refuge. Mandy or the mayor must've called for backup. Mitch didn't recognize anyone from when he had lived in Eagle Point prior to entering the service. Hard to tell with no one in street clothes. Not even his primary trauma team.

Mitch was glad Eagle Point's reporter suggested they wear scrubs for the ribbon-cutting to look official. Instruments in his lab coat had saved life-giving seconds. God had ways of taking care of them and patients in their charge. Like choppers being present. Therefore Mitch believed God would fix his acute staffing problem. *Lord, if You could do that STAT, I'd appreciate it.*

Lauren approached that instant and handed him a chart. Hmm. "We've cleared a room and pre-opped the next case."

"Would you like to assist me again?" He smiled.

She scowled. "Would you like a knuckle sandwich?" She sighed. Tilted her head. "Fine. If you need the help, I will."

"We have sufficient help now."

Her eyes widened. "Then why on earth would you ask *me?* I'm not cut out for this." Papers fluttered as her arm waved.

"Because *you* need to trust you." He took the chart and nodded toward recovery. "If they're okay in there, you're free to go." He left her with his words. No time to waste. The next patient was on the table.

Multiple surgeries later, Mitch exited the broken-in operating area and peeled off his cap. He stood beside his team, hand-washing in silence. "We tried, guys."

His words didn't mend Kate's melancholy or lift Ian's irritation. Ian glared at the ceiling, looking tempted to take the injustice up with God. "It's not right when the wrong one dies."

"Chin up. She could've been your daughter," Mitch said of the texting teenage girl who'd survived while her victim did not.

"No. Mine won't be texting when she's driving."

"How can you be sure?" Mitch leaned against an IV pole.

"Because she's not getting her license until she's thirty." A smile breached Ian's weary face.

"How's custody stuff going?" Mitch asked tentatively, knowing Ian was enduring a painfully ugly and disillusioning divorce.

Ian's jaw clicked. "Not in my favor."

Which accounted for Ian's rift with God. Ian's crumbled marriage cemented Mitch's belief that distance only ruined relationships. That also mutilated Mitch's last relationship when his girlfriend's unit moved to another area of Afghanistan.

Precisely why he should re-up his efforts to ignore an unexpected attraction to a cute, carrottopped Texan.

"Sorry, bud." Mitch wished he could ease Ian's pain. And prevent repeating his own, which made him wonder why he'd entertained an attraction to Lauren at all. Mitch shook his head. "Man. All my brain cells must've dehydrated in the desert."

"Nah. You have at least two left."

"Then one's hiding and the other fled to go find it."

Ian laughed. "Why you say that?"

"You don't want to know." Mitch's ridiculous attraction to Lauren was better off unmentioned. He'd just gotten over his girlfriend who broke up with him because they were long-distance. Lauren lived in Texas, which meant she was off-limits. Mitch wasn't looking to break his heart twice in one year. Safer to lean on the wary side while getting to know Lauren this summer. A feat, since Lem already exacted some pretty stealthy matchmaking maneuvers on them.

Thankfully Lauren was the furthest thing from interested in him, too. So jealous, she probably bled green rather than red.

Ian eyed him peculiarly then retreated to the staff lounge. Mitch ran a last patient round. As Kate stood in the hall updating Mitch, a rush of red hair caught his eye.

"Lauren?" Surprise coursed through him.

She leaned out of a linen closet. "Yes?"

"You're still here?" He approached Lauren slowly lest she unleash the anger he'd glimpsed earlier. Calm filled her face—and some other expression he couldn't place.

"Surprised?" She smiled.

"I am. Thought you left hours ago. You're free to."

She fiddled with the blanket. "I know."

He kept a gentle distance. She stepped away then turned back.

He readied for an explosion. Her face stayed thoughtful.

"Mitch?" Her mouth fumbled with words, which drew his attention to full lips. Bright red. Probably that color from dehydration, running halls for hours with nothing to drink.

He wrestled his unruly attention back to her eyes.

Finally she held his gaze. "I wanted to say thanks."

He nodded, not wanting her to have to explain.

By not giving her the chance to opt out of helping, he'd given her something unexpected. Had her confidence in her nursing skills been restored by this horrible accident?

"Lauren?" He liked how her name rolled off his tongue.

"Yes, Dr. Wellington?" She paused. Lovely profile.

"How many more patients might you go on to help now?"

"Tonight?" She looked haggard at the thought.

"No. We're done here tonight. I meant how many more patients…in life."

She blinked rapidly but didn't answer.

"Any?"

She bravely met his gaze and his question with an honest but vulnerable face. "Not sure. Jury's still out on that one."

"Would you reconsider my vacant nurse position?"

She looked shocked that he'd ask again. "I'm honored you'd trust me, but no. My life is in Texas."

"But your grandfather is here."

Scowling, she chewed her lip. "Thank you, Dr. Obvious."

Mitch chuckled. "We need an assertive charge nurse. I have it on good faith you can hold your own with bossy physicians."

She rolled her eyes. "My patient's blanket is getting cold. *Your* patient, rather."

Her answer far from pacified.

"Very well." He motioned. "Carry on."

Face lifted, she hugged the blanket. "It's for the texting teenage girl. I heard you lost her passenger. I'm sorry."

Mitch nodded. "We did everything we could."

She searched his eyes. "I admire you and your team. How do you do it? Lose someone yet never give up?"

"Because despite each one we lose, there's a slew to save."

She tucked her chin, as though trying to draw warmth from the blanket herself.

Not caring that his back bore Kate's insatiably curious stare, Mitch stepped close, his arms on her shoulders. "Lauren, I know this was horrific and hard. I didn't leave you much choice, but you held up as well as anyone. Sorry if I came across as rude and unfeeling before."

"You had a job to do and you were right...people were dying." She backed out of his grasp. "The last thing I want hanging over me is more guilt. I couldn't abandon you. Or your team." She nodded toward Kate, who nodded back. "Or them." Lauren indicated rooms of recovering patients.

Mitch stilled, respecting her need for space.

Good thing, because the beauty that unleashed every time she blinked was kicking his concentration to the curb. She had the most gorgeous green eyes.

Before she got out of hearing range he said, "Nurse Bates?"

"Yes, Dr. Wellington?" She appeared miffed every time he used the title. Like she knew he did so intentionally.

He leaned out of earshot of Kate, who'd be dying like an eavesdropping little sister to know what was said. "Please, call me Mitch. 'Dr. Wellington' makes me feel snobby and senile."

A gorgeous smile dawned. "Agreed. But only if you stop, and I mean this instant, calling me *Nurse* Bates."

"But you need to get used to hearing it." He grinned.

Her eyebrows pinched in a beautiful downward slope. "If my patient didn't need this blanket, Wellington, I'd be tempted to smother you with it."

His grin widened. "You definitely inherited your grandfather's temper."

"I can't imagine him ever being angry with you. You seem the best of friends."

There was no missing the sour tone that pickled her words.

"He hasn't been angry with me for twenty years anyway." Mitch chuckled, recalling the first time he met Lem, who dragged Mitch across a field by his ear for stealing corn. Made him work it off, too. Lem and that cornfield had been the best things to ever happen to Mitch. "But I have seen him come unhinged at a broken-down tractor or two."

She giggled. "He still kick tires when they break down?"

"Still does."

"I'm ashamed I never appreciated everything about him before." She slumped. "Anyway, time for vitals. See you later."

He could only hope. Mitch watched her departure, enjoying every second of her appealing stride.

Ian returned. "I'm— Wait. Why do you look sedated?"

Mitch shrugged and averted his gaze from the lovely Lauren.

Ian eyed him curiously. "Anyway, I'm heading out. See ya."

Mitch caught Ian. "Hey, what do you have going Saturday?"

"Besides staying in a coma?" Ian rubbed tired eyes. Mitch knew the feeling. His eyelids scraped like sandpaper.

"Lem invited the med team over for a Southern-fried feast."

"You making this famous chili we hear about?" Ian winked.

"Sure. We'll have a chili day at Lem's and just hang out. Refuge medical folks are covering our shifts here."

Kate approached, chomping on a delicious-looking apple.

His invitation lifted weight off Ian's shoulders. "Lem's it is then." Ian eyed Mitch pointedly. "Will Lauren be there?"

Wait…what?

Kate snickered then looked thoughtful. "You know…we need another nurse. Lauren did outstanding. Have you considered—?"

"Already asked. She said no. Not just no, but 'don't ask again or I'll throttle you' no."

Ian snorted. "When has that ever stopped you?"

"Point taken. I'll work on her as long as she doesn't do to me what Lem does to broken-down tractors."

His team laughed, but Mitch wondered how Lauren would take his familylike friendship with Lem. Daily breakfast with Lem would be interesting. Especially if he actively recruited her to be on his team, which would mean major life restructuring and relocation. Much as he wanted Lauren close to Lem and on staff, it wasn't his choice to make.

Help her make the right one, Lord.

But Mitch's gut knew. He eyed the ceiling. "Thanks. I'm commissioned to convince a hot-tempered redhead to uproot? This is one assignment I am *not* looking forward to." Especially if he had to continue to contend with this all-too-annoying attraction.

Mitch headed to look for Lauren and give her a ride home. And pester her a little more about at least being his part-time summer nurse. She seemed to enjoy scrub duty best and was good.

"Fine. I'm on it, God. But help me accomplish this mission with the least bloodshed possible."

He rounded the corner and ran smack into the object of his prayers. She returned his stethoscope.

He tried to hand it back. "You might—"

Her head shook firmly. "I won't need it again. This final cameo was nice for closure, but my nursing career is over."

Chapter Four

"She really said that?" Grandpa's laugh drifting from his kitchen drew Lauren from sleep the next morning.

"She really did." Mitch's deep, answering chuckle compelled Lauren to full wakefulness. Had she slept in? She blinked into darkness until her eyes adjusted and *7:00 a.m.* squinted back at her from Grandpa's antique dresser clock.

What was *he* doing here?

She rolled over to listen to the cozy male banter.

Grandpa harrumphed. "Well, it's not over until the Good Lord says so."

"Hate to say this, Lem, but she gets her iron will from you." Mitch chuckled. The invigorating sound lilted down the hall and lifted Lauren's head from the pillow.

She rubbed at scratchiness that the sleepless night had left in her eyes. If only she could rub away how raw his being here scraped her inside.

Who were those hooligans talking about anyway? Her? Sounded like it. In that case, she'd best be up and ready to defend herself. Grandpa's robust coffee should do it.

Lauren lifted her robe from the bedpost and snuggled her feet into pure comfort that Lem left beside her bed. Sentimental slippers she'd used here every summer since age ten. Ones that warmed her heart as well as her toes.

She traced fingers across calico star patterns embedded in the last quilt Grandma Bates made before she died. Lauren pulled it up, pressed it to her face and drew a sustained breath.

It smelled like home.

Lauren smiled, glad Lem left the quilt in "her" room. She felt touched that he remembered how she, Grandma and Mom toiled over the pattern together with lots of tangled thread and laughter. The quilt and its cozy memories tucked aside for later, she stepped toward her door.

"So if her stubborn streak came from you, who'd she get the luscious red hair and gorgeous green eyes from?" Mitch asked.

Lauren skidded to a halt and held her breath to hear.

"My daughter, her mama," Grandpa proudly answered.

"She must have been a looker. Lauren is beyond beautiful."

Mitch's heartwarming words washed through her. He thought she was beautiful? She pattered over, peered at herself in the mirror…and laughed.

Her unruly blaze of hair looked plugged into a live socket. Illinois's humidity poofed it out like mops-gone-wild. It was a crimson entity all its own today.

"No matter." Lauren wrinkled her nose at her reflection.

A handsome hunk thought she was pretty.

Despite the irksome fact that he was hogging her grandpa, Lauren stood what felt a foot taller. Which would still barely bring her nose to nose with Mitch.

His unwitting compliment melted off last night's stress and sleeplessness. Hours full of trauma images that had stalked her deep into dreams.

Worse was waking to find out that she'd actually experienced gladness and felt useful again caring for patients.

She remembered the respect that had multiplied in Mitch's eyes every time he'd sought her out last night, which had been often. She'd felt unequivocally in her element. Ian had even commented so in a hurried hallway. Kate, too, in surgery, said

Lauren looked to be doing what she was uniquely gifted for. Was she?

Lauren shook off the notion. It was nothing more than an acute case of memories or a major manifestation of jet lag.

Why was Mitch here anyway? She shuffled into the kitchen.

"Look who's awake!" Grandpa's explosive grin pushed tears to her eyes. He greeted her with a flurry of hugs that felt like five years' worth rolled into one.

When had anyone been this genuinely happy to see her? How she'd missed him, and the closeness they shared!

Which he now seemed to share with Mitch. The moment soured.

"Morning, Grandpa." She helped him to his chair and avoided Mitch's assessing gaze. Eyes that said he knew she struggled.

"Hope we didn't wake you." Mitch pulled out a chair for her at Grandpa's table, covered in a crisp red gingham cloth and place mats she'd made as a child. Homesickness overloaded Lauren's emotions.

As always, his kitchen smelled of cinnamon, her favorite toast. The kind she'd made for her parents that fateful morning.

She'd been so excited to show them that Grandpa had taught her how. Same toast she'd clutched in that irrevocable instant when she'd found the two most important people in her life barely breathing.

Life as she knew it had suddenly crumbled and fallen through fragile fingers.

Today the smell didn't repel because she equated it with Lem, her lifeline after her parents had died. In those days, Lem talked unceasingly about how heaven was the promise that she'd see her parents again. He told stories of what Jesus had to go through in order to whisper that promise to mankind.

Memories flooded back through a river of time and nearly swept Lauren off her feet. Every coloring page she'd perfected at this table, every dish she'd set and every summer meal she'd eaten. All with Grandpa. He'd become her mom and dad rolled into one.

How could she have abandoned him all these years? Yet hadn't he encouraged her nursing dream?

She swallowed a hard lump and ran her hands across the country tablecloth. How could one forget a rickety table meant for six, yet set for two, that housed a million happy memories?

"Never get rid of this, Grandpa," she whispered hoarsely.

Mitch looked up, eyes sharpening. Grandpa paused, and unlike Mitch, his gaze seemed to fade back in years. Perhaps to meet hers at a time and place where their memories mingled and played. Toys. Crafts. Food. Games. Baking. Devotions. Love. Life. Loss. Hard times. Happy times. Tears. Fun. Stories. Laughter. Learning. Faith. Family. A bond no two others shared.

Until Mitch.

And that upended Lauren's world more than he could know.

Slowly, Lem set a steaming plate of sausage and eggs in front of her. "Still like 'em scrambled best?" Gentle remembrance and solid knowing seeped into Lem's life-and-loss-wizened eyes. He'd been through everything she had and more.

He knew every tear she'd cried, every boy she'd liked, every stunt she'd tried and every piece of toast she'd ever burned. An unfortunate many.

No one knew her like Grandpa. In fact, no one knew her at all except Grandpa. Not even her Texas friends. Life suddenly felt very lonely. Yet had Mitch come to know her through Grandpa's gift—the power of story?

Suddenly Grandpa's vast love for books and storytelling held greater meaning. He loved words so much, he'd used Grandma's life insurance money to found and fund the local library, something Grandma had always wanted yet never lived to see.

What would become of Lauren if Grandpa died at seventy? Irrational or not, fear welled. Lauren had a tough time quelling it, even as Mitch and Grandpa eyed her with growing concern. Panic pulsed through her. She took deep breaths to calm down.

Didn't help.

"Yep, still—" For some reason, her throat clogged.

They'd shared so much. She and Grandpa.

No two people possessed the treasure of memories they cherished. Not even Mitch, who studied them gently now.

Yet Mitch and Grandpa had undoubtedly made their own trove of memories. Suddenly and without warning, she wanted in.

Back into Grandpa's life.

Grandpa shuffled contentedly to the stove to continue his domestic dance of eclectic hospitality. As his comforting and familiar clatter of pans resumed, Lauren sized up her foe.

Mitch stared at her with precision, proving he'd picked up on her envious vibes. Hopefully he'd see her need to resume her rightful place in Grandpa's heart and life and back off a bit.

If she thought she was determined, it was no match for the titanium will steeling his liquid silver eyes and chiseling stony angles in the jaw he tenaciously jutted.

Instinctually she knew he'd been a rock for Grandpa to lean on in her absence. Who was she to interfere or tear that down?

They needed to find a middle ground. Problem was, his devotion toward Lem made her feel even more irate. At Mitch, yes, but more at herself for letting things like her emotional distance with Grandpa get this way to begin with.

They continued to stare at one another silently but by no means quietly. His breathtaking eyes spoke of loyalty and love as he rose and took a territorial stance next to Lem. Hip reclined against the counter, Mitch's muscle-thickened arms folded across his broad chest. Not breaking eye contact, he leaned toward Grandpa with undeterred aplomb. Mitch's massive height and build morphed into a force of protective nature.

He was clearly afraid she'd run off and hurt Grandpa again.

Their challenge-wrapped exchange was protected from Lem

only because his back was to them as he whistled over sumptuous chocolate gravy bubbling in the pan. Lem was the only person Lauren knew who served dessert at every meal, including breakfast.

She doubted even Grandpa's sugary gravy could sweeten Mitch up this moment or erase the resolve on his face. It blared his thoughts. He wasn't about to lose ground just so she could gain it. He'd not alter his friendship with Lem for anyone. She knew this for certain, because he made no attempt to hide his expressive countenance and protective body language from her. Mitch's gaze drifted to Grandpa and softened in such a way to pierce her heart with a two-pronged spear of remorse and regret.

If one picture could say a thousand words, Mitch's face was a photo montage. Tenderness scrolled across masculine planes, and deep care swept into the valleys. Grandpa's incessant Mitch stories afforded her the ability to ascertain that Mitch's will to fight for a hold on Lem's heart stemmed purely from admiration, loyalty and love.

No doubt a by-product of Lem's reaching into Mitch's desolate childhood and pulling him, a broken little smudge-faced boy, out of the ashes of poverty and hardship and teaching him how to live and love, work and pray, play and laugh like a man.

So what was her excuse? Why were her feelings so unruly?

She returned her attention to Grandpa. Had he the slightest inkling that he was the invisible rope in this unspoken, territorial tug of warring hearts?

Mitch probably thought she was a flake and that she'd end up hurting Grandpa by leaving and not staying in touch. But he had no right to insert himself into her business. Unfortunately, Grandpa had given Mitch full right to insert himself into Lem's.

There was nothing she could do about that, but she could do her best to make up for lost time with Grandpa, with or without

Mitch. Preferably without. He was a multifaceted distraction, and one she could not afford in any fashion.

Grandpa set a gravy dish of cocoa goodness in the middle of the table. Mitch served them, starting with her. He ladled a heap of chocolate gravy over one of Grandpa's homemade biscuits she'd torn into quarter-size chunks over her plate.

She tried not to soften at Mitch's sweet Southern manners. Or notice the way his well-muscled forearm moved with motion that mesmerized. How many broken soldiers had those careful and caring hands mended? How many lonely days had Mitch's smile and presence brightened for Grandpa, who struggled with loneliness?

Tears pricked her eyes. She blinked vehemently.

She felt Mitch's militant intentional gaze on her again and remembered she hadn't brushed her crazy hair. Or finished answering Grandpa's question of many awkward moments ago.

Self-consciousness flitted through her. "What'd you ask?"

"You never did tell me if you still like your eggs scrambled best," Grandpa repeated with a spirit of patience.

She patted her head. "Yep. Scrambled like my hair this morning." She slid a sideways glance at Mitch. Maybe he hadn't noticed the big red mop.

Oh, he noticed, all right—because he stared right at it.

Mitch cleared his throat. "You have nice hair, Lauren."

Lauren wasn't sure Lem, fiddling again at the stove, heard. She also wasn't sure she liked Mitch being nice, or the merry way his flattery made her feel.

She leaned back and eyed herself in a shiny toaster. An out-of-nowhere laugh came from the back of Lauren's throat.

Grandpa turned faster than a man half his age. Mitch looked up with the most adorably confused expression.

"Nice?" Lauren held out her unruly hair. "Now I know he's as adept at fibbing as he is at interfering." She directed her comment to Mitch. His face colored as Grandpa chuckled and rejoined them at the table.

"Well, when you brush it it's nice." Mitch poked at his eggs. Had she offended him? Maybe he'd get a clue and get away from Grandpa. At least while she was here. She didn't need anyone distracting her from the reason she came to visit: to make up for lost time.

She refused to sit idly by while Mitch picked up where he left off before deployment—taking her place in Grandpa's heart.

Unfortunately, Mitch was the kind of man who was effective at whatever he attempted, which justified her jealousy. A little.

She studied Mitch. He still pushed his fork around his plate. Perhaps he'd cued in on her struggle with ill feelings.

Grandpa nodded toward Mitch's well-massacred eggs. "Uh, son, those are already scrambled."

Both men grinned. Lauren's faded.

Grandpa called Mitch "son." Dismay and fear disarmed her. Her heart thumped as though it wanted to be let out of her chest. Her stomach clenched and unclenched like a raw-knuckled fist.

Mitch and Grandpa were closer than she ever imagined.

What bothered her most was that she envied Grandpa this morning almost as much as she envied Mitch. Almost.

Thankfully her emotions came quickly to their senses.

Jealousy, she could contend with. Feelings for Mitch? No way. That would be the second stupidest thing she could do. Entertaining the annoying attraction had been her first.

The three ate in introspective silence. Lem looked from one to the other. His eyes circled Lauren's face.

The last thing she wanted to do was worry Grandpa. So how to wrestle her jealousy under a rug and remedy this? She needed to try to compromise. Be more understanding. Easier said than done, though. One solution was to strive to spend time with Grandpa when Mitch wasn't here. That meant rising before the crack of dawn and staying up late, like Grandpa-the-night-owl liked to, but so be it.

Whatever it took to regain the bond and have more time to cherish with him, like old times. Before Mitch.

"What's today's agenda?" Lauren asked politely to break the tension, ease Mitch's embarrassment and Grandpa's concern.

Mitch wiped his mouth. "I'm driving to the trauma center to check on last night's patients. Then returning to knock out some stuff on Lem's summer to-do list."

"For which I'm glad." Lem's arm draped over Mitch's chair.

Just great. More Mitch and less Grandpa.

She clenched her teeth until her jaw hurt.

Mitch stood. His height always took her by surprise. He carried plates to the sink. Grandpa nudged Lauren. She rose to help Mitch with dishes, even though she wanted to be nowhere near him.

Grandpa also tried to help. Mitch waved him back. "You cook, I clean, remember? That's the deal." Mitch grinned and shooed Lem to the living room.

It galled her all the more. Why hadn't *she* thought of giving Grandpa a break?

Lauren found herself glaring at Mitch before she could stop. Thankfully her back was to Grandpa. She peeked to be sure.

Lem eyed the television and didn't offer a clue that he'd picked up on Lauren's struggle. In fact, he looked overjoyed at the prospect of retreating without an ounce of argument.

Highly unusual for Grandpa, whose work ethic wouldn't let him see someone else working without stepping in to help.

Rather, he grinned all the way to his easy chair and appeared perfectly content to leave the two of them alone.

Keyword: *alone.*

His suddenly sturdy countenance depicted an inner well-being that left Lauren with a distinct impression. Perhaps Lem's fear of perishing at seventy had more to do with worry over her than himself? That made sense. Especially in light of Grandpa's grounded faith and trademark talk of the hope of heaven.

Dread gave way to a sick feeling inside Lauren. Did Grandpa

hope she and Mitch had a future together? And did that hope seem to invigorate and enliven Grandpa?

She studied Mitch and dearly hoped Grandpa's trust hadn't been sorely misplaced.

Chapter Five

What was she thinking?

Mitch would really like to know. He watched Lauren with magnified interest for the third chore day in a row after breakfast at Lem's.

"We got a lot done yesterday. Thanks for your help."

She shrugged. "No reason for me not to."

He eyed her attire and grinned. "Not many women can rock a vintage pair of farmer's ratty denim overalls. But you do."

Cheeks tinged, she quickly spooned scraps into the trash. Mitch was glad to know she became embarrassed as easily as him. Or maybe her skin was rosy because she was riled. He'd been here so much, chipping away at Lem's chore list before the trauma center got too busy for him to manage both.

Also for Lem's sake, he needed to keep peace with Lauren. She obviously had a problem with his friendship with Lem. Humor might defuse the situation. At least the immediate tension.

Wordlessly, she joined him at the sink. Her bracelet jangled as she slid it off and set it on the windowsill. Sunlight swept through the panes and painted a golden shine to her hair, woven in a loose, classy braid coiled over one shoulder. She batted and blew at flyaways curling into her face.

He turned on the water. "For the record, I like your hair even when it's misbehaving."

She paused while setting a dish in his soapy water. Met his gaze and smiled in a drawn-out way that made Mitch see a sharp resemblance to one of Lem's ornery impending grins.

"You don't expect me or my hair to stop misbehaving just because you're here this week, do you?"

Mitch chuckled and began scrubbing dishes. Fresh citrus scents permeated the air. "Hardly."

Something unsettling oozed out of him, like suds from the sponge he squeezed over a dish. She'd said "this week."

She must not realize his eating with Lem was an every-morning ritual, even when they didn't have a mile-long chore list. She was liable to go from zero to mad and stay there the second she found out. And she'd find out soon enough.

Days before Lauren told Lem she was coming, Lem had given Mitch the summer to-do list. Much-needed home-improvement projects, knowing Mitch had limited time before the trauma center took off full force in the fall. Mitch wasn't about to neglect Lem's requests, because in addition to worrying about Lauren, Lem fretted over things breaking down in and around his house.

Mitch regretted that her warmth would cool and her smile dim when she learned how tightly his life was twined with Lem's, but it seemed inevitable. Jealousy was the only reasonable explanation why her beautiful eyes radiated anger every time he interacted with Lem.

Didn't she know she didn't have to always live like the outsider or waste one more breath believing she didn't belong? How sad was that?

Mitch studied her as she dried the dishes he set in the drain. Water glistened off her hands as she rescued a spoon he missed in the rinse water before the disposal gobbled it.

She hit a switch and the noise faded. Citrusy clean scents permeated the kitchen. Horses clomped and pistols *pop-popped* from Lem's favorite vintage Western show on a TV Mitch had set up in Lem's living room.

She peered over her shoulder at Lem and smiled. It plied his heart like putty and softened it to clay.

Out of respect for Lem's care concerning Lauren, how could Mitch reach out and pull her in? Pulling away from Lem wasn't the answer, even though that's probably what Lauren would prefer Mitch do. Loneliness plagued Lem enough, and Mitch wasn't about to abandon him on purpose.

On the spurs of the rowdy Western show came a comedy, as evidenced by Lem's whooping laughter. The sound made Lauren's face beam like a thousand moons at midnight. Her iridescent eyes and effervescent expression mirrored happiness he felt inside.

Their gazes connected then darted to the floor.

She poured Lem a fresh cup of coffee. Mitch resisted the urge to tell her Lem preferred the red chipped cup. She'd learn.

Mitch's penchant for being helpful put him in trouble at times. Lauren obviously knew how particular Lem was about certain things. She stacked plates and organized dishes exactly how Lem liked it, which was "how he had always done it."

Coffee cups came and went, but the cherished never left.

Lauren would learn that in time. He refused to infringe on the sacred, and she and Lem had shared losses that immortalized them from ever letting the importance of one another go.

She was just insecure right now, was all. Hopefully.

The lower cabinet creaked as she opened it. Haphazardly stacked pans toppled out onto her toes. Mitch hunkered next to her to help restack the storage space.

"Thanks," she murmured.

"Sure." He lifted heavy pans as she held the cranky-hinged cabinet door. "I've been meaning to fix that. Time gets away from me."

"I know the feeling," she said softly, surprising him. Vulnerable eyes flitted to his then to where Lem cackled at the TV. Then her gaze lowered to the floor.

She needed to know Mitch wasn't a threat. He had no intention of stealing her grandfather away from her. He also had no intention of pulling back on the reins of his and Lem's family-like relationship just because it rubbed her wrong.

The solution was to share Lem. The problem was on her end. She needed to come to the realization of how irrational her ire was. Even still, compassion tried to take up residence next to Mitch's resolve not to let her anger influence his actions.

Disarmingly quiet, she hung the damp dish towel on a rack affixed to the wall then joined Lem. Mitch found a screwdriver. He grew intent on working the creaks and kinks out of the cabinet. And from this uncomfortably tense and trying situation.

Mitch would be here long after Lauren left. Lem needed stability in his life. Lauren had made it perfectly clear she didn't intend to stay past summer's end. That reality made Mitch sad for Lem, who desperately wanted Lauren close. Had she any idea how deeply Lem ached for her and her nearness?

Hopefully Lauren didn't have the kind of self-absorption that his ex possessed which led her to decimate important relationships in her life.

He shouldn't liken Lauren to Sheila. But the recent breakup still smarted. Perhaps he should withhold judgment and extend grace, as Lem taught him growing up.

Lauren reentered the kitchen with a funny expression. "Trash runs tomorrow. He asked us to clean out his fridge."

On the way to it, Mitch caught sight of Lem, sniggering over his coffee cup as he eyed the pair. "I'm sure he did." Mitch shook his head.

Lauren reached in and started checking dates on goods while Mitch peeled the lids of leftover dishes and looked with fear.

Lauren set about helping him. Only, she popped the tops off, poked her nose inside and smelled the contents.

"You are brave." He indicated the containers. "No telling how long some of that stuff has been in there."

"Ew!" Lauren's nose pinched as she clamped a lid back on a bowl. "I don't think those beets were supposed to be pickled."

Mitch laughed and tried not to enjoy her response too much.

She shook her head and surveyed the fridge contents. "I've never seen anyone with so many butter containers in one place."

"He likes using them for storage. Not just food. He has an entire garage wall lined with shelves of butter tubs. Full of batteries, bolts, nuts, nails and everything imaginable."

Her lovely smile dimmed, making him wish he'd kept quiet. Last thing he wanted to do was cause her to have to contend with more hurt. He was just trying to make conversation.

All these containers and no way to butter her up? Think, Mitch.

"Wanna help me wash?" Mitch lifted a dozen empty tubs.

"Of course." She also took an armload to the sink and they began doing the dishes. Again. This time the silence between them leaned toward sweet instead of stilted.

What gave him the nerve, Mitch didn't know, but he rested his elbow against hers as they worked together. Just as in surgery. Like a team. Surprisingly, she didn't resist.

Joy rose when she squeezed the detergent bottle and giggled. He loved the sound and intended to ensure Lem heard it more. Lem worried himself sick over Lauren.

Not only that, laughter seemed to deter her from the frank jealousy she possessed over his friendship with her grandpa.

Lauren stilled then stiffened. He peered at what she did.

Photos on the fridge. As many of Mitch with Lem fishing and doing other recreational activities as there were of her and Lem.

She narrowed her gaze, turned fiercely on Mitch.

"Yeah, we like to have fun," he said. "I don't see the problem."

"There lies the problem. You don't see." She swept her hand

toward the fridge surface as though tempted to sweep the photos away, but stopped and eyed Lem. Her hand dropped with defeated finality. "Fishing was *our* thing. Always. Just me and Grandpa."

"This isn't a competition, Lauren." Mitch touched her arm gently.

She jerked it away—not so gently. "He isn't *your* grandpa."

He was, though. Sort of. Not by blood maybe, but by tears and time invested and years of talks of dreams and fears. "How about next time we go fishing, you go with us?" Mitch offered.

"How about next time we go fishing, you stay home?"

Stunned by the amount of scorch in her words, Mitch formulated his own retort but scaled back the rudeness. "Lem's life will go on as normal. Period."

She'd have to learn to live with it. Lem had reached out like a dad to Mitch growing up, and he wasn't about to abandon Lem over mismanaged emotions and envy. Hopefully soon she'd see how irrational, abrasive and self-destructive her jealousy was.

Otherwise she was in for a miserable summer. So was he.

And so was Lem. Which is why Mitch needed to cool his jets and try. Attempt to reason with her instead of letting his sympathy wane every time she opened her mouth. Problem was, every third time she opened her mouth, acid spewed out.

He leaned in and softened his tone. "Look, if we don't nip this tension between us now, Lem will get wind of it and worry."

That seemed to snap her to her senses. Thankfully the anger didn't make an ugly encore, and envy managed not to rear its head. Mitch doubled his efforts to listen more than he spoke. It worked. Slowly they began less caustic verbal exchanges, sparring at first then funny and sincere.

It was obvious they were both putting their best foot forward. For Lem's sake, of course.

They had a second set of dishes done in no time flat, yet Mitch could have stood there talking easily with her all day.

Talking turned to laughing, which turned into total hilarity when Mitch kept pushing the plastic bowls down only to have them pop up again. She giggled every time it happened. He did, too. The shared humor drastically disintegrated the tension.

"Help me hold them down?" Mitch entreated after another bowl bobbed up and flung an airborne glob of soap in his eye.

"Think physics. You have to turn them sideways and fill them at an angle. See? The water and the air stop resisting one another and meet halfway." As she showed him, their hands touched. Their motions startled then slowed at the pleasant but wholesome sensation. Not only that, her carefully exacted comment about meeting halfway held unmistakable emphasis.

He met her gaze. "Meeting halfway sounds better than fighting constantly."

The depth of beauty and bravery in her smile plunged all rational thought into disarray. He had not expected it.

Seemed to him they took their time near the end of the butter bowl baptizing marathon.

Afterward Lauren washed the table. "Mitch, are you going to the trauma center today?"

"No. I'm going tomorrow after I come here and clear out Lem's gutters. I've already rounded at the center today."

"May I come with you tomorrow, to check on Mara?"

"The texting teen?" He hadn't meant it to come out so abrupt. But seriously, what was Lauren's draw? The girl killed someone with whatever string of words she'd felt too important to pull over for. Talk about a death sentence.

Mitch's annoyance regained ground.

"Yes." A wary expression accompanied Lauren's answer. Perhaps his ire was a little overdosed. Yet hadn't his dad's life been snuffed out by an equally distracted driver?

Mitch scrubbed the opposite end of the table with fervor. "Suit yourself. But just to warn you, Mara's still on a ventilator, unconscious. There's also a possibility I'd get held up at the center because the other surgeon who's been graciously covering for me is on call at Refuge Memorial, his primary hospital."

Mitch really did not want Lauren getting attached to Mara. Nothing good could come of that. Right?

The stubborn set to her jaw resembled Lem's when things— like tractors—didn't go his way. "I'll take my chances."

Chapter Six

One hour into their trauma center visit the next day, Mitch guessed Lauren regretted saying that.

She took her chances coming in, all right.

A bus of summer-camp teens overturned shortly after Mitch and Lauren arrived, which filled the center with victims.

"Eighteen and counting," Ian informed Mitch. "No way to divert." Ian referred to the fact that the center was diverting low-risk patients to other hospitals until Mitch and Ian secured a second trauma team. Today that wasn't possible.

Kate handed him a chart. "Want me to call help in?"

Mitch nodded then faced Ian. "I need to get on the ball putting together another full-time trauma crew."

"Yeah. You've been tied up at Lem's, though."

"Not enough hours in a day to get everything accomplished that needs to be, this summer."

"Let me know how I can help."

"I will." Yet he knew Ian was already strapped for time with his divorce, court hearings, housing and custody stuff.

"Where's Lauren?" Mitch asked Kate, passing by with an armload of ice packs.

"Your new director assumed Lauren came to help. She assigned her to triage to treat non-emergent wounds which, thankfully, she did graciously. She's doing awesome, Mitch."

Still, he'd better go check. Mitch found Lauren and assessed her for signs of panic. None whatsoever, but he should ask anyway. "Are you okay?"

"Are you absurd?" She looked down the hall of writhing, wailing, wall-to-wall youth and laughed. "I'm not about to abandon you to the fate of all this teen angst. I'm the last person you should be worried about right now, Mitch. Your director, however, is having a total freak-out."

"So I heard. She's not used to trauma care."

Lauren made the funniest face. "Uh, hello? Neither am I."

Yet he didn't see her screeching down halls and complaining in front of patients and their families, as he'd received reports of the director doing. His mistake. Some applicants looked good on paper, yet they had no people skills.

"Point well taken, Lauren. I trust you. Unequivocally. I just wanted to make sure you weren't feeling overwhelmed."

"I doubt there's a staff member here who doesn't feel overwhelmed. Twenty patients hit the floor in two hours' time."

He grinned, loving the fire in her eyes. "You're made for this. You are."

"What I am is annoyed at the prospect of being babysat over a busload of mostly bumps and bruises. Now shoo!" But she smiled when she said it.

Satisfied she was okay for now, Mitch viewed X-rays. Then casted an ankle, miraculously the only bus-wreck fracture.

Between patients, he went to check on Lauren again.

She waved him toward another incoming gurney. "I'm fine. Check on that one. He looks kind of critical." She smirked then righted herself before anyone but Mitch could catch it.

When Mitch found nothing but a nosebleed on Gurney Guy, he realized two things: One, Lauren had a gift at triage. Two, she knew when it was okay to use humor to cope. Something he felt crucial to anyone in trauma care. Otherwise stress and burnout would run off the best ones.

After earnestly convincing Gurney Guy he wasn't bleeding

to death, Mitch held an ice pack to the kid's nose and issued fatherly hugs. Like Lem used to whenever Mitch had some kind of accident.

"Ever had a nosebleed this bad?" Gurney Guy asked him.

"Actually, yes." He nodded at Lauren, bandaging a wound nearby. "I nearly broke my nose crashing a new bike her grandpa got me. Refuge Community Church had pitched in on it."

"That's cool," the kid said.

"Not really." Mitch laughed. "Considering I'm probably the only kid in Southern Illinois to have an entire congregation present to cheer me on when I learned to wreck and ride it."

"You still go there?" The young man looked up to Mitch.

"Yep. That church has prayed me through med school and safely home from two wars. I have to say, though, that we didn't have the distinct pleasure of experiencing a bus crash."

That evoked the youth's laughter and erased tension from his features. Mitch pivoted and caught Lauren, within hearing range, watching them with an adoring expression.

"She your girlfriend?" the kid asked.

Mitch caught himself before he reacted sharply. "Nope. She's my nurse." But he could hope.

"She *could* also be your girlfriend. Maybe even your wife."

He could hope that, too. If he was hungry for more heartache. No, thanks. Still, the kid's words circled around his head, stalked his brain and mocked his steely resolve.

If Mitch were smart, he'd refuse to entertain the innocent suggestion at all. Instead he dwelled on how to get Lauren to join Refuge Community Church this summer, as Lem had requested of him. Refuge lived up to its name and was where Mitch met the PJs who had become his friends.

After releasing the now-calm nosebleed fellow to his mom's care, Mitch checked on other patients then the rest of his crew, including Lauren. Or maybe he just liked watching her work.

Her efficient yet calm body language revealed she'd picked up on the fact that the bus driver and chaperones had blown this wreck way out of proportion. Yet Mitch didn't blame them for being scared. He was thankful it wasn't worse.

It could well have been because they'd had to call Refuge's pararescue team to help firemen extract teens who were in reality more frozen with fear and panic than physically trapped. Still, God had evidently had His hand over the kids and the bus. *Thank You, God.*

The bus patrons had non-life-threatening injuries, but Mitch wanted everyone assessed nonetheless. That, along with parental worry and teen drama, made for a long, interesting day. By the time they had finished, dusk's velvet-purple evening winked at them through the trauma center's windows.

Lauren approached. "Mitch, some off-duty PJs are here."

"Probably checking the status of bus teens they helped rescue."

"They also offered to man the center overnight so your current crew can make like platelets and regroup."

Mitch laughed. "Is that how they put it?"

Lauren grinned. "Pretty much."

The group of elite men came down the hall like a formidable force, prepared to strong-arm Mitch's crew into a much-needed break should anyone protest. He knew those guys well.

He also respected his personal limitations, plus the well-being of his overworked crew. "No argument here. Let's give them a report, turn over the floor and head out."

One of the PJs, Brockton Drake, approached. "You look whooped. Go home, man. Get a good night's sleep."

Mitch stretched. "I will but I have a unique date first."

Lauren's head popped up from behind a computer chart she took notes on. He couldn't discern her expression, but knew it was one he'd never seen on her face before.

She blinked a couple times then closed the computer and walked off. Weird. He might've imagined it. Nope. Brock stared at her then faced Mitch. "Who's she and what's wrong with her?"

Mitch watched Lauren retreat like a soldier under fire. "She's Lem's granddaughter, visiting for the summer. She's also a nurse who's helping here sporadically. Name's Lauren."

"Why'd she walk off like that?"

"I'd like to know that very thing."

Brock refaced Mitch. "It's good to have you back in the States. Sorry your engagement with Sheila went south."

"Thanks. We never actually got engaged, though. She turned me down even after I bought the ring she picked out."

"Man, heartless. What happened?"

He shrugged. "She moved with her unit and moved on from me at the same time. Fell for another guy."

"That bites. But, hey, better to have it happen now. I hear Ian couldn't talk his wife out of a divorce."

"Yeah. He's having a rough go of it. Deployment and distance decimated a lot of relationships overseas."

"Not all of them, though. And you have a date, so it seems you're bouncing back okay."

"Actually, the date is with one of Lem's tractors. Specifically Lauren's tractor, Bess."

"Lauren's the girl you're into?"

Mitch handed Brock the patient roster. "I'm not into anyone. Especially not her. She lives in Texas."

"What's wrong with Texas? Part of our training's there."

"I have nothing against Texas. I love it, in fact. I just have a problem with being attracted to someone so far away."

Brock grinned. "Yeah, that's what I thought. You like her."

Did he just say that?

Brock tapped papers on the desk. "We have training ops the next couple weeks, but let me know if you need help after that."

"Might take you up on that. Lem added fixing Bess to my already-tight summer to-do list. I don't mind though, and would never want him to regret asking or feel like he's a burden."

"I hear he's done a lot for you."

"More than I could list in a lifetime. Anyway, he says Lauren loved to ride the tractor. So he asked me to make fixing Bess my top priority. I want to oblige Lem, even though it's another unexpected time-sucker."

"I hear ya."

"Hopefully fixing her tractor will put her in a good mood about my being at Lem's tomorrow."

"She has a problem with it?"

"Pretty much. It boils down to us both having lofty summer goals yet little time. Plus our plans clash on all fronts."

"You're innovative. You can figure out a way for them not to."

"In theory. In reality I won't be able to get Lem's stuff done once the center hits full status in the fall. The way we're getting slammed now, I only have this summer to do projects I put off due to deployment."

"I don't get what Lauren's problem is."

"I have to be at Lem's to do the chores, and Lauren wants uninterrupted, undistracted time with her grandpa."

"Doesn't sound feasible."

"It's not. She's struggling emotionally, so I'm giving them the space I can. But I need to be there most of my spare time or projects won't get done."

"I can help with the time-sensitive stuff a couple days before I leave and more when I get back. What all is there?"

"Might be easier to list what doesn't need repaired." Mitch chuckled. "I have a feeling some of it is Lem wanting me to be there when Lauren is."

"Cupid's arrow?" Brock laughed.

"Totally. Anyway, in addition to misguided matchmaking, Lem has a leaky roof, basement flooding and a rickety porch all the way around. I'm afraid the railing will give way and he'll take a tumble."

"We'll get that stuff knocked out when I get back."

"Awesome. Thanks, Brock. I appreciate you and your team stepping in to help."

"Keeps our paramedic skills up. I'll call you later about helping at Lem's."

"I owe ya one, buddy." Mitch clapped Brock's shoulder. With Brock being the only unmarried member of his pararescue team, he probably needed to keep busy anyway.

"Nah. Just pay me back in chili. I hear Lem's is kickin'."

Mitch laughed. "It is. Sounds good. See ya later, Brock."

Mitch twisted his watch then peered around. Where had Lauren gone? Probably with Mara, the texting teen. He really wanted to go work on Lem's old tractor as promised so Lauren could ride it. No rest for the weary. And no romance for the wary. Cupid could kiss off. *Hear that, bowhead? Abort mission. This arrow won't fly.*

Mitch talked with a few PJs, signed patients off then located Lauren, quietly stocking surgical rooms. "Ready?"

She didn't meet his gaze. "Sure."

"Something wrong?" Mitch asked in the truck. She hadn't spoken since leaving, and Lem's place was now a few miles away.

She shrugged. "Thanks for dropping me off." She fidgeted with his dash. Nervous gesture? If so, he wished she'd get her fingers away from the bad memory bound up in the glove box.

"Sorry to infringe on your date time." What? He scrambled to remember any conversation that might've led to the assumption. Then it hit him.

Mitch burst out laughing. "The date I mentioned is with a farm contraption named Bess. *Your* tractor, to be exact."

Lauren's cheeks reddened. "Oh!"

He decided neither to press nor tread.

By the snarky gleam entering her eyes, her thoughts about the misunderstanding must be too caustic to mention.

* * *

He did *not* want to know what she was thinking. He'd conclude her as a cross between the ultimate curmudgeon and ambivalence at its finest.

She'd completely shocked herself by experiencing disappointment that he was interested in someone. *That* sure came out of left field. It had so rattled her, she'd had to power-walk halls until her head had cleared. But then the saner part of her had kicked in—the part that preferred he had a date. It meant more opportunities for her to have quality time with Grandpa.

Would Mitch intrude on their time all summer? The more she got to know him, the more caring he seemed. Couldn't he see it bothered her not to have all the time she could with Lem?

Time to start dropping heftier hints.

"Need to stop anywhere on the way home?" Mitch asked.

Home. The word startled her coming out of his mouth. The ambivalence flared both because he thought of Lem's as home and because Mitch's use of *home* put him in a sudden domestic light.

"I'm dying for a cola." Grandpa normally kept his fridge stocked with her favorite goodies. This was the first time he hadn't. Of course she had dropped in with little notice. "I've taken too much for granted."

Mitch eyed her keenly. Compassion grew evident. Surely he'd be considerate of her need for time with Grandpa. She didn't want to smite Mitch's feelings or make him feel unwanted. She knew how that felt and didn't want to inflict it on others.

Still, he was beginning to really step on her proverbial toes. Thinking that made her wiggle her real ones, which ached from all the work they'd done.

She flexed her ankles. "I definitely need better shoes," she said at a gas station he pulled into.

Mitch's gaze found her feet. "Those look sensible."

Sensible? Lauren eyed her foot attire. "Hmm. I wonder when I went from stilettos to Dr. Scholl's."

He laughed. "Lem said you love to dress up."

"Not anymore." Fairy tales were made only to destroy little girls' dreams. She unlocked her seat belt.

"Really?" He lent his hand, helping her from the truck. Warmth trickled up her palm and her wrist.

Once down she swiped her hand across her leg, but the feeling didn't go away. "Occasionally I used to dress up and go out with my girl pals on weekends."

His eyebrows lifted as they headed in. "Used to?"

She shrugged. "Too much going on. I let my social life dwindle." Her dating life, too, thanks to her reclusiveness since the lawsuit. Another reason she didn't want to be around Mitch.

Everything about him reminded her of what she'd lost or given up. A career in the medical profession she'd dreamed of since a childhood tragedy took her parents away. Then the loss of her young patient that took *that* dream away.

Not only had her patient's death in childbirth left a newborn motherless, Lauren knew what it felt like to grow up without a mom, which is why she clung all the more to Grandpa.

Plus Mitch's closeness with Grandpa put her mind in a dark place and brought to light just how far she'd drifted away. After all, Grandpa's pantry was loaded with Dr. Pepper, which Mitch drank. Not the Pepsi or Coke she liked.

She didn't blame Grandpa for filling the void, but at least he could focus on her a smidge more than Mitch during her stay here. But Grandpa seemed oblivious to the idea for some reason, which admittedly stung. And scared her.

Were his mental faculties slipping?

Grandpa used to know her like the back of his eyelids during sleep. He had always perceived her feelings and soothed them.

Something had changed. Shifted.

And it was as depressing as school on a snow day.

When she reached the counter with her fountain soda, Mitch

was waiting with a case of Coke and Dr. Pepper. "I got this." He included her soda in his bill, then leaned close at her befuddlement. "Don't protest. Just say thanks."

Making matters worse, Mitch smelled like a man, smiled like he meant it and stared at her like she could someday mean something to him. Despite that she'd been intentionally cranky.

In short, he sounded, looked and felt like family.

But she wasn't about to be stupid enough to tell him.

"I insist!" Lem said upon their arrival.

Mitch and Lauren's gazes collided. They cracked simultaneous smiles. No doubt they were thinking the same thing. There was no arguing with Lem after his mind was made up.

"Okay, Grandpa. You can make us dinner." Lauren's wink did funny things to his pulse. Lauren's gaze glittered. His lingered. He felt stricken with how, in moments like these where Lem's one-of-a-kind quirks surfaced, he felt magnetically drawn to Lauren.

No matter how much they disagreed, their mutual love and admiration for Lem became an unexpected bond for them.

He snuck Lauren's case of soda into the pantry. Lem was probably too preoccupied with house repairs to ponder his usual special touches. A tiny reminder couldn't hurt because the twinge of pain in Lauren's eyes each time she had to move something of Mitch's over in the pantry or fridge was beginning to undo him.

Lem gave a grand arm wave. "In fact, you should've brought your entire trauma team. I imagine they're hungry after all that hard work."

"I invited them, but Ian's helping Kate move. She found an apartment, though it's farther from the center than she had wanted."

"Well, let 'em know they're always welcome here."

"They know, Gramps." Ugh. Lauren stiffened every time Mitch used the title. Yet Lem was the one who had requested

Mitch call him that. Maybe he hadn't expected the hurt it caused Lauren.

If Lem knew how much it bothered her, he'd probably dissuade Mitch from referring to him that way while she was here. But old habits die hard. He needed to dial it down this summer—for Lauren's sake. Lem had an affinity for bringing people together and pulling fringe dwellers into the fold.

"At least let us help you cook." Mitch bent to haul out the heavy-duty saucepan, but Lauren lifted a lighter one instead.

"He uses that one for spaghetti," Mitch explained before thinking. The fallen look to her face hit him hard.

He hadn't meant to tout how much more familiar he was than her with Lem's current domestic dealings.

Head dipping in a dispirited manner, she pushed the pan back into the cabinet and raked silky hair behind her ear.

Mitch drew close. "Hey, sorry. I—"

Her upshot palm abolished his apology.

At first he thought she was too mad to listen or speak. Yet the gloss surfacing in her eyes and rapid blinks hinted of hurt and unspeakable pain. His heart dropped through the floor, squeezed with concern then swelled with empathy and compassion.

Amid the rush of emotion, he almost reached for her. No telling what stopped him.

She schooled her features as Lem clomped back in with a sack of potatoes. Mitch rushed to take them, which earned a dirty look from Lem, who muttered something about being capable of carrying taters. Lem's protests elicited a fragile smile from Lauren.

His guilt eased, yet his concern for her deepened. Maybe he needed to be more sensitive?

Likewise, in time perhaps she'd be less sensitive.

Something more than simple jealousy had fueled it. He was determined to find out what.

Moonlight slivers shone when Lem held back the curtain.

"Since it's dark, I suggest we wait until tomorrow to mess with cantankerous Bess."

Mitch helped carry serving dishes to the table. "Remember Brock, one of the Refuge PJs?"

Lem nodded. "The brawny, strapping, amber-haired one?"

"Yeah. He's coming over here tomorrow to help me out with some projects on that to-do list."

"That's right nice of him. I'll have some lunch in the fridge for you, how's that?"

Mitch smiled. "Brock loves hard work almost as much as he loves food. So that'll suit him just fine. He mentioned chili."

"I'll thaw a big batch then. Lauren and I have a special day planned tomorrow. Don't we, carrottop?"

She looked nervous, like Grandpa might bring Mitch into it. "Yes. I'm looking forward to it."

"I'm looking forward to getting some stuff done here," he said to alleviate her fear that he'd try to intrude on their day. Little did she know he was working on a project for her benefit. Not just for Lem, but Mitch found himself looking forward to seeing the joy on Lauren's face when Bess fired up.

Bess the tractor had refused to run for years. Four and a half, to be exact. Lem said Lauren loved to tinker around on her.

He'd had no reason to run Bess since Lauren moved away because he had other tractors that were more dependable and less sentimental.

Bess pretty much ran on her own terms, kind of like Lauren. He knew because Lem had confided generously.

Maybe that accounted for why the bond he felt with Lauren seemed stronger than the norm for two people who'd recently met. Lem had been telling them stories of one another for years now.

Mitch would be better off to leave the bond alone. Feeding the romance brewing between them would be foolish on several fronts. Among his old heartache and new work responsibilities that gave him pause, Lauren lived too far away for going further to feel safe.

Chapter Seven

Lauren couldn't remember looking more forward to a day. "Turkey and Cheddar Jack's my favorite." She tucked the sandwiches she'd made into a picnic basket on Grandpa's table.

"Mine, too. Except I prefer provolone." Grandpa set a thermos of coffee near their cooler basket.

"Since when? You're the one who got me hooked me on Cheddar Jack."

"Since Mitch turned me on to provolone."

Familiar slices of jealousy cut through her. She fought it with a vengeance and a prayer. *This day is too important to let unruly emotions ruin special time with Grandpa. Lord, please help me.*

"Let's go outside and pick us some fruit for the day. We'll be in the boonies and out late, so let's stock up in case we get stranded hunting abandoned mansions to explore, like old times."

They headed out with a bowl and plucked apples, peaches and pears from Lem's few fruit trees. While he didn't have a lot of trees, they all yielded an enormous amount of fruit.

"Grandpa, we need to pick these peaches or the branches will crack. They're bowing and will be brushing the ground soon."

"We'll do that when we get back. How's that sound?"

"Good. What will we do with all those peaches?" She wondered if Mitch liked cobbler or pie best. Then she wondered why she was wondering so much about Mitch today. His genuine smile yesterday upon hearing of her and Grandpa's excursion had been the first thing she'd pictured upon waking this morning.

It had solidified in her mind how caring Mitch really was. He truly did have the best interests of others at heart. Yet he also had an air of strict self-protection that she'd really like to breach in order to better understand him.

What would a man that amazing have to be afraid of?

"Let's let the rest ripen." Grandpa started back inside.

Lauren followed, carting two bowls of fresh fruit. "Did you remember to set out chili for Mitch and his friend?"

Why was her mind so focused on Mitch today?

"Almost forgot. You do that and I'll whip up a batch of corn bread. Mitch likes it with his chili."

Lauren pulled out the chili and eyed Grandpa. "Mind if I make them some dessert?"

"That'll be dandy. Mitch loves cobbler like crazy. And from what he tells me, Brock eats anything that doesn't move."

She laughed. "Cobbler it is." As they prepared cobbler and corn bread side by side, an elated sensation wove into her. A deep sense of companionship and belonging seeped in, as well as the strongest feeling of contentment she'd had in years.

She tried not to acknowledge how good it made her feel to make dessert for a man. Specifically a man like Mitch.

Just when did the desire to bless and please him creep in?

Nevertheless, Grandpa loved cobbler, too. He always doused it with ice cream, a staple in this freezer.

Memories swarmed her. Good ones that made her smile inside and out. How could she have forgotten all these little nuances and details about life with Lem? "I love you, Grandpa."

He paused and grinned. "What brought that on?"

"Things like this just make me realize how much I miss

you. And how much I've missed by not coming to spend time with you."

"Well, don't you worry. We'll make up for lost time this summer. Like today. If I can keep from getting us lost."

Lauren laughed and let herself enjoy having something to look forward to. "That's what you always used to say. Yet you never once got us lost."

"Well, I'm not driving today. You and that QRS are."

She giggled. "GPS. It's a satellite navigation system."

"If you say so. There's Mitch with his truck now."

Her heart gave a little flutter at the sound that had become familiar in mornings. Mitch's truck door closing. He stepped in and handed her his keys. "Wanna see where my truck's navigational and safety stuff is?"

"Sure." She tried not to notice how his worn charcoal T-shirt and jeans showcased his impressive physique.

Mitch accompanied her out and helped her attach the GPS to the dash. "Here's the emergency brake. Here's how to put it in four-wheel drive. Try it."

She got in and fired up his truck. They drove across Grandpa's yard. Lauren listened while Mitch explained where all the important controls, knobs and buttons were.

A hilly snatch of terrain that couldn't be resisted loomed. She gunned it a little then eyed Mitch, expecting him to scold her for the momentary orneriness.

Instead, he grabbed a ceiling handle. "Go for it."

Wow. She did not expect that. "Really?"

A slow grin crept across his face, giving it even more appeal. She slammed the pedal to the floor, and the truck peeled out and ramped dusty hills. Mitch *whooped* like Lem, making Lauren laugh.

Grandpa was probably wondering what all the dust was about, so she drove back to the driveway like the well-behaved granddaughter she wasn't.

Lem stood on his porch, shaking his head and laughing.

"He's something, isn't he?" Mitch eyed Lem fondly. Then faced Lauren. "You have more of his traits than you realize."

"What, his penchant toward orneriness?"

Mitch chuckled. "Well, that, yes. But I mainly meant his uncanny ability to handle life's problems rather than let the problems handle him."

Her grin faded. "I think you're mistaken. That's not me."

The gleam in his eyes grew fonder, and firmer. "Oh, yeah. It is. You'll see. You're the kind whose nettle surfaces the more they're squeezed. Some strengths shine in weakness, Lauren."

"If you say so."

No one said anything for long moments. She was taken by how comfortable it was to be alone with him. Did he feel the same way?

"Thank you, Mitch, for doing this. I know I haven't been the nicest. So it's supersweet of you to loan us your truck for the day." She cut the engine, missing the fun of riding around.

He smiled. "No problem. I hope the two of you have fun."

"I'll be careful with your baby."

He stiffened and paused. Then peered toward the glove box, then away. He nodded more stiffly. "I know you will. I checked all the fluids, oil, transmission, wiper. And she's gassed up."

When a downtrodden look accosted his face before he could mask it, she felt sudden remorse over not inviting him along. Should she?

"What chores do you have planned today?" she asked.

"Knocking out another couple items on his to-do list. Fixing the fence and replacing his screen door. Which I need to get out of here." Mitch reached into the back of the truck and hefted out a solid wood-and-glass carved door as if it was cardstock light.

She eyed the price tag he ripped off, and…wow.

"Do you need help paying for that?"

He shook his head. "Lem went in half. Or thinks he did. He insisted so I kinda fibbed and told him it was only a couple hundred bucks. I didn't want him to have a flimsy door since he lives alone. This place doesn't have a high crime rate, but it's better to be safe."

"Thanks, Mitch, for all you do for him." For some reason, she felt supersentimental about it today. "You could go with us if you want."

He rose slowly after setting the door against the siding. "Thanks. But I think I'll hang here. Brock should be over soon."

Wow. She did not like the letdown she felt at his answer. She had wanted special, extended alone time with Grandpa. Mitch was making that possible. She should be happier than a raccoon in Grandpa's cornfield right now.

So why wasn't she?

Mitch accompanied her inside. His eyes landed on the corn bread and cobbler. His face erupted in elation.

"Lauren made that." Lem indicated the cobbler.

Mitch's face lit up in surprise and delight.

Her insides turned to mush as he peered at the cobbler then back at her with deep appreciation.

What if he didn't like it? Her nerves quivered.

He took a piece to taste and pretended to melt to his knees as he savored it. He liked it!

"Now, that's perfection right there." He took a second bite and fastened her with another long look of surprise and approval. "I'm touched and impressed. And my taste buds are very, very happy right now."

She felt too giddy to speak, so she just nodded and smiled then turned to wash the already-clean counter so he wouldn't see the blush and ridiculously gargantuan grin taking over her face.

Lem came back into the kitchen. "Ready to go?"

Hmm. Just where had she left her brain? "Yep. Let's hit the road."

Mitch loaded their basket in the truck. "Call if you have trouble." He gave her a paper with his number on it.

This made Lauren's insides feel even more giddy. "We'll be really late getting back."

"Not a problem. Brock's coming to help before a training op. He's giving me a ride home after we get some stuff done. Ian will drop me back off here tomorrow to get my truck."

"Thanks, Mitch." Gack! How many times would that sentiment bounce out of her mouth? Maybe she thanked him profusely out of guilt? She'd been so ornery to him. Gratitude overwhelmed her for his giving—and forgiving—heart.

"Have fun." He patted the truck then stepped back.

Lauren and Lem waved as Brock passed them outside Lem's driveway. "That's nice of him to help."

"Yeah, those PJs are something else. They've reformed this community of Refuge."

"I have a feeling Mitch and his trauma crew will do the same for Eagle Point."

"The unemployment rate was sky-high. The center definitely boosted morale. I feel terrible taking time away from his trauma work. I guess he didn't really expect the place to take off the way it has…so fast anyway."

Nor did Lauren expect her pulse rate to take off at every mention of Mitch. Only, today her respect for Mitch and growing intrigue with him overpowered the troublesome jealousy and envy.

She knew Mitch had to be sick and tired of her repeated mishaps and missteps of giving in to envy. He saw the jealous reaction, sure. But did he see her angst about it after?

Why all of a sudden did his opinion of her matter so much?

"I know for a fact he doesn't mind helping you, Grandpa."

That must've comforted Lem because he stopped chewing his cheek.

Lauren and Lem spent the day driving along the Mississippi exploring historic towns, museums and libraries. They stopped at a peach orchard and ate scrumptious homemade cobbler topped with vanilla ice cream.

"This isn't as good as yours," Grandpa doted. "Mitch thought so, too. I know there won't be a drop of your cobbler left when we get home tonight."

She smiled, remembering Mitch's genuine reaction.

After having their fill of orchard goodness, they headed to the southernmost tip of Illinois to visit a monument where some of their ancestors from Civil War times were buried.

They stopped and perused in an historic bed-and-breakfast shop known for its authentic period antiques.

Lauren purchased Mitch a statue of a doctor holding a little boy's hand while a nurse gave a shot. When Grandpa eyed her funny, she quickly found a trinket for Brock, too, lest Grandpa get any ideas that she was growing fond of Mitch.

She absolutely wasn't. Though tingles walked up her spine, it was best to ignore it.

"What now, carrottop?" Lem asked once back on the road.

"Want to go for a hike at one of the state parks nearby?"

"Wish I could. I can't go more than a few miles, though."

"Oh." Last time Grandpa could hike circles around her. Could a person age that much in five years? She needed to have a private conversation with Mitch about Grandpa's health.

"It's too hot to hike today anyway," she said to make Grandpa feel better about his lost stamina. They drove at leisure along a scenic route and spent time perusing specialty shops before driving through a wildlife refuge. "I enjoy seeing the familiar birds, animals, trees and foliage that makes Illinois more beautiful than I remembered."

Lem smiled and nodded.

Memories of times like this with Grandpa also added to its beauty and appeal. Now she'd have new memories to draw upon. The thought of time with Grandpa being reduced to rare memories instead of daily experiences brought a profound sadness upon her. And disconcerting dread. *Please don't take him anytime soon, God.*

Lem adjusted his seat belt. "Remember when we used to drive to the riverfront mansions and pretend like we lived there?"

"I do."

"Let's."

"Today?"

"Sure. Why not?"

They drove to a gas station, and Lauren filled Mitch's tank. Then they purchased a jug of homemade tea from the village café.

"I can't believe we're doing this." A little later, they arrived at their favorite abandoned mansion. Lauren felt like a miscreant, squished between two ivy-colored fence panels. She helped Lem and giggled.

"What? Pretending isn't against the law."

"No, but sneaking onto private property is."

"This is public property. It's bank-owned. Besides, we won't harm anything. We'll just eat in the courtyard and pretend we live here."

"Don't be surprised if the cops show." She laughed at the thought of Mitch having to bail them out of jail.

Once on the brick patio, they dusted off a wrought-iron table and two chairs. "Mitch has a similar set at his place."

Lauren pursed her lips. "I wouldn't know." Lauren spread a tablecloth on the table then put their food on it.

"The deeper the South, the sweeter the tea." Lem pulled out the iced-tea jug.

They enjoyed lunch in the courtyard amid a symphony of singing birds, cicadas and chirping crickets. Two curious baby squirrels kept them company. Their acorn antics provided comic relief. A watchful mama squirrel occupied a branch above the patio. "Mitch would have loved watching all these critters frolic."

Lauren ignored the feelings bubbling up with Grandpa's mention of Mitch. She viewed the abandoned mansion. "I can imagine this place in its prime. It's sad they've let it go to ruin."

"They need money or someone to renovate and repair it. A lot of these Mississippi river mansions have been let go."

Grandpa inspected artistically carved eaves and whistled. "Mitch's carpentry skills could do wonders with this place."

Lauren set down her water. Every ten minutes of their trip, he'd mentioned Mitch this or Mitch that. It hadn't bothered her until now. A yucky feeling hit Lauren that jealousy had somehow stowed away in the truck and accompanied them here after all.

It continued a little later on the road as Lem marveled at four huge funny farm silos they passed. They'd been painted with life-size, to-scale *Flour, Sugar, Tea* and *Coffee* logos. "Take a picture for Mitch. He'll get a kick out of that."

"I'd like to give Mitch a kick, all right," she muttered.

Grandpa put his hand on his ear. "What's that? You'd like to give Mitch a kiss?"

Her face warmed. "No. That is definitely not what I said."

Grandpa scratched his cheek and pushed back his cap. "Then I need to get my hearing aid checked. Maybe the battery's croaking out on me. What *did* you say?"

"Nothing important." Somehow, even without Mitch present, this trip turned out to be all about him.

Man, was she selfish. To even hear her own thoughts disturbed Lauren to the point she couldn't stand it anymore. "Grandpa, I have to confess something. I lied to you."

"Oh? Well, obviously something's bothering you, go ahead."

"I have major issues with Mitch. Well, he's not the problem. I am. I am very jealous of your attachment to him."

"I'm sorry, love. You mean the world to me. Ya know?"

"I know. I'm sorry. I just guess I need reassuring right now. How pathetic is that?"

"Not pathetic at all. We have a God who delights in reassuring us and reminding us of His love and care. His thoughts toward you are always good, Lauren. Even when your mind and heart act a little unruly. He understands your insecurity."

She laughed. "Thanks. But it's more than a little unruly."

"A little or a lot unruly, He still loves you. So do I."

"Mitch could do without me, though."

For some reason, Grandpa smiled slowly.

And didn't utter another word for miles.

"Pull over up here," Grandpa said as they drove through a gorgeous state park, lush with cyprus and other area trees. Thousands of purple, yellow, white and orange wildflowers carpeted the foot of gorgeous rock faces jutting into blue sky.

She pulled over to the scenic view area, and they got out of the truck to stretch. Something in the field caught her eye. "Oh! Elderberries. Let's pick some. Maybe can them together."

"Good idea. Mitch's been wanting to learn how."

Her smile deflated. "I meant me and you, but I suppose I could stand him being in the kitchen, too."

Grandpa's mouth curled in and his eyes sharpened. She couldn't tell if he was perturbed or pleased. She sighed. "See? I'm hopeless."

"No, but you are capable of controlling your response to hard things."

He was right. She let herself soak in the surroundings. Sounds. Smells. Sights. The texture of velvety flowers, scratchy branches and marble, smooth rocks. Birds serenaded them with forest tunes that reminded Lauren of animated cartoon movies.

Lem leaned against a weathered fence. "It's peaceful here."

"How'd you find this place? It's off the beaten path. Wait. Let me guess…Mitch brought you here."

Lem eyed her, head bent and eyebrows squished. He started to look a little like a charging bull.

"All right, to my credit, I *did* think good thoughts about him the whole time we were in that military cemetery in Mounds. He must have sacrificed a lot in order to serve our country."

"More than you know." Lem turned a pinecone over and over. It suddenly resembled a wooden grenade. "What do you mean?"

"His girlfriend dumped him for another doctor after having him fork over a fortune for an engagement ring. So you can understand why he's a little gun-shy of romance right now."

Whoa. Why would Grandpa bring that up? "Fine by me because I'm not interested in him like that."

Grandpa laughed so hard his throat whistled Dixie.

"What?"

"I think part of why your emotions are so out of whack is because deep down, you *are* interested."

She blinked.

He chuckled. "I'm serious."

"So am I."

Lem sobered. "I just want you to be okay, carrottop, in the event something was to happen to me."

"Don't talk like that."

"I have to. I want peace of mind that you'll be all right."

"Don't worry about me. I will be fine. And so will you. If Mitch says you're healthy then you need to trust him."

For some reason as they picked more berries along the road, Lauren couldn't get Mitch's breakup off her mind. "How long ago did that heartbreak go down with Mitch?"

"About the same time as yours. Which I find interesting, seeing as how I was praying for God's will for both of you in a future mate." Grandpa placed the berries inside their picnic basket, which Lauren carried.

"You're reading too much into it. Does he talk about her very much?" Lauren asked as they headed back toward Mitch's truck.

"Those details are his to share."

"Well, that's not fair. You tell him everything about me. Yet hold his secrets sacred?"

Grandpa scratched his head. "Nah, I don't. Do I?"

She planted hands on her hips. "What about your stories in the truck on the way to the ribbon-cutting that first day?"

"Well, I suppose I do share a lot about you with him. But that just proves I think about you as much as I do him, if not more. If something happened to me, he'd take good care of you."

Sudden stark desperation in Grandpa's eyes unnerved her. She rested her hand on his cheek. "God will take care of me."

"Who says He might not use Mitch to do it?"

She started to open her mouth, but frankly, had no retort.

Because in truth, she'd been thinking steadily about Mitch all day. And admittedly, she missed his presence today more than she wanted to admit to anyone. Especially herself.

"I can see why he means so much to you, Grandpa. He's a truly special individual."

"One you'd be smart to pay attention to, heartwise."

The last thing she ought to do was ponder what Grandpa might mean by that.

Yet the two-hour drive home was filled with nothing but pondering Mitch. No matter how hard she tried to think of other things, his face kept cropping up in her mind.

This simply would not do.

Especially since Grandpa hadn't mentioned Mitch since leaving the park.

Yet Lauren's mind continued to want to wrap itself around the strapping doctor whose heart and manners were sweeter than the Southernmost tea.

Chapter Eight

When Mitch arrived at the center early on Monday morning he discovered it eerily sedate. Good. He could work on staffing and recruiting trauma team members.

He found Kate huddled over a cup of coffee and the morning paper. "What gives?" He didn't want to say the words *quiet, calm* or *slow* because then they'd get slammed.

She set down her pencil and stretched. "That amazing administrative clerk you hired is brilliant. She had the fabulous idea to try traveling trauma nurses and rent-a-docs."

"So Nita is working out well?" She was the wife of a medic on Mitch's team who was still deployed overseas.

"Very well. Unfortunately, the director you hired isn't on my Employee Honor Roll list." Kate scowled.

"So I heard."

"I don't have a good feeling, Mitch. Keep an eye on her."

He nodded, explicitly trusting Kate's instinct. "I regret that the center's unexpected early opening hasn't afforded me the kind of time to hire key office people that I'd like." Kate's newspaper crinkled as he pushed it aside to sit.

"Look at the bright side. You're taking special care to hire staff to do direct patient care and triage."

"True." Mitch admired how Kate was great about pointing out the positives. That had been invaluable in combat care.

She turned to go, but before retreating, said boldly, "The halls feel empty without Lauren."

What a coincidence. Mitch felt it, too.

Fortunately his feelings didn't lead him around on a leash.

With everything going on, he needed to be commandeered by common sense right now. Kate studied his reaction intently.

Nosy girl was baiting him for information. Not inclined to bite, he made his features stoic.

Kate groaned. "You disengaged yourself from this conversation faster than flame follows mortar," she said with levels of annoyance that made Mitch laugh.

"First off, this wasn't a conversation. It was a stealthily exacted interrogation session and you know it."

Kate laughed.

"Secondly, I'll make my lack of intel up to you by giving you the rest of the day off with pay."

"Lovely. That downs my excuse for not unpacking boxes."

Humor and renewed thankfulness hit Mitch over his team's willingness to uproot their lives to help start this center. Would Lauren ever uproot hers to be near Lem? He couldn't get past feeling that she completed his team. Until now, he'd been successful at ignoring how often she'd crept into his mind this early in the morning.

Mitch needed a distraction. He met with the director about staffing and applied for grants. Then he organized with media and city officials a community call for trauma center employees. Eventually Ian sauntered into his office with two cups of coffee. He put one in front of Mitch.

"Thanks. What's the status of staff and patients?"

"Most have been transferred out or were discharged except the few, like Mara, who are too unstable for transfer."

"Thankfully Refuge and visiting staff have stepped in to cover shifts until I can hire more floor nurses."

The voice-mail alert on his phone beeped. He replayed it.

Lem's voice, inviting him to stop over for breakfast, as was customary. Ian dropped off Mitch in Refuge later than usual.

He and Ian could've gone earlier, but Mitch was really trying to give Lauren and Lem as much space as possible and still have enough time to get the list done for Lem. Ian dropped off Mitch in Lem's driveway, then Mitch strode to his truck to retrieve the keys Lauren had left in the ignition. As he reached for his folio, which contained notes on Lem's projects, a letter fell out. He didn't recognize the writing until it was too late.

"Dearest Mitch, this is the hardest letter I've ever had to write…"

A sick feeling fisted his gut. He clenched his hand around Sheila's Dear John letter and thought about torching it. He didn't fancy blowing up his truck though, so he popped open the glove box and crammed the note in. He felt around. The pricey ring was still there. He refused to bring it into his home.

That ring cost what a small home might. Yet Mitch couldn't bring himself to take it out of the glove box where Sheila had left it…along with this letter.

Why was it out? Maybe Lem had to get into the glove box for a flashlight or something. He took a moment to compose himself before leaving the truck…and the memories of that unexpected heartbreak behind.

He tucked the folio under his arm and went to pull out his tool box. His hand wrapped around something papery. Lifting the handle, he peeled a note of a different sort, taped to it.

Unlike the handwriting on the last letter, he didn't recognize this one at all. He unfolded it.

Hi, Mitch. Just wanted to say thanks for letting us use your truck. We had a lot of fun and made some great new memories. My only regret for the day was that you weren't included in the memories, too. I'm sorry about how I've been acting. I don't know what's wrong with me, but I do know you're not to blame for how I feel.

Thank you for being in Grandpa's life. Once I go back to Texas, I'll rest better knowing he has someone as special and strong as you watching out for him.
Love, Lauren.

Love, Lauren?
The two words pressed his mind with relentless force.
Love, Lauren.
The concept hadn't remotely entered his mind until the two words ambushed him.

Sheila's note had ended with *Regards, Sheila.*

The difference between the two letters and how each of them made him feel was something that taunted him all the way to Lem's porch. He couldn't shake the inner sense of a growing attachment to Lauren. This simply wouldn't do.

He'd thank her for the gesture but get rid of the letter. Keeping it could endear him to her in ways that would matter to his heart. He went back to the truck, put Lauren's letter next to Sheila's and closed them up where they belonged.

Lauren met him inside Lem's door. "I heated your plate."

A childhood flash of Mitch's mom meeting his dad at the door with hot dinners each night accosted Mitch out of nowhere.

He stared at the plate then met Lauren's gaze. "Thanks."

She had no idea the sweet but forgotten memory she'd just evoked. Unfortunately that memory also bore the intriguing association of what life with Lauren as a wife might be like.

Nonsense. He had more pressing things to think about than flimsy daydreams. Because her home was in Texas. And his heart was here in Illinois, with the trauma center. And he wasn't willing or ready to set it out on another high-risk wall, like Humpty Dumpty.

"Everything okay, Mitch?" Lauren eyed his untouched plate.

He forced himself to poke the food around. He didn't have the heart to tell Lem he'd already eaten. Plus, for some reason, thoughts of Lauren leaving at summer's end obliterated his appetite. For Lem's sake, of course.

"Still a little tired. Haven't caught up on sleep." Not a lie.

She nodded, but the concern etched into her extraordinary features was palpable enough for him to diagnose doubt.

He noticed something else, too. Her makeup appeared fresh. "Did you and Lem go somewhere fun this morning?" he asked, because he was really interested in her answer.

Her eyes darted toward the floor. "No. Just, you know, fiddling around the fields."

Which equated to her putting on makeup merely for his arrival? Mitch couldn't discern why that both pleased and uneased him.

Midway through the day, she got a call from her building contractors. Then one from the friend she went into business with. Both calls left Lauren visibly upset. Not that she was demonstrative about it. He knew her well enough by now to be able to tell with very little outward emotion on her part.

"What's wrong, carrottop?" Lem asked over the counter.

"Nothing to worry about."

Then what put the glisten of tears in her eyes? It was enough to worry Lem too because he gnawed the inside of his cheek like he always did when he was worried. "You can tell us."

She eyed Mitch, then Lem.

Mitch straightened. "I think I left something in the truck." He made swift strides toward the door so Lauren could feel free to talk about whatever went down during the phone call.

But as he passed Lauren, she snagged his sleeve. "You can stay." She eyed Grandpa funny. "The contractors are trying to pull a fast one and delay the timeline in our contract. My friend may need me to come home sooner. Grandpa, I'm so sorry."

Lem's countenance fell. "How soon?"

She looked like she was unsuccessfully swallowing a brick. "M-maybe as soon as next week. For sure by next month." Her chin quivered and she hovered on the edge of tears.

Lem froze at the stove. His motions became fidgety then twitchy. He gnawed his cheek and roiling tongue the way he did when he was at high-fret level. "Do what ya gotta do, I reckon."

"It'll work out," Mitch blurted, disappointed for them both. This threw a wrench in everything—for everyone.

"Mitch is right," Lem said. "We just gotta have faith." He tugged Mitch's sleeve. "Come 'ere." He met Lem in the hall. "I need you to run me to town right quick. She likes cola and it dawned on me this morning that I don't have a drop in the house."

Mitch put a calming hand on Lem. "I got it. Don't worry."

Now Lem's eyes glistened. "Maybe if I paid better attention to her instead of being so scattered and obsessed with winterizing this house, she wouldn't want to leave." He trembled.

Mitch thought carefully about what he was going to say. "Lem, to be completely honest, I don't think she wants to leave."

"You think?" His countenance lifted, and trembling abated.

Mitch nodded. "God's at work." He smiled. "Just trust."

Lem blinked. "You remember?"

"I remember every phrase you taught me because I began to live my life by your word and God's. Let's eat."

Lauren observed them in a subdued manner as they returned to the table. Lem said grace then rubbed his palms. "Dig in."

Mitch fingered a flower petal on the table. It felt velvety rather than plastic. "Wow. Those are real."

"Lauren brought them for me." Lem's voice had grown thick.

Lauren's head dipped with a semiguilty look.

Mitch leaned over when Lem went to the restroom. "What?"

Her lips pursed. "I took them from his flower beds."

Mitch laughed. "He doesn't know?"

She shook her head. "He has so many. He'll never miss them."

Mitch nodded. "So which one of you likes fresh flowers?"

"Me. But he got me started picking them when I was little."

As Mitch imagined Lauren's life with Lem, he felt a little like an intruder today. The feeling didn't shake off well.

After he ate, Lauren insisted on washing his dish. Then the three retreated outside and went to war with Grandpa's most ancient tractor, affectionately called Bess the Beast.

Lauren eyed the tractor's bumps and bruises. "She needs more repair than Monday's marathon of trauma patients combined. I like to tinker on these old tractors."

"Me, too," Mitch admitted. "Now, whether they run or not afterward is a different story."

The three shared a laugh then set about fixing Bess. Lem began finding random reasons to leave the two of them alone. Mitch watched him go inside for the umpteenth time to look for another "whatchamacallit." Last trip in, it was to search for a "doohickey" and the time before, a "hoopendiker," whatever those were.

"I'll give him credit, he's creative with excuses."

Lauren's eyes widened, proving she was as surprised as Mitch that he'd acknowledged Lem's matchmaking maneuvers out loud.

"You noticed his matchmaking penchant, huh? We need to help Grandpa see that a summer romance between us would never work."

"Yeah, because that's all it would be." When he played, he played for keeps. None of this temporary stuff. He was far from ready to hand out his heart again, and she was not only Texas-bound but highly annoyed at Mitch's intrusion in Lem's life.

"I'd hate for Lem to get his hopes up, only to be disappointed. The sooner we convince him to disable Cupid and confiscate his ill-aimed arrows, the better," Mitch stated.

Lauren laughed. "Good luck with that. You've no idea how stubborn he can be."

Though Mitch did know, he smiled. "Should I be scared?"

Her eyes shone vulnerably for a flash. "Very. So should I."

They shared a laugh, yet a trepid element resided in it.

Midway into lunch at Lem's the next chore day, Mitch received a frantic phone call from Nita that her brilliant plan wasn't working so well today.

He got off the phone and explained to Lem and Lauren, "Nita feels it best if the regular staff trickle back in. The center's heating up with complicated patients. The traveling staff isn't as familiar with where things are, which lessens efficiency and safety."

"We understand," Lem said. "Seconds matter in trauma care."

A concept which disturbed Mitch more than he cared to process when Lauren didn't offer to come to the center with him. After all, she was more familiar with where things were than all the traveling nurses and rent-a-docs combined.

Yet it wasn't her fault Mitch had come to depend on her despite her warnings she would do it only temporarily. Her same code of ethics that kept her at the center the bus crash day kept her seated now. He knew by the stubborn look on her face that she was still fearful of the more complicated cases, which apparently the center had today.

Fine. Maybe she wasn't the perfect person for the job, but she was better qualified than the crew there now. Still, he'd put her in a position she hadn't asked for, and a lack of preparedness on his part shouldn't constitute an emergency on hers. Bottom line: he needed to hire someone for her position rather than wait and hope she'd take it. Right?

Lord, grant me guidance and wisdom.

Mitch left for the center fighting frustration over not getting more done at Lem's. Perhaps if he'd gone over earlier today and yesterday, he might've made better headway on the work.

Yet he'd wanted to honor Lauren's wishes to spend uninterrupted time with Lem. Her contagious laugh still echoed in his ears long after leaving Lem's.

Once at the center, Mitch poured his heart and skill into

the cases that captivated him. All the while, he did his level best to fend off other images bent on captivating him. Those of Lem's granddaughter. Of fiery hair that matched her temper. He didn't mind if she never tamed both.

Ian approached. "What's that look about, Wellington?"

Mitch shook his head. "Trust me, you don't want to know." He kept intentionally busy the rest of the night.

When relief came on shift the next morning, he returned to Lem's to help finish the tractor. Mitch hated to begin a project and not finish, but sleep was essential, too. Thankfully he'd been able to catch some z's in the trauma center doctors' lounge between cases. Plus, he'd promised.

"You look haggard and worn," Lem commented when he arrived.

"I was on call all night."

Mitch only slightly regretted that Lauren looked remorseful. She hadn't offered to help and Mitch hadn't pushed. He wanted to tread lightly and give her an opportunity to take the initiative. "Let's go fix old Bess." They headed outside.

"She's my favorite." Lauren patted the tractor's gills next to the engine they'd spent many hours repairing.

"Ready for a ride?" Lem asked her.

"You don't have to ask me twice." Lauren climbed the tractor like an outlaw would a getaway horse and fired up Bess.

"Away she goes," Lem said as he and Mitch watched Lauren bump and plod along the road and then to a field.

Lauren eventually circled back around and peered expectantly at Mitch and Grandpa from beneath sun-shielded eyes. "One of you handsome gents care to join me?"

Grandpa muttered something about needing to water his vegetable garden and shoved Mitch forward, causing Lauren to laugh. Mitch loved hearing it and seeing the deep-seated tension leave her face.

He climbed on behind her. Lauren pivoted to face him, yet nodded to Grandpa. "He has no vegetable garden this year."

"I know." Mitch grinned like the tractor grill as it bumped across the road and into the track she'd carved in the field and, as fast as she gunned it, into the wind.

Comfortable silence fell between them. She didn't startle when he rested his chin on her shoulder as she maneuvered Bess around fields that probably hadn't felt tractor tread in years.

To Mitch, it just felt like the right thing to do. Maybe he was right because her back relaxed into him in a way that made him hopeful he could earn her full trust. The tractor bounced over a rock and jostled them. Alarm screamed through him.

She'd almost bounced off the seat.

Pulse returning to normal, he surveyed the coming landscape and brought his thighs in, snug against her hips. Stiffened, she peered over her shoulder, eyes asking his intention.

He grinned and raised innocent hands but kept his legs against her like buffers. "To lessen the likelihood of you sliding off the seat when we jolt over big ruts."

Kind of like in life.

Lauren must've felt safe with his answer because she relaxed again. Even when he took the next step of planting his palms atop his thighs in order to brace his arms around her like a shield. Better yet, she let herself lean deeper into him, proving he'd earned another measure of her fragile trust.

"Lauren, your hair smells like strawberries and sunshine."

She smiled. The curve to her mouth became all too inviting. So he looked away.

You never liked strawberries much anyway, he tried telling himself. Yet the essence of her appeal never fully went away.

Chapter Nine

She shouldn't be enjoying this as much as she was.

Lauren peered around to find Mitch's eyes averted. His grin elicited hers and left her with a contented feeling.

It wasn't every day she got to wreak havoc in Lem's fields with an irresistibly handsome rider.

Lauren steeled herself against silly notions and simply enjoyed the sun's warmth.

Sure, he was cute and this felt a little cozy for comfort. But being out here on Bess was so relaxing, she couldn't bring herself to end the peaceful ride.

However, she could bring herself to make the moment last as long as possible.

She drove Bess up a perfectly inclined hill and cut her engine. It ticked to a stop. Every sound became absorbed by the silence around them.

"Those are his old pastures?" Mitch asked her.

Lauren figured he already knew the answer but was being polite. There was little about Lem that he didn't know. He didn't tout it today, however.

She had to give him credit. He was trying. She should, too.

She pointed to the land their hill stood over. "His horses used to chase escaped rabbits back to their hutches." Lauren took it all in. If she squinted, she could almost see where the hutches had been. She climbed down to get a better look.

"Lem always warned me not to get attached to the rabbits. That they were for eatin', not pettin'. But he never butchered a one. The next summer I came back, we had another fifty rabbits."

Laughing, Mitch got off the tractor and tossed a dirt clod. "I took care of those rabbits one winter. The hutches were wooden and they had chewed through the walls to get to one another."

"I know. Those critters multiply faster than a fourth-grade math class." She walked alongside him on the ridge. A gentle breeze brushed hair into then out of her eyes, beating Mitch to it.

His hand lowered. "Lem's land is filled with beauty."

Mitch was right. She sighed as she looked around at what Mitch must be seeing. Crape myrtles, her favorite Southern Illinois shrubbery, painted the perimeter with bright fuschia flowers. Crabgrass danced between the house and barn. Wild trees dotted sporadically over purple-and-yellow-wildflower-strewn fields.

"It's breathtaking," he said in a voice octaves deeper.

Lauren pivoted to find Mitch's eyes on her, not the landscape. He quickly looked away and cleared his throat.

Silly girl. You're imagining things.

She climbed back on Bess and refocused on her surroundings, not including a certain distractingly cute doctor.

"You must have memories that rest on every square mound of earth that makes up Lem's property."

"I do." There wasn't an inch she hadn't traversed as a child and young adult.

The familiar landscape afforded her the ability to look back and remember good times. Being with Mitch afforded her the ability not to delve into the hard stuff that led her to spend every summer at Lem's.

"Grandpa will wonder where we are."

For some reason Mitch snickered. "I doubt that."

She smiled against her will. "You're probably right."

They chatted companionably until Lauren lost herself in telling Mitch stories of her and Lem.

She eventually eyed her watch. "Oh! I lost track of time. We should head back or the mosquitoes will carry us off."

"I suppose so." He chuckled. "I had fun, Lauren. After the few hectic days I've had, I appreciated how relaxing this was."

"Hectic how? As in at the trauma center?" Guilt nibbled.

He raked a hand at the back of his neck as though he regretted saying anything. "I'm used to it, though," he backpedaled.

"I should have gone to help."

"Nah. You need to be spending time with Lem. Especially if you end up leaving early. For the record, I hope you don't."

While he surely meant that only for Grandpa's sake, her face heated as his eyes bore into hers. She averted them to the crazy circle eights they'd carved into fields. "This was fun and relaxing for me, too."

Yet he didn't say they should do it again sometime. Probably for the best because of how giddy being with him today was making her feel. Especially when they remounted Bess. Maybe it was her imagination, but it seemed as if he sat closer than before. Kinda scary—felt odd not to be sparring with him.

Yet every time Mitch moved or said something interesting or insightful, her ears and heart melted toward him.

The last thing she needed was to feel conflicted over a man who lived too many miles away.

Especially not the one she felt she had to fight for her own grandfather's affections.

Their lovely day was merely a joint effort to get along for Grandpa's sake—despite Grandpa being nowhere in sight.

They just needed the practice for when he was.

Yeah. That was it.

* * *

Wow. Mitch couldn't get over her switch from rude to nice. While he didn't like sparring with Lauren, he'd prefer that to fighting with the errant thoughts striking his brain every ten minutes.

When he got immersed in her facial expressions as she told him stories, ones he'd mostly already heard from Lem, he had to remind himself of all the reasons he shouldn't be interested. She began telling stories of Lem's antics.

Mitch laughed. "Lem probably never would have pushed me on this ride if he'd known."

"What? That I'd tell stories of his more ornery moments?"

"Yeah." Mitch chuckled again, remembering some of them.

"Serves him right for trying to set us up." Lauren smirked.

"Definitely. Plus now I have new ammo."

Her eyes rounded. "To go back and tease him about?"

"Sure," Mitch agreed.

She giggled. "Make sure I'm there when you do. I wanna see him squirm. Fess up. You probably already heard most of the things I told you." She swallowed as though she hoped he hadn't.

So he shrugged and adopted a dense expression. "Nah."

Only partly true. Some stories he hadn't heard before. Or at least not her version of them. Mitch appreciated her opening up. It was beautiful to watch. Like flowers blooming around them. Only flowers evolved in slow motion. She'd opened up far faster than he expected. Not that he minded. Just surprised him. Maybe she struggled with loneliness like Lem?

Any time *flowers* and *female* came together in his mind, his heart ended up in trouble. "We should start back. He might worry."

"Yeah." She fired up Bess and they trudged a less-forgotten path.

After they ran out of field and excuses to ride around together, Mitch eyed his watch. He needed to get cracking on

Lem's long to-do list again. In fact, Lem had added a few more items. Mitch wondered if Lem really wanted that stuff done, or if his additions to the list were chores to keep him and Lauren together.

Lauren drove to Lem's yard and cut the engine. Bess sputtered down in protest.

The seat creaked when Mitch shifted. "I know the feeling, Bess. I'd love to ride around in fun, carefree circles all day, too." Especially what felt like a carving of new tracks, not only in Lem's latent fields, but in all of their lives.

Strange. Yet he couldn't shake the sensation.

He patted the tractor. "Bess, ole girl, it's been fun, but work awaits."

Lauren smiled sweetly at Mitch's interaction. "I feel a personal connection with her. Bess was Mom's favorite tractor."

"That explains why Lem added her to the top of his to-do list."

She pivoted. "Did he really?"

"Yeah." He leaned in to whisper, "But don't tell Bess she didn't appear on the list before you got here. She might be mad and quit on us because she didn't make the original cut. I'd hate to have to walk all the way back from some remote field."

Lauren laughed, and the sweet sound swept through him, brushing the week's stress away. Felt good to be a little silly. They peered at the expanse of Lem's property. Nostalgia danced in the air alongside dandelion particles. Their tiny parasol-shaped feathers whirled and swooped like little ant-size parachutes, whisked by a refreshing breeze.

Mitch shifted. They rested on Bess's sun-cracked seat out of respect for the moment. Basked in the warmth of solar-kissed skies and fond memories, distant in time but close to the heart.

A slight breeze whispered from nowhere and rustled strands of Lauren's hair. So silky. Mitch became instantly afflicted with the urge to touch it. His fist clenched against the compulsion. His mind recoiled. His unruly imagination could take a hike…off a one-way cliff.

"I'm rounding at the trauma center tomorrow. Care to join—"

"Not on your life." She aimed a wrench at his nose that she pulled from under her seat. "Nice try."

Undeterred, he smiled. "Just checking." He climbed off the tractor and lent Lauren a hand down.

When her feet planted squarely on the ground, Mitch tugged her close enough to widen her eyes. Her gaze skittered to his hand, holding hers firmly. Intentionally. To keep things affable. He didn't want hostility to return. She couldn't give in to envy again because frankly, Lem didn't need the worry.

"See you tomorrow, Lem's table?" he said as a heads-up so she wouldn't feel as though he was barging in or intruding.

Lem invited Mitch. Mitch never invited himself.

Her face masked. "See you tomorrow."

"I regret that I won't also be seeing you at my operating tables."

She groaned. "You're incorrigible."

"I'm seriously short staffed tomorrow."

Her expression sobered. "Dangerously so?"

"Depends on what comes in."

She nibbled her lip. "Can't you hire someone?"

"My director is scrambling with interviews. Meanwhile, we've been getting slammed."

"I wonder why? It's not like this is a big-city E.R."

"No, but our trauma center sits straddled between two major interstates. Eagle Point is also home to one of the Midwest's largest recreational state parks with tempting caverns, climb-friendly rock faces and hiking trails that are magnets for extreme sports fanatics."

She nodded. "And we're at the height of hiking season."

"The center's become busier than anyone anticipated."

"Proving you were right to build it."

"I could really use more nurses familiar with where things are." He let his shoulders slump and feigned a fatigued yawn.

The moment her face softened, he knew he was winning. Maybe.

Him and God.

At least for the moment.

Chapter Ten

"Carrottop, I'm gonna ask you to do something for me." A long *zzzssshing* sound broke predawn stillness on Eagle Point Lake the next morning as Lem zipped a fishing line over his head. The lure plunked in the water thirty feet from where their boat bobbed leisurely on glassy sapphire water. "It might be tough."

Excitement welled in Lauren like the sunrise about to break over the lake. Maybe he'd let her tackle some of the items on the to-do list he'd given Mitch. Then she'd have more time with just Grandpa. And lighten Mitch's load. "Anything. Just ask."

"Anything?"

"I'm pretty handy with a hammer, and I wield a mean wrench."

He chuckled. "I know. But the only kind of hammer you'd need for what I'm gonna ask of you is one of those little rubber ones you bang on people's knees with."

Her heart thumped hard, paused then thudded back into rhythm. She cast her fishing line. "Oh?"

"I want you to seriously consider taking up nursing again."

"Wow. You drive a hard bargain."

"I know you have it in ya. You're a good nurse. Mitch even calls you exemplary, and he's a man of sky-high standards."

Hearing that did not help matters. "Grandpa, why do you care about his opinion so much?"

Grandpa reeled in his line. "Because he cares about me."

Well. What could she say to that?

"I suppose he does. Do you care about him more than me?"

A scowl came across Grandpa's face. "Of course not. That's not a fair question to begin with. And it's silly for you to assume."

"Sometimes it seems like you do."

"Lauren, you mean the world to me. All these projects I'm having him do, all this maintenance and upkeep, is for you."

Dread filled her stomach. "Why? What do you mean?"

"We both know my pa and grandpa died soon after seventy."

She stood. The boat wobbled. She promptly sat. "You're not gonna." Tears flooded forth. "I forbid it."

He chuckled then grew serious. "Carrottop, if anyone could stop it, you could. But stubbornness and love aren't enough to keep a person here if God thinks it's their time to go."

"I think you should stop assuming He does."

"I'm just planning for your future."

"My future won't mean anything without you in it. Grandpa, I promise I will come see you every few months from now on." Her voice had been reduced to begging, but she didn't care.

She needed him. Who else on earth did she have? Her business partner and best friend, but that was a tough one since she was also sister to her ex.

"I won't be here forever. I want to make sure you're left all right. I'm leaving part of the property to you. The house'll be yours, too. I hope you never sell it because the memories won't mean anything to anyone else. I never could change my cabinet doors because you cut your teeth on them, and the itty bite marks are still there." Now he blinked tears.

Overcome with emotion, Lauren set aside her pole and knee-scrambled across the boat to hug the stuffing out of him.

Tears flowed freely down both their faces. Emotion welled to the point that hiccups tried to convulse her throat.

Never in her life had she felt so confused and dismayed.

She'd planned her future all out to be in Texas, with plans to simply visit Grandpa. But more and more, the thought of leaving him caused panic, depressing thoughts and profound sadness.

How had she gotten her life in such a mess?

Rash decisions. That's how.

"I don't want to come to this lake, your house, your property if you're not here, Grandpa. That'd be too hard."

"Which is why I'm willing part of the property to Mitch."

She gasped. "He's not family. Your sister'll throw a fit."

"Let her. She never treated you right and you know it." His eyes looked about to boil, and his false teeth clacked like a war drum.

She slowly sat. "You know?"

"Yes. Your cousins filled me in. Had I known how miserable you were and how she never treated you kindly, I'd have fought for full custody and raised ya myself. But in my blind grief, I didn't see the whole picture. I will always regret that. I wouldn't have been a half-bad dad, ya know."

"You *were* a dad to me, Grandpa. You were everything I had. I always felt loved and secure with you."

"Then come back. Live here. Work as a nurse with Mitch."

"I wish I could. But even if I did, Mitch and I aren't compatible." To her dismay, she discovered she really meant what she said about wishing she could stay. Furthering that dismay was her sudden dislike for how incompatible she and Mitch were.

If Grandpa knew, he'd flip out of the boat and swim laps around the lake with joy as his lone propeller.

"He's just hurt right now, Lauren. Mark my words, once you two bleach out your stubborn streaks and let your guards down, you'll be amazed at just how compatible you are. I love the two of you more than anything, and I want you both to be happy."

If that was meant to make her feel better, it didn't. Because Grandpa was essentially saying Mitch was equal to her in his eyes. Equal care. Equal love. Equal receivers of property.

She didn't want to be Mitch's equal. Not in Grandpa's eyes.

"At least consider it." Lem brought in his pole.

She reeled in hers, too. "What, Mitch?"

"All of it." He peered at the sun. "We'd best get back. He'll be arriving soon for breakfast and to work on the deck before he has to round at the center."

At the dock, Lauren helped Grandpa onto it. "Be careful." Once he made it safely to land, she secured the boat.

"You be careful too, carrottop. Flooded rivers have flushed out snakes." Grandpa eyed the ground diligently. "Watch your step."

She would. Not just with snakes. She'd watch her steps with Mitch, too. Because if she weren't careful, one of Cupid's arrows might get through and make Grandpa's words come true. Mitch could be charming, for sure.

She popped open the fish bucket. "Look! Enough for a Friday-night fish fry." Seeing Grandpa's grin at their catch made her feel better. She wanted to make him happy. Ease his worry.

"Grandpa, I can't believe I'm saying this, but I'll try."

"Try what?" His face beamed as he lifted the tackle box.

"To work as a nurse. At least while I'm here for the summer."

"That's it?" He frowned.

She gave him a wry look. "That's all I can promise for now." She had responsibilities in Texas, and in fact needed to call her contractors today to check in with them. See how renovations were going. Which reminded her that her life was in Texas.

Fishing with Grandpa this morning had almost made her forget. If she weren't careful, Grandpa would talk her into moving back. She couldn't let her friend down. Lauren had given her word, which was her honor. One of many things Grandpa had taught her. To have integrity, a hard work ethic and, most importantly, to never, ever, go back on one's word.

"I can't believe I'm doing this," Lauren muttered to herself after Mitch came in later from repairing a good portion of Lem's deck. Mitch tried his level best not to grin while Lauren glared at her nursing certifications printing on Grandpa's fax machine.

"Hey, where did the other day's good mood go?"

"It flew the coop the second your truck pulled up. You intruded on my morning with Grandpa again." She grinned.

Lem poked her shoulder. "Whoa, little miss. Where'd those manners that I taught you go? It just so happens I invited Mitch to breakfast. So if you're gonna have a hissy, have one at me."

She let out a long-suffering breath, yanked Mitch's stethoscope from his pocket and draped it around her neck.

Mitch could *Yeehaw!* the corn out of Lem's field. He restrained himself lest she become annoyed and change her mind.

"So you'll send for your permanent Illinois license?"

"Temporary. I'll help out today. That's it."

"And if you enjoy today, you'll drop by the office to apply for a vacant nurse position?" He treaded carefully.

She flipped around and issued the same stare Lem did right before he kicked tractor tires. "Don't push it."

His hands flew up like two wise white flags. "Fine. I'll take what I can get." Some of his inward smile must've escaped.

She narrowed sharpening eyes at his sudden vigor. "And why do you look suspiciously not dead-dog tired anymore like you were when you dragged in this morning?"

He shrugged. "Lem's orange juice kicked in?"

"Uh-huh." She inclined her head. "Just how much time did you spend sleeping in your call room last night as opposed to operating on trauma patients? Hmm?"

He grinned and politely evaded her question. "Thanks for helping today, Lauren." He didn't call her Nurse Bates because he really was thankful and didn't want to rile her out of helping today.

He had Refuge helpers he could call on. But his gut said to keep after Lauren. He just hoped his gut was hearing from God. Otherwise this could get mighty messy.

Because, for Lauren's disillusionment with nursing and her laying down her calling and walking away, it was life or death. This was it.

Mitch knew it. And so did Lem, who was not shy about saying how he felt. And he felt Lauren was still meant to be a nurse. One more reason for Mitch to keep chipping away at her about it.

"Grandpa, I'm going with Mitch to help at the trauma center," Lauren said when Lem stepped outside with a drink tray.

"Oh! That news is sweeter than this sun tea!"

Mitch didn't know if Lem was happier about Lauren going with him and the two being together, or Lauren utilizing her nursing skills again. Maybe both, if Lem's hefty grin as he handed them two glasses of tea before they left was any indication.

"Kate has extra scrubs in her locker," Mitch reminded her when they arrived at the center after a half hour of awkward conversation in the truck. Mitch attributed it to a combination of his in-your-face attraction and her nervousness at helping today.

Mitch took every opportunity to reassure her and answer any technical or logistical questions she had.

"I promise, I'll be right there with you," Mitch said.

"That's what I'm afraid of," she said, then laughed.

He didn't know what to make of that.

When Lauren returned, she wore a new pair of scrubs and a scowl. "Your circulating nurse decided to leave me a gift." She plucked the hem of a uniform top he'd never seen on Kate.

Understanding dawned. "Kate bought that for you?"

"Yep. Left it with a key to what she assigned as my new locker and a *very* interesting note."

One that obviously left Lauren perturbed yet contemplative.

"I'm dying to know what the note said."

She pointed to a corridor no one liked walking. "Morgue's that way."

In other words, she wasn't giving up the info.

And after withholding vital information from Kate, he highly doubted she'd miss this opportunity to torture him with the aggravation of dearly wanting to know what was said yet not having the satisfaction of finding out.

Yet. He *would* find out.

Ian approached. The look on his face meant Mitch wasn't going to like this. "We have a motorcycle crash victim on the way. You okay handling it?"

Mitch felt the familiar suffocating sensation that came over him every time an injured biker was mentioned. "I'm good."

Ian nodded. Lauren peeked up but kept counting instruments. She looked scared but willing. He realized just how confident he was in her nursing skills. Did she?

It suddenly hit Mitch how brave Lauren was. Every time she helped at the center, she faced her fears. He drew strength from knowing her as the pre-op crew rapidly wheeled the patient in. Mitch pushed the past aside and poured every bit of grit and skill into giving the young man the future his dad never had.

Not only had the accident been life-or-limb damaging, the surgery was going to be dangerous. Did Lauren know how much so?

Her hands weren't quaking, and she wasn't nearly as ashen as he imagined he'd been when the word *motorcycle* had come out of Ian's mouth. So she'd be fine. Plus Kate was here, and another crew slept in the call room should complications arise.

Thankfully, they didn't. Mitch helped the orthopedic doctor close incisions they'd made to repair multiple fractures.

"I'm confident he'll make a full recovery," Mitch said.

"Indeed. Thankfully he had his helmet on," the orthopedic guy replied while finishing, before meeting Mitch's gaze with professional respect. "Fortunate for him this center was right here. Otherwise…" He trailed off when Ian shook his head in a withering motion. Mitch and Ian were close—like brothers. They had each other's backs, both here and on the battlefield.

Mitch nodded his thanks to Ian. The third doctor looked from one man to the other.

Kate cleared her throat. "Mitch is the last person who needs to hear how minutes matter. His dad was in a motorcycle crash and made it to Refuge Hospital mere minutes too late."

"My apologies." The doctor's tone carried respect anew.

Mitch nodded his acknowledgment. Gratitude overwhelmed him.

Lord, thank You for leading us here. Bring capable help and funding so we can expand to meet the full needs of this community. Mitch finished the prayer as the last suture went in.

The O.R. door swung open. "Don't go anywhere. We've got another bone trauma en route," the director said.

The crew scrubbed out, then back in, and regowned. Lauren didn't seem fazed, though this surgery took longer than the last. Afterward Mitch faced Lauren. "Meet me in the doctors' lounge when you're done?"

She nodded and continued to carry out her tasks with Kate, who smiled like an elated little sister at the pair.

Mitch flashed Kate a visual warning. Yet he couldn't deny that the blush on Lauren's cheeks above her mask drained the strain and fatigue out of his tired muscles and feet.

"Orthopedic surgeries are slower than molasses," Lauren said once in the lounge after surgery. She stretched her back.

Mitch resisted the urge to rub the knots out of her neck. He was physically and mentally drained, and this room was quite secluded and dimly lit. Recipe for disaster. "Ready to go?"

She nodded and gave him back his stethoscope. Which made him frown. And made her laugh. "You need it more than I do."

At least she didn't say she'd never need it again.

Progress, right?

"Thanks for giving me rides home, Mitch," Lauren said as he helped her into the truck.

Mitch smiled because she'd said *home*. Every time before, she'd referred to it as *Lem's*. Maybe her heart's roots were deepening for Southern Illinois? That would be fine by him. Maybe by her, too, because the closer they got to Mitch dropping her off, the more she fidgeted and seemed to want to say something.

Likewise, Mitch wished to draw out their time together.

"Do you want to—?"

"How about we—?"

They both laughed at their simultaneous questions. Lauren tucked her hair behind her ear. "Want to go for coffee and feed the geese at Refuge Park?"

Mitch smiled and headed to the bread store. "That sounds fun." Right now—the way she and her sparkly eyes and gorgeous grin made him feel—she'd make a trip to the dentist for a root canal fun.

They got coffee to go from the bread store, then parked near a cluster of geese. When Mitch got out of the truck with the bread bag, he was mobbed by winged critters.

"Haven't you fed them before?" Lauren asked, giggling, after rescuing him and the empty bag.

He led her to a picnic table, laughing, despite having been pecked. "No. Here's your coffee."

She took a sip and grimaced. "Gross. How can you drink this stuff? It's pure sludge."

"I hadn't noticed." He peered into his half-empty cup, realizing she was right. He looked back up at her and scooted closer than a friend would. "All I noticed is how lucky I am to be in the company of someone so beautiful and brave."

"You mean, the geese?" Her cheeks tinged as she smiled and lowered her gaze.

Mitch raised her face because he needed to look into her eyes to say this. "No. I mean the fearless knockout who rescued me from them."

Chapter Eleven

"What gives?" Lem handed Lauren a cup of caramel mocha coffee one morning the next week after they came home from another early morning fishing excursion. "You're all dolled up."

"Oh, nothin'." She cleared her throat and eyed the window.

"You wanted to don your war paint before Mitch got here."

Lauren glared at her grandfather, but kept silent.

"Don't worry. His smile will be worth it." Lem chuckled. "Admit it. You think he's cute."

Lauren sighed. "I can't pull any kind of wool over your eyes, can I?"

Grandpa chuckled. "Not in this lifetime."

"Speaking of lifetime, Grandpa, you look healthy enough to hit a hundred." *Please, God, let it be so.*

"I do feel smidgens better now that you're here."

"Good." What could she say? She wasn't here to stay. Would he worsen after she left? Thankfully Mitch's truck rumbled up, sparing her from guilt.

Mitch stood at the door with a riveted expression. "Wow."

Lauren fumbled verbally, but no words would emerge.

Mitch stepped in, canvassing her. "Glossy hair. Movie-star makeup. Outfit too dressy for a cornfield. What's the occasion?"

Grandpa grinned. "Just you, Mitch. Just you."

Heat blasted Lauren's face. "Grandpa!" Was nothing sacred in this house? She shook her head at him.

Lem's eyes twinkled as he headed to man the stove.

Mitch watched the two of them and didn't crack a smile.

She could just die of embarrassment. Thankfully Mitch spared her by picking up a drill and going to work on the deck. As soon as he was out of sight, Lauren trudged toward Grandpa. "I wish you'd cut the matchmaking already."

Grandpa chuckled over ham he seared in a pan for tonight's beans. "Looks like he could use a hand. It's supposed to rain today, so I'd appreciate it if you'd go help him."

"I'd appreciate it if you'd let me *really* help him by handing me a tranquilizer dart."

Lem poked a spatula at her nose. "That, young lady, was uncalled for. Now *git* yourself out there and lend him a hand."

Whoa. Grandpa never used *git* or any other Southern slang words unless he was perturbed.

Well, he could join the club. Lauren's teeth gritted until she saw through the window how much work the deck still needed. She eyed Grandpa. He peered out his side of the kitchen window at clouds, then at Mitch with a worrisome gnaw to his jaw.

"Quit eatin' your tongue, Grandpa. I'm going." She grabbed her work gloves and headed out, knowing that this time, Grandpa was merely looking out for Mitch and not trying to be a matchmaker.

"Hey," she greeted Mitch on approach. "How can I help?"

He peered up, then to his work area. "Let's cut these before the weather unleashes on us. I want to get this electrical stuff inside before it starts." He nodded at vicious-looking saws.

Mitch and Lauren worked together until Lem peeked his head out the deck door a while later. "Lunch is ready. Come on in."

Mitch eyed the darkening clouds, then Lauren, then the deck. She read his concern. "I'm not hungry yet," she fibbed. "You?"

"I can wait, too." He pulled his cheek, the way Grandpa tended to. "So which one of us is gonna tell Gramps?"

Lauren laughed. "I'll do that piece of dirty work."

An hour later, and Grandpa's seventh trip to tell them food was getting cold, Mitch stood. "We can finish this another day. I'll drag the saws into his garage if you wanna bring board remnants and the nailer."

They packed up the work area, and Lem stepped out onto the deck. "Wow. You two work fast. You nearly have it done."

Mitch nodded to Lauren. "Thanks to her help. She's a hard worker. Good with power tools, too." His proud grin sent zip lines through her tummy that left her exhilarated and light-hearted.

On the way to the table, Mitch slipped her a fistful of flowers in passing. "Peace offering."

"Awww. Thanks!" He must've had them hidden. Wait… "Did you steal these from Grandpa's yard?"

"Yes, ma'am. Learned from the best. Shhh," he said with whispered breath and a finger to his mouth, which drew her attention there. What was meant as a kidding gesture captivated her.

And aggravated her to no end.

"Thanks. I think." She groaned inwardly. "I can't believe I've influenced you to lift bounty from his prized flower beds."

Mitch smiled. "I confess it's not the first time I have. He has plenty and gets a kick out of me snitching them."

"I hear you're still adept at getting corn by a five-finger-discount, as well," she teased in reference to Grandpa's Mitch stories this week. He'd recited them nightly, with great animation, after Mitch went home or to the trauma center.

The departure always plagued Lauren with guilt. But he needed to secure permanent staff and get used to the idea that her help was only temporary.

Lauren enjoyed Grandpa's renditions of good times with Mitch. She'd also realized how much Mitch did for Grandpa.

Mitch flashed a handsome grin her way.

Her traitorous pulse went aflutter like a rebellious butterfly.

She lifted the flowers and thought about whopping him with them. Instead, the floral scents of lavender and rose beckoned. She inhaled deeply. Unfortunately she also caught whiffs of his cologne. Hints of sandalwood and the outdoors made her slightly dizzy. "He also said you help plant the corn when you're not deployed."

Mitch handed her a vase. "He told you that?"

"Yep." When she went to push flowers into the vase, some stems didn't make it in. Mitch came to the rescue by wrapping his fingers around the flowers.

They both drastically slowed their motions. Drawing the tender moment out.

She was enjoying immensely the warm contact of their hands meshing together to mend a barely living thing. Like in surgery. *Like we are meant to be.*

Caught completely off guard by the out-of-nowhere thought, Lauren looked up to find Mitch watching. Had he read her mind?

Perhaps they were fueled by the romantic childhood storybooks that Lem still kept in her room and had read to her every summer. Reading and fishing with him were two of her favorite pastimes.

Placing the flowers as the centerpiece, Lauren helped Mitch set the table. Something suddenly hit her. "Mitch, if I spent summers with Grandpa and you grew up here, how come we never met before?"

"Probably because I was shipped away for summers."

"And I spent every off-summer season at relatives' houses."

Mitch leaned in. "Lauren, you should know that Lem once told me he agonized over discovering how unhappy you were by moving around. Had he known at the time, he would have sued for full custody." For some reason, Mitch's own words stiffened him.

"What's wrong?" Lauren asked.

"Ian's facing a painful custody battle. His marital problems began during deployment. Which cements my assumption that distance only mangles a marriage."

"Kate said they had problems beforehand."

"Still, I'm convinced absence does *not* grow hearts fonder." His expression sobered.

"Sounds like you know from personal experience."

He shrugged and dragged a sip of coffee from his cup. Then averted his gaze. After an introspective moment, he tipped his forehead toward Lem as he returned. "Your grandpa and that cornfield were the best things to ever happen to me. It's when I learned about choice and consequence."

"About sowing and reaping," Lem added as he sat.

Mitch eyed Lem with fondness and respect. "Took me under his wing. Taught me faith in Jesus and how to make a mean pot of chili. Became like a second dad. A spiritual father."

Lem patted Mitch's forearm. "And I consider you my son. I don't know what I would have done all these years without you. Even when you weren't here, you made sure I was taken care of."

Mitch laughed. "So you know about all the people I had checking in on you and doing things for you?"

"Wasn't tough to figure out. They came like clockwork. You must've formulated a schedule of revolving folks or something."

Mitch smiled. "I'll never tell."

Mitch's doting over Grandpa like a son pressed Lauren's blood pressure to dangerous limits because her face flamed hotter by the second. Anger at herself, too, for not seeing to it that Grandpa was looked after. For not even considering that he might need to be. Her self-absorption made her as mad as Mitch's intruding into what should be her second chance with Grandpa.

She rubbed her chest but the sudden tightness would not go

away. Anxiety? The invisible claw that Lem's obvious care for Mitch clenched her shoulders with wouldn't release her. Neither would the jealous envy she struggled against.

She should have that closeness with Grandpa. Not Mitch.

She used to. Why was Grandpa letting Mitch replace her? Did loneliness make him desperate enough to do something so drastic?

Her appetite fled so she methodically stabbed her food as if it were the cause of her emotional quandary.

Lem didn't even notice. Rather, he beamed at Mitch's tender words and seemed to stand taller. Then tapped an ice tong atop Lauren's shoulder as if knighting her. "It's good to have someone looking out for me. Then Lauren can go about her life."

His statement devastated her.

"Ain't that right, carrottop?" Lem rustled her hair then whistled his way back to the stove. But looked back when she didn't answer. To Mitch's credit, he looked apologetic.

Lauren nodded to be polite because what else could she do with that influx of information? She'd process it later. For now, she'd try to fight the hurt and bitterness inside her heart. "I'm glad you've been there for him." She tried to mean it. Maybe if she said it often enough, it would be true. "You've obviously been a bright spot in his life."

He laughed. "Yeah, like a bad sunburn at times, I'm sure."

That gave Lauren an unexpected laugh. While he annoyed her, she enjoyed his unexpected transparency and well-placed humor.

Lem left the stove and joined them. "He was quite a handful in his youth." He squeezed Mitch's shoulder. "But he turned out all right." Lem let them carry the serving dishes to the table.

Mitch maneuvered Lauren's chair then draped a linen napkin over her, which sparked an extra twinkle in Grandpa's owlish eyes. "We're glad you joined us today without getting paged away." Lem elbowed Lauren when she didn't answer. "Aren't we?"

Lauren gave Grandpa a wry smirk. "Of *course* we are," she said through a clenched jaw.

She forced herself to curtsy, then sat. "You must be giving the debonair fellow chivalry lessons, Grandpa. If so, your prince of a pupil deserves an A-plus."

"Then you, my princess, should attend my library event with him."

The shock on Mitch's face would have made the world's most hilarious social-network profile photo.

"Grandpa, may I remind you I'll be gone at summer's end or earlier."

"And the event is six months away," Mitch added coolly.

Yet as Lauren relaxed at Lem's table, she couldn't get past feeling like a front-row observer at the heart of an epic rebirth. Of new memories being made. Of faith. And of a God-woven, willfully reconstructed family.

What was up with *that?*

Mitch cast concernedly cryptic looks her way before dipping his head toward her plate. "Better eat. We have a long day."

"We?"

He nodded. "I need you to run some errands with me."

Lem aimed a butter knife at Mitch. "He's up to something sneaky. Won't tell me what, though."

Lauren pivoted to study Mitch. "What errands?"

"You'll see." Expression purposely vague, he winked at her then ate another bite of the food Lem piled on his plate.

Suspicion rose like the lemonade he refilled in her cup.

"This doesn't constitute an errand," Lauren said an hour later as Mitch pulled into the trauma center lot.

Mitch parked his truck near the entrance but kept the engine running. "I didn't say you had to go in." He grinned.

She refused to let it melt her. "Good. Because I'm not."

She had to set boundaries; otherwise he'd finagle her into helping full-time. Arms folded, she turned to admire a floral explosion of color lining the parking lot, courtesy of ornamental shrubs.

"Suit yourself."

"I plan to."

He looked about to say some snarky phrase, but his mouth flattened into a determined line instead. Which made her wonder like mad what he was thinking.

She'd probably be better off not knowing.

And she'd *for sure* be better off not to notice the fluid way his muscles moved when he walked. Nor should she be remotely intrigued by how intent his expression became whenever he shifted into trauma work mode. Yet she was.

With more difficulty than she wanted to admit, she forced her gaze and musings away from him.

She studied hummingbirds flitting in feeders next to a garden area. They held her attention for only so long.

After a conflicted moment, she stared at the entrance.

Looked away.

"I'm *not* going in." Her eyes veered toward the front doors again. "I mean it." Tearing her gaze away proved tougher this time. She studied the beauty of the building…only to catch glimpses of staff scurrying about inside.

They looked busy. Lauren looked away.

Her thoughts stayed. How were the in-house patients? She fought wonder. Her eyes strayed to room 24, Mara's, the texting teen's.

How was she today? Still comatose? Lauren shouldn't speculate. Especially since she had no intention of going back in there and involving herself in Mara's care. Images of the girl became too vivid to fight. Lauren found herself twisting to get any glimpse of movement inside room 24. Nothing.

Lauren's heart began to thud. Had Mara perished in the night like Kate had feared and Ian had said she deserved? What painful part of Ian's life caused him to say such a heartless thing?

Sweet Mara, such a mess you've made. One choice. So much chaos. And she may never know. Her family hadn't come. Why? How horrible was it to die utterly alone?

Something broke in Lauren. Perhaps the last frayed strands of resistance. She cut the ignition and jerked out Mitch's keys. The medical emblem on his key chain caught light and brought home the nursing creed she'd excitedly vowed on her licensure day.

And she lost the battle.

"Fine. I'll go in. But only for a minute."

As she checked on Mara, Mitch joined her at the bedside. "Still unresponsive, yet improved on the coma scale. We haven't been able to transfer her to another facility because she's so unstable. Merely moving her up in bed caused her to code."

Lauren turned. "When?"

"One day when you weren't here. She had a bad few days."

"All on days I was gone?"

Mitch seemed to think hard a moment. "Yeah, actually."

Lauren always spent time talking to Mara. "Do you think my not being here adversely affected her?" Lauren could scarcely bear the thought of that.

She met his eyes. The tense look in them said it all.

"She hears me, doesn't she? When I talk to her and hold her hand and tell her I'm here, she knows it, doesn't she?"

He nodded. Which meant Mara might also know when she wasn't. Lauren trusted Mitch's integrity. Knew he would never use that to manipulate her to be here. Yet he could have.

Maybe there was more to Mitch than met the eye. Maybe he didn't merely have his own interests at heart. If he was as focused on others as his discretionary act of refusal to use manipulation hinted, that changed the game from every court. Even the home front.

Respect increased for him, as did compassion for Mara.

Lauren took her hand. "Mara, it's Nurse Lauren. You're still in the trauma unit. You're never alone, okay?"

She squeezed Mara's hand and could've sworn she felt a minuscule tremor in the girl's finger. Nah. She'd probably imagined it for wishing. *Please wake up.*

Mitch stepped rapidly closer to the bed. He had the most intense look of concentration as he angled his chin sideways. "Talk to her again, Lauren."

"God watches over you always. Especially when we humans have to step away to work on other people."

Mitch leaned closer and pointed at Mara's eyelids, which fluttered every time Lauren spoke.

Hope and tears welled. "Mara, I hope you wake up soon. You have to see what a very cute doctor you have taking care of you."

"Look." He nudged his chin toward Mara's monitors. "Her heart and respiratory rates elevate with your voice."

"Which means?"

"She knows." He grinned.

Lauren giggled. "She knows what? That you're cute?"

His ears reddened. "No, silly. That you're here and that you care." When the nurses came to change Mara's dressings, Mitch offered to do it instead. Lauren assisted him, then they exercised Mara's legs to prevent blood clots and the like. Afterward, Ian came and checked on her vent settings and cleared her airway with a suction tube. Mara's numbers reached alarm point, but they got her calmed down with medication.

"She's agitated and tired. We wore her out. Let's allow her to rest." They reluctantly slipped from her room. But not before Mitch bent and brushed a fatherly kiss on Mara's forehead. "Get better, kiddo."

Lauren almost fell flat on her face in love right then.

Mitch wasn't as hard-hearted as he'd like her to believe. Therefore her heart had better be on its best behavior and quit trying to defy her resolve not to fall for him.

Chapter Twelve

"I have no intention of leaving Texas." The second Lauren drove that metaphoric tractor over his chest, Mitch woke with a start. Gasping and drenched with sweat, he sat up.

Then realized it was a dream.

Yet Lauren's words still rang in his ears. *No intention of leaving Texas.*

"And I have no intention of letting myself fall for you," he hollered to the air, then immediately realized how ridiculous he sounded.

The complication of romance would be the *worst*-case scenario in his life right now.

Plus, with her home being in Texas, he refused to even consider it.

But why was he sitting here arguing with himself over it? It was, after all, just a dream.

Mitch flipped covers off and tried to figure out if he looked forward to this day or not.

Unfortunately he might have to contend with this annoying attraction until the day she left. Because no matter how much he tried to ignore it, the feelings wouldn't wane.

Breakfast this morning was going to be an unpleasant, uncomfortable experience.

But he refused to stay away from Lem or neglect their friendship because of Lauren.

She'd get over her envy. Eventually.

When he arrived at Lem's, Lauren was still in bed with no apparent inclination to get up. Maybe the whole attraction ordeal was giving her nightmares, too. Served her right for running a tractor over his chest. He still felt annoyed about it.

Then he heard noises from Lauren's bedroom. Since her door was open, Mitch stood respectfully there. "Something wrong?"

"What's *not* wrong?"

He waited for her to vent because it looked like she needed to. If he was getting to know her as well as he thought, she'd share if he stood there and kept quiet instead of offering solutions.

She swiped hair out of her eyes. "For one thing, the whole world seems intent on destroying my time with Grandpa. You're taking over my life with him. Then the contractors called today during our fishing time—" Her voice quivered. She stood up. He stepped back to let her through.

But she paced right where she was. "They aren't abiding by our renovation terms. My friend is freaking out. And I'm not there to oversee it."

He bit his lip against giving advice.

She flopped back onto the bed in a comical motion. "She wants me to come back and deal with it. I want to spend the summer here."

"So set boundaries. Spend the summer here."

She groaned and shoved a pillow over her head but looked as though she'd much rather shove it over Mitch's and hold it there.

Lem joined them. He leaned against her doorway. "I think you should be patient. Things will come around."

"I think you should move to Texas so I can have you to myself without interference." She shot Mitch a look.

Lem crossed his arms. "I think you should quit moping the

morning away, get out of that bed and off the rude horse you seem intent to ride this morning."

Lauren lowered the pillow. Grandpa wasn't smiling.

Mitch turned and eyed him funny. "Wow, Lauren. He's looking kind of fierce. Like he could kick a tractor tire. You should probably obey." Mitch delivered his much-needed tension-diffusing smile.

"I just don't want her pouting her life away and wasting the gifts she has." Grandpa scowled so much that Lauren laughed. She also knew he was right.

"Wow. Grumpy today. You tired?" Mitch asked Lauren after Lem retreated to the kitchen to begin the breakfast ritual.

She yawned. "I didn't sleep well last night."

"Join the club. Someone ran over my chest with a tractor." *What?* She blinked. "Huh?"

He shook his head. "Never mind. It's not important."

"I'm worried about Mara."

He looked slightly annoyed now. "I think she'll recover."

"I don't mean that, necessarily. I mean socially and emotionally. The girl never has visitors. Her foster family all but abandoned her. I'd like to find a decent family member who'll take an interest."

"I'm pretty sure she has a grandmother who cares about her. Just no transportation. She calls more often than you realize."

"You act like the grandma might be offended because I'm spending so much time with her granddaughter."

"That would be an inaccurate assumption. While I do have strong concerns about you growing attached to Mara, I realize you're just projecting your own anger into the situation."

"What anger?" She sat at Lem's table and pulled a bowl of potatoes in her lap, then started peeling.

"Because I'm closer to your grandfather than you're comfortable with."

She swung both feet over the chair and stood so fast, Mitch

stiffened. She set down the potatoes and managed to resist the temptation to assault him with the peeler. Tension grew so thick in the room, not even a scalpel could slice through it.

"I'm irritated with the situation in general. Dealing with disappointment over how I envisioned this summer going, yet it's not. Also, it rubs me the wrong way that you oppose my desire to reach out to the girl everyone else has written off."

"I do have compassion for her, Lauren, but you seem to forget something. She made a choice. It took a life."

"Like the person who killed your dad, Mitch? Seems I'm not the only one projecting my ire into the situation."

That one stung because his face flinched. She felt bad throwing that out there, but she had no other way to make him see she wasn't the only villain here. Yes, her jealousy warts needed removing, but she and God were working on that.

He wordlessly left the room, probably to cool down before he knocked her in the head with a potato. In his absence, Lauren confiscated Lem's to-do list. If she could finish some of it, that would help everyone.

Problem was, Grandpa kept adding more and more to the list.

Mitch stood after the three had breakfast, during which Lauren and Mitch did their best to be congenial. "Is this all you need?" Mitch slid Grandpa's shopping list closer to him.

Lem donned his spectacles. "Yeah, only, go ahead and grab a couple of big watermelons, too, while you're at it."

Mitch tucked the list into his chest pocket. "Will do."

"Going with him?" Lem asked Lauren.

When she started to shake her head, he all but shoved her out the door. "Mitch might need help with those melons." Lem winked at the two and retreated to his chair.

"Right." Lauren gave Mitch's bicep a playful squeeze. "I can see he needs help."

Mitch's laugh eased the tension. They shook heads all the way to his truck.

"He's ornery." Lauren adjusted her seat.

"That's an understatement." Mitch maneuvered winding roads connecting Eagle Point to Refuge.

"We go out to eat Sundays after church. You should join us."

"Grandpa will expect me there soon, huh?"

Mitch grinned. "Probably so. You know him well."

Her head snapped up. "Why wouldn't I? He's *my* grandfather."

Not yours.

Mitch's forehead wrinkled, but he stayed silent. His lively eyes dimmed so perhaps he perceived her prickly thoughts.

Remorse slammed her. What possessed her to spew that? She placed her hand on his. "I'm sorry, Mitch. That was uncalled for. I don't know what's wrong with me lately."

"Long hours with Lem? Stress? Lack of sleep?" He smiled.

"No, this is more deep-seated, something further back."

"No offense taken or meant. I know you don't need to be reminded that you've been gone from Lem a long time. You're having a hard time coming to terms with it." He shrugged it off.

And forgave her just like that? Her heart melted another measure toward him and all he stood for. Wondered against her will what other amazing things there were about him. Stuff she'd never discover living in Texas. Away from Grandpa. Why, oh, why had she set down roots so far from the one person she wanted to be near?

"Maybe not reminded, but I should be taken out and whipped with a willow switch." She meant it, too. "Stupid loan."

Mitch sailed a kind look her way as he merged onto the main road. "Don't be so tough on yourself."

"There's nothing I should know about his health, should I, Mitch?"

"No. He's healthy despite his fear of turning seventy."

"So you know about that?" Relief rippled through her.

Mitch nodded. "That's partly why I came over to sneak you

away. To discuss a few things about Lem. I've run every test imaginable. I don't think he's anywhere near death."

"But sometimes they just know."

"True. But in his case, I think it's mostly fear-based."

"Mostly?"

He seemed to want to say something else but decided not to.

"*Mostly* doesn't make me feel good. What're you not telling me?"

"First, it's no secret I want you on my trauma team."

"Wow. Blunt as a bulldog clamp."

He laughed. "I say that to be up front because I think the biggest part of Lem's problem is loneliness."

"But you're here now and you seem close." She plucked madly at her hem. "Plus he has his library crew and church buddies."

"He misses *you*. You're his closest living relative."

"Actually, he has a sister and a nephew not far from here."

"Lauren, I meant that you're the closest to his heart. He loves you like nothing I've ever seen." Mitch's eyes grew tender, as though his soul carried the full weight of empathy for Lem.

Lauren looked down at her hands, wringing like wayward pretzels in her lap. "I know. I regret moving away. But I'm bound to my shop building." Distress over her decision waylaid her.

Mitch inclined his head. "Are you sure about that?"

Increasingly nervous, she thumbed the glove compartment. "It would take a lot to get me out of that loan."

Mitch smiled but kept his attention on the hairpin curve he was navigating. "I know Someone who specializes in that."

She aimed her finger at his chiseled cheek. "If by the grace of God I am able to quickly pay off the loan, don't get any ideas of trying to turn me back into a nurse."

He adopted a militant expression. "I can't turn you into something you already are." They pulled up to a train crossing and stopped as one passed.

What could she say to that? Nothing. Because other than Grandpa paying for her initial schooling, she had no idea why she'd hung on to her Texas license after the lawsuit. The judge had deemed her nonnegligent and had said all evidence proved that no amount of medical intervention could have saved the patient.

So why did Lauren still feel responsible?

She met Mitch's gaze head-on. "Another thing you're not considering is I have to leave sometime anyway. I live in Texas, remember?" Stress pressed her fingers hard into the glove box. The button clicked, and it tumbled open, spilling out a velvet box. Lauren eyed the floorboard. The box had popped open, and resting between its ridges shone a sparkly diamond solitaire.

She reached for it. "Whose ring is—?"

Mitch beat her to it. Snatched it up in an iron grip that reminded her he was a combat vet. He tossed the ring box back into the glove compartment. Train gone and bars lifted, Mitch proceeded.

Lauren saw that beside the ring sat her note. Crumpled.

Upon seeing her startled reaction, he schooled his posture. His slowed motions didn't smooth the jagged look on his face.

"Okay, I gotta know. What's with the ring? Whose is it?" she asked as they entered Eagle Point.

She expected Mitch to take on his hallmark lighthearted grin. He didn't. Rather, hurled an irate glare at the glove box, closed like the conversation. Why did he harbor a ring he hated?

She'd obviously opened a wound. Remorse and an unexpected surge of care for Mitch rose within her. "I'm so sorry, Mitch. Please accept my apology," she said in a small but sincere voice.

Mitch eyed her, then the glove box, and visibly relaxed.

He stayed silent until they stopped.

"So what all are we getting?" she asked tentatively, having a childhood flash of Lem's sister yelling at her when she asked her to remember a certain sewing stitch Lauren's mom had shown her. Her great-aunt had practically yelled her into next week.

When Mitch relaxed rather than tensed at her voice, Lauren's fear of him screaming at her dissipated.

"I'm picking up stuff for Lem's chili cook-off tomorrow. We rescheduled the others due to trauma calls."

She sought a subject for small talk. "Ian's coming, I hear."

"My entire crew is," he said flatly. Yet the soft look never left his face. He seemed…disappointed somehow. In her? A bad feeling went through her about the way he worded his last phrase. Before this, Mitch had always included Lauren when he mentioned "his crew." Not today.

Had he already begun to distance himself from the idea of having her on his team? Wasn't that what she wanted? Then why did his words nick like a scalpel?

He faced her. "Look, I overreacted. I've been meaning to tell you thanks for your note."

She scoffed. "Yeah, looks like it really meant a lot."

He sighed. "Lauren, come on. Don't be like that."

"I made a nice gesture and you smooshed it."

"I said I was sorry. I *am* sorry. It's just complicated."

She rested her hand on his arm. "It's okay, Mitch. I understand *complicated*. But I don't understand why you trashed my note."

His jaw clicked. "I can't tell you that." His eyes tendered. "Okay, fine. For what it's worth, I do like you."

What? How did he like her? The thoughts went swirling in her mind because there were only two possibilities. And she didn't know which scared her most at this point. Him liking her romantically, or just as a friend.

Oh, boy. She might be in real trouble here.

At the store, Mitch chose a cart. "Need anything?"

To see you smile. "Maybe." She giggled as girls passed.

He peered delightfully down at her. "What's so funny?"

"You're oblivious to the fact that you're the sort of man who whirls women's heads wherever you go." Giddiness engulfed her. Elation bubbled at the thought that Mitch liked her. She tried to tamp it back down, but like Lem's buoyant butter bowls in the dishwater that day, it kept bouncing back up.

"I don't whirl yours," he said wryly. Then peered at her with an almost-vulnerable expression before refocusing ahead. His breakup must've shattered his self-esteem.

She cleared her throat and hauled up courage. "That's because I'm walking alongside you, going the same direction. If I were passing you, trust me, my head would whirl. But don't get all egotistical about it."

That almost wrought a smile. "Lem says it's been a while since your breakup. He thinks you've been too busy hiding behind Texas sewing machines to socialize or date." He bumped her elbow, but left his arm in contact with hers while they walked.

She did not know what to think, so she just rolled with the lovely flow. Plus hid an impending blush by heaping mass amounts of dark chocolate in the cart. And a yogurt.

Mitch eyed her goodies and grinned gorgeously down at her. Finally. Relief spread through her. He wasn't still mad at her insensitivity before.

Even better, he settled his arm against hers again after she broke contact to retrieve items from shelves.

Once they had their items in their cart, plus things from a list that looked like Grandpa's, they headed to the check-out.

"He hates shopping," Mitch said as she eyed the familiar scratchy scrawl of half cursive, half print, slanted up the page.

She nodded, feeling heartsick for unrecognizable reasons. "He still does, huh?"

"Yeah. Although he's capable, he'd rather delegate it." Mitch spoke more tenderly than the words required. He was obviously acutely aware of her fear regarding Grandpa.

She dug out her wallet. "My treat," he countered. She attempted to protest, but he squared wide shoulders and issued his *this is doctor's orders* look.

"Thanks." Her laugh made his eyes sparkle. "How embarrassing that I filled the cart with chocolate!"

"That's okay. I fully expect you to share. It's my master plan to sweeten you up." He had a decidedly handsome smirk.

She pressed hands to her hips as they exited. "Sweetened? Why? What are you conniving?"

He raised his hands innocently, but grinned wildly. "I'm batting around the idea of giving Lem a surprise party since his birthday is in a few months," Mitch said once they were back on the road.

"Great idea," she forced. While she was grateful Mitch was mindful of Lem, she should have thought of it first.

"You know he's restoring the old truck he has, right?" Mitch asked once they pulled into Lem's driveway.

"Surprisingly, yes." Why had he asked, anyway?

"Lauren, sorry. I didn't mean it as an insult."

"I know. You're good for me, Mitch. And as envious as I am of the closeness you share with Grandpa, I'm thankful you're in his life. I'd never want you not to be." She gritted her teeth.

Mitch paused in the driveway. "But?"

She shook her head, unable to finish yet. She hugged her ribs, heaving emotion for everything she'd forfeited in the past five years. Every lost minute with Grandpa. And for what? "I'm scared of losing him and scarred with regret that I let time go by without seeing him more," she managed to say until her voice fractured.

She wasn't prepared for how fast Mitch moved or how strong and safe and warm his arms felt as they curled around her and pulled her firmly in. "You haven't failed him, Lauren."

She swallowed against his chest. "I hope you're right."

"You get up early just to spend the sunrise with him every morning, then fish for hours before breakfast. You have talk time every evening. I know because he tells me everything. He wanted you in nursing school. It brought him joy."

"That makes me feel worse for quitting, then."

"It's not too late, Lauren. Do you miss it?"

She nodded. "A lot. I love nursing."

"Then stay."

"That's what Grandpa says."

But the vulnerability in Mitch's eyes extended past asking her to stay for Lem's sake.

Lauren broke off the embrace because the last thing she needed to do was grow dependant on Mitch...and because it felt far too wonderful to take refuge in him.

In fact, his arms felt more like home that moment than Texas.

Chapter Thirteen

"Perfect," Mitch said to Lauren on the Saturday morning of the chili cookout. He enjoyed the graceful way her hands moved as she sprinkled garlic into his stockpot.

"Let's see." She passed him a ladle the way she did instruments in surgery. Did she realize how naturally they worked together? "I find this interesting."

"What?" He stirred the spices in with the peppers stewing in the chunky sauce.

"All this." She gestured to Mitch's pot, then across the yard to Lem's. Her smile wattage could light up the yard.

Mitch turned the heat down and eyed Lem, manning a separate simmering pot. "That we have chili cook-offs?"

"Not that, per se. Just the fact that you're making it your life's mission to recreate his recipe when he won't give it up."

"True. Lem's like the ultimate vault when it comes to that recipe." Mitch smirked playfully.

She aimed a spatula at him the way Lem often did. "Don't you dare tell me he gave his coveted secret recipe to you, buster."

Mitch laughed. "Hardly. I've tried for years to replicate it, to no avail. No one makes chili better than Lem."

"You could always try to search his house and steal it."

That made Mitch laugh. "I hope you're kidding." The

fiercely determined look on her face made him think she wasn't.

She tasted a spoonful of Mitch's chili. "You're getting close. It nearly tastes like his. Although I need another bite to be sure." She poured a ladleful into a tin cup then blew on it.

Mitch leaned. "Your sampling will leave none for guests."

She shrugged and grinned past the tin cup he'd sipped many slop soups from while stationed overseas as a combat surgeon. "Warn me if you plan to fire me as your official taste-tester."

"Ha! You'd just sneak over there and sample his." Mitch nodded toward Lem, hovered protectively over his chili pot.

"Probably so." She giggled, then looked up at Mitch in an admiring way that made his insides feel all warm and bubbly. Like the chili sauce. "Don't you know any military interrogation techniques we could use on him to uncover the ingredients?"

Mitch laughed. He really liked engaging her in lively conversation, and even the camaraderie of having her at his side. In the operating room and here, in a domestic setting. *Domestic.*

The word prickled over him. Perhaps they were getting a wee bit too cozy. Or maybe he should just give in to the attraction and court her instead of expending all this energy fleeing from it.

He took a smart step back.

Probably not his most healthy coping mechanism, but that was how things had to be for the time being.

Too risky otherwise. Too much to overcome. For the first time, though, fighting off his growing feelings felt less appealing than contemplating courting her.

He needed a distraction. "Tell me something I might not know about you and Lem."

"Right. Like that's possible." She smirked.

"Seriously. Try me."

"He started cook-offs in my honor." A nostalgic look piggy-backed Lauren's words. "Chili was always my favorite meal."

"Was?" He bumped her shoulder. "Don't talk like it's past tense. It's not too late. You'll be around from now on."

She shielded her eyes from the sun and peered up at him in a feeble way that made him hope he was right. "How do you know?"

He captured her gaze and held it firmly. "Because I know."

Emotions began pulling at all corners of his heart the same time cars began pulling up in the driveway, ending the conversation. And hopefully the good way she was making him feel right now.

Yet for a moment Lauren didn't take her eyes off him. Just studied him like a researcher staring into a microscope.

Until meeting Lauren, he'd been sure his heart had been irrevocably broken. But now, he got to thinking maybe his heart was whole again.

Thankfully a slew of cars quickly ran over any crazy thoughts of romance. He could never let himself forget that miles and distance were the masterminds behind a busted heart and broken engagement.

One look at Lauren's face, and he knew her smile was capable of saving it. Which put him at risk of love and loss again.

He wasn't ready.

And she was worth more effort than he was capable of giving right now.

Plus, all his energy needed to be poured into the trauma center and the details involved.

"Come meet my friends," Mitch said in an agitated tone, even to his own ears.

Her eyes widened as she looked up, so she had noticed.

He turned the burner off with a finality that sent dread through him at the thought of hurting her.

Were their hearts already becoming invested in each other?

Stiffly, they walked together until joining Lem, headed to meet the cars as people exited, bearing smiles and scrumptious-smelling side dishes.

"Lauren, this is my pararescue buddy Nolan. He's married to Mandy, also known as Dr. Briggs, who you met at the center," Mitch said.

She nodded. "Nice to meet you, Nolan."

"And you remember me telling you about Brock?" Mitch indicated the friend who'd helped with Grandpa's repairs.

The PJ, a heavily muscled military guy whose height rivaled Mitch's, stepped forth and shook her hand. "Nice to finally meet you after hearing so much about you. Keeping this guy in line, I hope." Brock nodded to Mitch, who watched Lauren carefully.

Sure enough, as the implications of Brock's innocent words sank in, Lauren blushed.

Obviously Brock's words gave away that Mitch had mentioned her to his friends. Which meant, whether he was ready to admit it or not, she was becoming important to him.

As though picking up on it, her grin exploded out of nowhere. His face burned. A blush? Or chili he'd managed to hijack from her spoon?

Mandy faced Lauren. "Mitch tells me you help at the center."

"Some. Thanks for your help there, too, Dr. Briggs."

The woman smiled. "You, as well. And it's Mandy."

More people, some who'd also helped at the trauma center, arrived. Townspeople scuttled about, doting over Lauren and how grown-up she looked. Some she appeared to recognize, some not.

Mitch derived simple joy out of watching her interact with the range of people. "Lauren, you have uncanny warmth and a gift to be approachable by all. I like that about you."

She dipped her head and didn't say anything for a moment. Then she shifted to peer up at him. "Thanks. I'm glad to know there's one thing you like about me."

She had no idea. Neither did he until the moment those words left her mouth.

There was a lot he liked about her. More and more things in fact.

"Let's eat!" Lem exclaimed. "Mitch? Do the honors?"

Mitch relaxed and thought about what to pray for.

What was he most thankful for today?

"Lord, thanks for bringing Lauren home. For time with Lem. Bless the food and Lem for his hospitality. Help him stop being stingy with that chili recipe. Amen," Mitch finished amid chuckles.

Lem's was loudest as he clapped a weathered hand on Mitch's shoulder. "Nice try, son. God's the only one who could convince me to hand over that recipe before it's time."

Wow. Mitch noticed Lauren didn't flinch when Lem called him "son." When did that change of heart happen?

"And when will it be time, Grandpa?" Lauren licked a spoon and appeared to let Grandpa's mystery chili languish on her tongue.

Lem grinned. "At the readin' of my will."

"Grandpa, don't say that! I'd rather have you than your chili." Lauren became visibly upset, which wiped the smile off Lem's face.

Mitch had noticed a tear in her eye at the end of his prayer and felt her lift her face when he'd taken care to mention her in it. He'd meant every word. Minus the chili part.

Like Lauren, he'd rather have Lem around than the best chili in the world. Mitch cast a warm smile her way. One that intentionally lingered. He dipped his head toward the food. "Chili's ready. Shall we?"

"We shall." Her smile lingered, too. "In fact, I think second helpings are going to be in order."

Mitch had the strongest urge to tuck his arm through hers while they walked and talked together. "I like how you think—"

His emergency beeper went off, interrupting his words.

Ian's phone rang. So did Kate's, who'd just added a delicious-looking green bean casserole to the table.

The trauma crew eyed one another, then looked apologetically at Lem. All conversation stopped as they returned calls.

Lauren bit her lip and watched Lem for signs of disappointment, as did Mitch.

Thankfully, Lem seemed to roll with the punches and didn't appear upset at all.

Not even when, after taking the hectic caller's report, Mitch clicked his phone shut and set down his uneaten chili. "I'm sorry, Lem. There's been a trauma alert. They're calling us all in."

Lem shooed them toward their cars. "Go on then. Food'll be waiting when you take care of business and get back here."

Mitch couldn't describe the disappointment he felt when he walked away from Lem's yard, and Lauren didn't come forward to offer to join his team.

He'd dearly wanted her to step up on her own this time instead of him having to ask.

Granted, she volunteered if she were assured the situation was low risk. He understood why she was skittish. Especially with the complicated cases.

The problem with that was, in trauma care, one couldn't choose. You took what came in, and therefore he needed her either all-in or all-out.

How much longer could he wait for her to jump all-in? Would she ever?

He desperately needed to know he wasn't wasting his time.

Chapter Fourteen

"**I**'m sorry, Grandpa. You went to all this trouble," Lauren said the next afternoon as she stared into Lem's overloaded fridge.

"Searching for dark chocolate?" Lem peered beside Lauren.

"Yep. But all I see is chili." Unfortunately the team had been unable to return yesterday. "There's a ton of food left."

Lem reached in and pulled out a chocolate bar. "Oh, piffle. We have noon cookouts every Saturday. Leftovers go to needy folks. We eat chili once a month." He handed her the candy bar.

She broke it and tried to give Grandpa the bigger half. "You do? I'm glad you stay social."

Lem went for the smaller portion. "Try to. Don't much like being alone all the time." He scratched his head and seemed confused for a second. Cleared his throat and looked away. Then cleared his throat again.

She peered at him. "Grandpa? Are you crying?"

His face squished up, but when she went around to face him, tears definitely pooled in his eyes. He cleared his throat again. "Ah, just my allergies botherin' me."

No. Those were unmistakable tears. And that was undeniable loneliness hovering in his eyes next to the tears.

She couldn't leave him alone anymore. How dare she?

Yet her life was in Texas. The binding weight of her verbal

agreement and the huge loan she'd taken out suddenly sat on her like the issuing bank's three-ton armored truck.

She wrapped arms around him despite his bristle at her doting. "Grandpa, I've made many wrong choices the past five years." *Like every time I didn't come visit when you asked.* "But I promise to make those wrong things right and redeem the time."

He hugged her back, seeming stronger than moments before. "Ah, now. Don't go rearranging your life for me."

"Grandpa." She set her candy aside and put her hands square on his shoulders. "You *are* my life." *Starting now.*

Building loan or not. She'd somehow make it work. She'd learn to love flying. She could visit often that way.

Yet somehow the thought of only visiting Grandpa depressed her. "I want to move here, Grandpa. Let's hope it works out."

He blinked back emotion then swiped a hand, equally strong and wrinkled, over his eyes. "Don't go all sentimental on me." He draped an arm around her, and for once in a long while seemed to hold her up instead of the other way around.

Perhaps her visit, and the promise of her being around more, restored some of Grandpa's strength?

"Tell ya what, carrottop. What say me and you go for a drive? Deliver us some chili to a few hungry folks at the trauma center. They must be starving."

"Surely they've eaten."

"Doubtful. Mitch texted to say he wouldn't make it to breakfast, and in fact probably won't be able to leave all day. They've been going nonstop since lunch yesterday."

"Trauma patients?"

"Yep. And Mitch pulling double duty securing staff. I told him we'd pray. But let's put feet on those prayers and take lunch over, too?"

She grinned. "How do you propose we get there? By tractor?"

He smiled. "I got my old truck in the shed. We'll take it."

"I was looking forward to a ride on Old Faithful or Deere John. Those are the other tractors you still have, right?"

"Yeah, the pair of them plus Bess the Beast, and Clyde, my one-of-a-kind combine."

"I admit that breakfast this morning wasn't as fun with Mitch's empty chair staring dismally at us."

For the first time ever, Lauren *really* missed Mitch not being at Grandpa's. Even digging in to the chocolate bar didn't make it better. Not that she'd tell him so.

But according to Grandpa's grin, he might. "Don't tell."

His face went ultra-innocent. He shuffled outside faster than she could catch him. "Grandpa, I mean it."

Effectively ignoring her, Lem opened the barn door, surprising Lauren with the superb shape his antique Ford was in. "Mitch's been helping me restore it. We're supposed to pinstripe and paint it this week. You ought to help us."

"Be glad to. Then maybe I can borrow it to go see Mara, and Mitch won't have to drive me back and forth."

"He likes giving you rides. Gives him time to talk to you."

"How do you know?"

"He told me so. But you can drive the truck when it's ready, if you insist." He smiled like he had a big secret.

She set the chili pot in the floorboard and went to help Grandpa in, but he scowled at her. "You quit that. No lady should open a door for a man." He prodded her around to the driver's side, then, hand to elbow, helped her up instead. "Say, does Mitch open doors for you?"

Smiling, she started the ignition, which purred. "Always."

"Good. I taught him well, then."

She'd have to agree with Grandpa. Mitch had superb manners.

"Grandpa, after we drop off the food, will you tell me about Mitch on the drive home?" Lauren should probably be concerned that she was curious where Mitch was involved. But she just couldn't be this time. And she had no idea whether that was good or bad.

Lem buckled up his seat belt. "What do you want to know?"

"Ummmm…pretty much everything there is?"

"For starters, huh?" Grandpa sniggered on and off about this the entire trip to the trauma center. Once there, he opened the door before she had the truck fully parked.

"Hang on to your horses." She shook her head at his sudden lithe movement and the surge of energy boosting him up and out.

He swung his head around. "Chili's getting cold. C'mon. No. Wait. You sit." He scurried around to open her door. He took the chili from her and slid a sidelong look. "I might be getting old and decrepit, but I can still open doors for a lady and bring a pot of food to the hungry."

She nodded accordingly. "You certainly can." She followed him in, opening doors for him and ignoring his scolding look when she did so. The nurses' station was dead silent, other than phones ringing incessantly.

"Should I answer that?" She eyed the trilling phone. Call lights flashed like carnival lights along the corridors, too.

Where was everyone? She peered down the halls. Her heart rate sped. Every operating room was full of flurry and people.

She rushed back to the desk and picked up the phone. "Eagle Point Trauma Center. May I help you?" Lauren poised a pen to jot notes, but the caller's words spilled too frantically for understanding. Something about 9–1–1. Signal was poor. She scrambled to string every third word together. "Ma'am, what did 9–1–1 tell you?"

"I couldn't…through! My cousin fell…bluff! He's hurt! We need help! We…help!" Expletives and sobbing came next.

Lauren stood. Signaled Lem. "Grandpa, get 9–1–1 on another phone?"

He did as asked and Lauren relayed the information and location to the dispatcher. She hung up, feeling frazzled and inept, yet as though her nerves were juiced for action. "Apparently a nearby hiker fell pretty far." She scooped up the paper and ran to find someone, anyone, to let them know the ambulance would probably come here with the hiker.

She poked her head in the first O.R. Ian observed her, then pointed to his mask. Mortified at her break in sterile technique, she scuttled backward, slammed the O.R. door and smashed a mask to her face before opening the door again. "We came to drop off chili. Grandpa's manning phones and calling reinforcements," she said, explaining to Ian first why she was here.

"Thanks. That all?" Ian eyed her carefully.

"No. There was a call of a fallen hiker nearby. I imagine they'll bring him here rather than Refuge."

Ian nodded. "Do me a favor, let Mitch know? He's in O.R. Three."

"Will do." Lauren really hadn't wanted Mitch to know she was here. Because then he'd probably order her to help.

To her surprise, he didn't. When she explained the situation, he simply nodded and thanked her. How odd.

Probably for the best. Otherwise Grandpa'd be stuck here.

Grandpa updated her about the ambulance service call.

Mitch came out and washed up. "Any other info?"

Lauren brushed hair from her eyes. "The ambulance service asked permission to come. We told them yes. Hope that's okay."

Mitch eyed the rooms. "Yeah, we're about done here. We'll get this one moved out then ready the room in case the hiker needs exploratory."

We. By that, did he mean her? Or just his crew? He didn't say, just pressed a mask back over his mouth and reentered the O.R. suite, presumably to give the crew an update that another patient was on the way.

Did Mitch want her help? He hadn't directly asked. She went back to the desk and found Grandpa, relieved that Nita now manned the phones.

Had she been thrust into answering call lights? She had less training than Lauren. Poor Nita!

"We may as well put the chili in the fridge," Nita said to Grandpa. "Doesn't look like we'll have time to eat anytime soon."

Lauren nibbled her lip.

Lem eyed her pointedly. "They're busier than that angry hornets' nest I knocked down last week."

Lauren's gaze turned toward the O.R. bays. And the blinking call lights going unanswered. Nita rushed off to answer them. Her face was so flushed, Lauren grew concerned. She knew Nita would never put Lauren on the spot and ask her for help.

Yet Nita would also never stand here and watch others sink.

"I wonder how Mara's doing," Lauren whispered.

Grandpa stuck hands in his pockets and tilted his head. "You should go check then. Maybe stay and help."

The expectation in his face matched the conviction pulsing through her heart. Lauren looked back down the hall and saw the state the harried staff was in. "I should."

"I can hang out on Mitch's fishin' boat 'til you're done."

"I don't want you out fishing alone. It'll be dark soon."

"I got a nearby buddy I can fish with."

"Promise you'll be okay for a bit?"

"I live by myself, don't I?" And he didn't look too happy about it, either.

"I suppose you do."

He shooed her. "Go on, child. They need you worse than I do at the moment." His grin was back.

It bolstered her courage as she walked up to Kate, who approached the desk with her head down, frantically sorting through surgical papers.

Lauren approached her. "Is something I can do to—?"

Kate's head surged up. She grasped Lauren's shoulders. "Oh,

yes. Please! A nurse was a no-call, no-show. We are very short staffed." Kate shoved her toward O.R. Three. Mitch's room.

What if Lauren did something worse than forgetting to put on a mask before entering the O.R.? Her mistake had rattled her.

Kate fell into step beside her. "They need a scrub assistant in there. Mitch's circulating nurse is trying to be two people right now, and she almost left a clamp in a patient."

"Not good." Yet it almost made Lauren feel better that she hadn't made the only nursing mistake today.

Lauren changed into surgical garb and scrubbed her hands with a sponge, then stepped into the O.R.—

To find Mitch already prepping to operate on a patient. Mitch looked up when she entered. Acute surprise, then, as she gowned and gloved, stark relief on his face flushed all fear and doubt away. "Lauren" was all he said. Then gestured to the spot right beside him. As though she naturally belonged there.

"The hiker?" She nodded at the patient, already asleep.

"Yeah. Thanks for taking the call." His hip settled against hers. She hadn't seen him stand that close to any other nurse.

"We brought chili over."

"And stayed to help?" Delight brightened his amazing eyes.

She nodded, lowering her head in hopes he wouldn't see the blush flaring past her mask and goggles.

Fondness washed across eyes that suggested he knew how hard it was for her to do this.

Mitch held out his hand, but she rested a scalpel there before he could say the word. She could tell by the way his cheeks lifted above the mask that he grinned.

She loved the transformation of lighthearted Mitch to serious surgeon. Yet he never lost his trademark humility. Confidence crucial to his job and leadership, yes. But no shred of an inflated ego existed in him.

Lauren busied herself organizing surgical instruments, feeling all eyes on her. She looked up to see Ian's eyes crinkling at the corners as he observed her. The circulating nurse also smiled and appeared to melt with relief. They seemed really happy to have her.

God, don't let me mess this up. More prayer surfaced in her mind. *Help me deserve their trust and keep me as competent as this patient deserves.*

"Retractor," Mitch said after his initial cut.

Lauren eyed the instruments and picked up something resembling a shoehorn. "Retractor," she repeated and placed it where he indicated in the surgical site.

"What happened?" Lauren asked after Mitch got through the intense portion of the surgery and into wound closure.

"Rock climber not properly geared for the terrain."

"He's lucky," Lauren said, then eyed Mitch. "Had you not built this center..." She trailed off, remembering that even under anesthesia, patients' hearing was the last sense to go.

Mitch's expression finished her sentence.

Had this center not been here, this young man would not have made it to another hospital.

It dawned on Lauren what Mitch reminded her of when he entered into surgery-mode. He operated on each and every patient as though intent to give the person the life his dad never had.

Compassion welled up for him. She knew how it felt to grow up without a dad. Yet hadn't God provided Lem? How odd that she and Mitch never ended up meeting until now. She handed Mitch his next-needed clamp.

Ian arranged respiratory tubing. "Cardinal outdoor rule. Never hike or fish alone," he said to no one in particular.

Alarm screamed through her. "Mitch, does Grandpa have a fishing buddy close by?"

"Not that I'm aware of. Why?"

Lauren broke out in a cold sweat. "Then I may need to scrub out and go check on him. He came with me to drop off chili. When I was needed, he said he was going fishing with a friend."

Mitch met her gaze. "He's safety-conscious. I doubt he'd go alone. We're almost done here. Let me go with you to be sure."

Lauren didn't like the concern swimming in Mitch's to-die-for eyes. Or the intensity and speed with which he worked now to suture a wound.

A terrible sense of panic enveloped her. Mitch's expression didn't circumvent it.

No, she didn't like it at all.

Chapter Fifteen

Not until two military search-and-rescue helicopters hovered over the trauma center with pararescuemen scampering down ropes did Lauren realize how worried Mitch was about Lem.

She raised her voice above rotor buzz. "PJ friends?"

"Yeah." Mitch bent to exchange his surgeon shoes for combat boots. "I called in a favor." He winked at her, but tension carved a determined edge into his face she'd never seen before.

One she guessed he'd honed overseas while operating with bullets zinging over his head. She knew because Grandpa told her, which added to Mitch's appeal. Which was the last thing she should notice right now with Grandpa MIA.

Lauren stared at her phone screen and felt like growling. "Why isn't Grandpa answering his cell phone?"

Mitch drew near. His very presence calmed. "Probably because it's sitting at home on his stereo, where he leaves it every time he walks out the door." His tone went wry.

Lauren looked up. "Sure he knows how to use a cell phone?"

Mitch unfolded a lake map. "Yes. I made sure of it."

"You got it for him?" She instinctually knew the answer. A man like Mitch would.

"Yeah. Hooked it up, paid the bill and taught him how to use it. But so far haven't managed to get him to take it with him when he goes somewhere." Mitch ran hands over his buzz cut and walked with her to meet the camouflaged men.

"Thanks for coming, guys. He's been gone an hour now," Mitch said to the group of PJs as he led them to a picnic table. "I went out with binoculars but didn't see any sign of him or my boat, which isn't in my pole barn. I can't fathom him being out in this kind of heat."

Mitch was right. Ninety degrees lasted into evening. Lauren fought fear and images of all that could go wrong with a frail person. He could become disoriented. Fall in the lake. He could—

Ugh! Being a nurse was a curse sometimes as far as making one imagine the worst.

"Is he alone?" Brock asked.

Mitch motioned to Lauren. "She mentioned he was going to fish with a friend."

Lauren put her hair in a ponytail. "I'm not sure who the friend is. Grandpa didn't give a name or address. He didn't take water or anything, to my knowledge." The words sounded ridiculous coming off her tongue. How could she have let him go without getting more information? Still, he was an adult....

"He said he had a fishing buddy." Welling panic threatened to choke her. She coughed. Mitch handed her a swig of water. She didn't want a drink. She wanted Grandpa to be okay.

Why had she let him venture off alone? Yet the grandpa Lauren remembered taught outdoor safety to Eagle Scout kids. If anyone knew not to traverse the terrain alone, it was Grandpa.

"I am fairly certain he is fishing with a friend. I hope we're overreacting," Lauren said to Mitch's rescuer friends.

"Still, it's better to be safe." Mitch planned a search grid with the PJs while Lauren paced.

"Please pray," she whispered desperately to Mitch, drawing from his strength before he headed out to search.

When he came back with no sign of Grandpa, she crumpled into a garden bench overlooking the lake.

Mitch rested a sustaining hand on her. "Eagle Point authorities are also looking. We'll find him, Lauren."

"But in what condition? I let him go, Mitch. Me. I did this." Her voice cracked. She looked up, expecting a scolding. Deserved it. Instead, strong arms braced her and mercy emanated from beautiful eyes.

"Keep praying," she pleaded, and yearned for his faith.

"Sweet Lauren." He pulled her up and into a big hug. "I have been. Won't hurt matters for you to say a few, too."

She set her cheek against his throat from where warm strength and pure comfort wafted. She nestled closer. It was the right thing to do. Lean on him and let God flow between.

Mitch pulled back without severing the embrace, his sturdy gaze tentative yet tender. That moment she knew several things.

He *really* cared about Grandpa. So did God. More than she and Mitch put together. She also knew Mitch understood what Grandpa meant to her.

Their joint love and concern for Lem bonded them beyond human time and reason.

Mitch's mouth moving against her temple told her he prayed beneath his breath for Lem, and probably for her.

He shouldn't have to pray alone. Her faith surged. "Please bring Grandpa back safely. And his friend, if there is one. And teach Grandpa to take his stinkin' cell phone with him."

Mitch chuckled at her ending prayer and echoed her "Amen." He hugged her again. Profound realization hit that she didn't want to leave the strength and surety of his embrace. Ever.

Mitch broke contact, but not completely. "We'd better go house to house. Ask if anyone has seen him. Surely the friend lives along the lake. If we don't find him there, we'll expand the search." He kept an arm around her, undoubtedly to provide support as she walked. It meant nothing more.

She'd be a fool to hope for more.

This was one guy even the strongest-willed woman would

have a tough time not falling for. She'd mentally joked about liking him, but this—this was becoming the real deal.

Lauren had no idea how her mind could grapple with Mitch and forever with Grandpa missing. Except maybe subconsciously she knew if something happened to Grandpa, she'd have no one.

Other than Mitch?

The thought of something being wrong with Grandpa caused Lauren to hyperventilate. One of the PJs brought her a bag. Mitch helped her to breathe in it until she calmed down.

A local first responder spread out a neighborhood map on the table. Mitch and Lauren sat opposite the rescuer.

A whistle behind them brought them up. They turned to find Brock sprinting over. "Found him."

Lauren rushed him. "Safe?"

Brock pulled Mitch aside, which incited Lauren. "He's my grandfather. I should be kept in the loop."

Whatever Brock said made Mitch brace an arm around her.

"He's safe…for now," Brock assured.

"For now?" Her body became one gigantic cold sweat.

"Yes, he was bitten by a venomous snake."

Lauren felt like heaving. Mitch upheld her. "Where is he?"

Mitch led her to the center. "Headed to the trauma room."

"What happened?" Mitch beat Lauren asking Brock as they ran. "Most poisonous snakes in the area are defensive and like to be left alone. Lem must've accidentally stepped on it or something. Never would he provoke one."

"All I know is he was fishing with a friend, but on his way back to the center, he was bitten."

"What kind of snake?" Mitch seemed breathless, yet not from running. He was as worried about Lem as she was.

"Copperhead or cottonmouth by the looks of it. They're giving him antivenom now."

"Who found him?" Lauren asked.

"His lady friend. When he didn't call to let her know he

made it back to the trauma center, she went looking for him. Found him nearly unconscious and called authorities."

Lady friend? What lady friend?

Brock continued as they sprinted toward the center. "She thought he'd had a stroke because his eyelids drooped and his speech slurred. But he was able to communicate that after leaving her dock, he walked into a snake's path and somehow was stricken. That part's unclear."

"Call off the crew. We found him. He's mostly okay," Mitch said as they passed the search party leader, who relayed the message into a fancy radio as they reached the double doors.

Brock held them open. "I'll finish updating searchers."

Lauren rushed inside the center with Mitch. "What room?" she asked Kate breathlessly, who met them at the door.

"With Ian in Trauma Three." Kate ushered them to the room. Lauren stopped short. An older woman stood by Lem's bedside and held his hand. Her forehead pinched in worry.

Lem looked like a bloated baked potato with sausage arms.

As Grandpa and the woman stared caringly at one another, they both wore devoted expressions and floppy sun hats.

Matching sun hats.

The sight froze Lauren speechless on the spot.

Mitch hunkered at his bedside. "Heard you lost consciousness after the bite. Did you see what kind of snake it was?"

Lem shook his head. "We were both trying to get away from one another but he took a swipe at me anyhow." Grandpa grimaced and writhed. Lauren knew his high tolerance. He was in excruciating pain.

Her heart squeezed with fear and compassion. Able to move now, she leaned across the bed and hugged him. Her tears wet his gown. "I'm grateful you were found in time to get help."

No one commented, which ramped her into outer panic. She eyed the doctor. "He *did* get found in time for help, right?"

Mitch raised his chin and eyed her sternly. *Calm down.*

Right. Okay. She needed to not lose it. Otherwise Grandpa's pulse would soar and the poison would travel faster. She reached for Mitch's offered hand beneath the bed. He squeezed. The minor tremor in his fingers told her that while he was doing a better job than her of hiding it, he was seriously scared for Lem.

She gave his hand a good return squeeze this time, still under the bed rail and out of Grandpa's sight.

It felt good to draw strength from Mitch and to impart it.

"Thizzziz lady." Lem aimed a groggy grin at the woman.

Mitch reached across and shook her hand. "You look familiar. You're the new local librarian, right?"

She nodded and nibbled her lip as the antivenom specialist reentered. "Folks, if I could ask some of you to step out. We need a little more room to work. One of you may stay."

"Tight quarters," Lauren said and scooted back, annoyed that the hat woman and Mitch stayed plastered to Grandpa's bedside as though family. Lauren was Lem's blood relative, yet the doctor kept asking Mitch for the legal and medical permissions.

Lauren gave the woman an abrasive stare. "Excuse me, but I'd really like to have time with him, too."

The woman's eyes widened, making Lauren realize how rude she sounded. "Yes." She stepped back but her eyes filled with tears. "By all means. I'm so sorry."

Remorse riddled Lauren as she spent time with Grandpa and tried to ignore the sniffling behind her. Either the woman was very attached to Grandpa or very hurt by Lauren's outburst.

Lord, maybe Mitch should just suture my mouth shut.

Lem eyed the lady, then Lauren sternly. "What'd you say, urchin?"

"Nothing, Lem. She's fine. Let her be," the lady said.

Lauren blinked and offered a kind smile. Genuine this time. The woman didn't have to defend her. Lauren didn't deserve it.

"We'll step out," Mitch said to Lem's lady friend and ushered Lauren out, to her further dismay.

"Mitch, are you Grandpa's power of attorney agent or something?" Lauren blurted out as they stepped in the hall.

Mitch's eyes narrowed in an assessing manner before he spoke. "Yes. I hope that doesn't bother you."

Her eyes narrowed back, giving him a plain answer. Of course it bothered her. Why hadn't Grandpa asked her?

"Lauren, he needed someone who'd be physically present in order to make decisions in events of emergency. Like this."

"But you've been overseas."

"We just signed the papers a month before you decided to drop in with little notice."

"Yeah, well, I'm sorry to crash your and Grandpa's lives."

"You know I didn't mean it like that. Why are you angry?"

"Because it should be me."

Mitch enunciated clearly, probably so the frustration he felt building inside would not cause his teeth—or hers in her axe of jealousy—to grind. "It still can be."

She hated when he was right. "So I suppose you know also about the new library Grandpa's founding in Eagle Point?"

"I know everything about Lem. Except this." Mitch grinned at the elderly pair through the doorway.

She socked his arm. "They could just be friends."

Mitch leaned in. "Pretty cozy for 'just friends.'"

"Let me see." She shouldered him aside. "What's cozy?"

Mitch pointed over her shoulder. "Look. Grandpa's elbow is brushing hers," he whispered.

A sudden thought perfused her face with warmth. Clearly, Mitch thought Lem's brush of elbows meant more than friends.

What, then, did it mean when Mitch did the same while they worked surgical cases side by side?

Or had Mitch simply used that contact as a means to infuse courage to Lauren because he knew she felt ill-equipped?

Lauren studied him, but his face gave nothing away.

Something else hit. What Mitch said about knowing everything about Lem. Indeed he did. Except maybe the thing

Grandpa told her on the way here. "Mitch, did you know that Grandpa is donating this year's Library Fun Day proceeds entirely to the trauma center?"

His expression didn't waver. "He mentioned that."

"You seem intimately acquainted with all his dealings." Her tone sounded sour to her own ears, but she couldn't help it. Was there any aspect of Grandpa's life Mitch wasn't involved in?

Mitch eyed her funny but didn't say anything.

He didn't have to. The scowl forming over his eyes said enough. He was plenty tired of her jealousy. She was growing sick of it, too. Sick of the struggle of not being able to let go and lay it down.

"Do you know what this year's Library Fun Day will entail?"

She clenched her jaw. "No. Do you?"

"Hey, cool your jets. I asked out of curiosity. Not to incite you."

"Grandpa never shares what the Library Fun Days are to be until a few weeks out. He likes surprises. And don't tell me you already knew that, or I might have to box your ears."

Mitch almost smiled at that.

Maybe she was on to something here. Maybe humor could defuse some of her envy.

Mitch's place in Lem's life, however innocent, irritated Lauren beyond reason. Perhaps her mind's wonky way to prevent her heart from finding one more reason to like Mitch?

"Quarter for your thoughts." Mitch watched her carefully.

"You seem to know more about Grandpa than I do." Jealousy stabbed its ugly blade in Lauren's heart again. She fought it.

After all, she had had a chance and she'd chosen Texas and nursing school, then a shop, over Lem and making a life here.

Mitch knew. He could see the fight in her eyes. The regret. Jealous envy. Remorse. Guilt. Irritation.

All rooted in her fear of losing Lem.

No doubt his disappearance and unknown whereabouts these scary couple of hours gushed it all to the surface for Lauren.

He needed to distract her from fear. "Lauren, will you help me plan Lem's surprise party for summer's end?"

She shrugged. "Sure. I plan to stay until his birthday."

At least she didn't sound as jealous. He refused to apologize for being there for a man who was there for him when he had needed a dad. Yet her angst over Mitch's closeness with Lem seemed to scrape against her like a cheese grater.

"Let's make time for just you and me to plan it," he said in a lower voice as Ian walked their way. Mitch didn't want Ian to know he was interested in Lauren. Admittedly, he was. Their bonded fear over losing Lem had blown his cover and brought his feelings to light. He told Ian everything. But to mention this would be insensitive, right? Ian was going through a painful divorce.

Memories of Ian's agony slammed to the forefront how distance destroys relationships. Memories of his own pain made Mitch wary of falling for someone again so soon.

His guard needed to be all the way up in resisting Lauren's unwitting charm. He scooted a distance between them now.

Lauren must have mistaken his motion as ill thoughts toward her because shame cloaked her face. He could kick himself. She wasn't to blame for his past relationship pain.

Yet the last thing he wanted to do was repeat it.

Lauren struggled enough with self-abasement. He didn't want to add to that. But she was destined for Texas anyhow. Safer for them both to resist the draw he didn't like admitting was there.

"How often did you and Grandpa talk when you were deployed?" she asked, confirming his suspicions that she'd taken his cold-shoulder maneuver personally. How to remedy this?

"I checked in with him daily when I could. Some weeks I could only check in a few times."

Lauren's countenance dipped more. A physically ill look came over her. "I hate that I let time get away from me. That I only managed to talk to him once a week."

"Fridays."

Her face lifted. "What?"

"You called Lem every Friday evening at seven sharp."

"How did you know? Never mind. You know everything about him." In a blur of flailing arms, she stood, left the center and fled to the lake's edge. Mitch had followed, yet stood back. She paced the beach, not seeming to know whether to be mad at Mitch or glad she'd been consistent in calling at least.

"Mitch!" Ian waved them inside. They sprinted. As soon as they entered and saw staff scrimmaging around Lem's bed and how much more swollen he was, Mitch knew what was up. He pulled Lauren back. "Let the specialist handle it."

She puffed air, her breathing ragged. "What's happening?"

"Antivenom reaction." Mitch braced her shoulders while the team worked to reverse or lessen Lem's reaction.

"The medication was supposed to make him better, not worse."

"Sometimes it happens." Mitch rubbed hands along her arms. "They'll handle it, okay?"

When she looked up at him with the same fear his mom had had the moment she had gotten the call that Mitch's dad had been in a wreck, Mitch broke inside. He pulled her around so her face would be hidden in his chest. She didn't need to see everything. "It's okay. He'll be okay." Mitch watched the team to be sure.

Ian intubated Lem, and the specialist gave antidotes through Lem's IV. Mitch eased Lauren into the hall amid the flurry.

Her face stayed pressed to his chest the entire time. He held her too, drawing strength himself. They prayed together until Ian called them back in. "Coast is clear. He's stabilizing."

"Close call." The specialist waved them to the bedside. "He's resting now but he'll have a longer recovery than expected. Let's keep him overnight."

Lauren nodded. "Where did his lady friend go?"

"She left for the evening."

"We should probably let her know."

"I'll take care of it," Brock offered.

"Thanks," Mitch said. They went to Lem's bedside and bid him good-night. He was so sedated, Mitch doubted he comprehended. "We'll be in the waiting room," he told Lem's venom specialist.

The man nodded. "We'll take good care of him. Go rest."

"His leg looks like it'll have cellulitis," Lauren said.

"I wouldn't doubt it. He'll probably need help the next couple months as the infection clears. He may not be so mobile."

She sighed. "One good thing about this. It brought my priorities front and center. At least what they should be. No matter what it takes, I'll stay as long as he needs me."

Mitch thought Lem would always need her, emotionally. Physically, it would be touch and go for a while. "That's probably not a bad idea."

He walked with Lauren to the waiting room, but resisted the urge to hold her again, though everything in him screamed to.

The last time wreaked havoc with his emotions.

They settled in the waiting room. To his delight, she sat next to him on the couch and rested her head on his shoulder. So much for resistance. Mitch just couldn't. He wrapped an arm around her and they lounged in quiet under subdued lighting.

The Bible on the table kept him centered. "Lauren, just so you know, Friday evenings were his favorite time," Mitch said when some moments of reflection passed. "He'd wipe everything off his schedule for you, because he knew that's when you'd call."

"Still, I feel bad and wish I could redeem the time."

He hugged her for emphasis. "You can."

"Can I?" She stood and wrapped her arms around herself.

Paced then stepped close, as if needing to read proof in his face as he rose. She shook her head. "Not without that help from God you and Lem are bent on believing in."

Forget his bruised heart. Lauren's was wounded far more critically at the moment.

He breached a personal sense of honor to guard his heart like a high-security military compound, braced his hands on her shoulders and hauled her in for the hug of a lifetime.

Mouth against the silky hair nearest her ear, he whispered, "Then perhaps it's time for you to start believing in them again, too."

Chapter Sixteen

Maybe Mitch was right.

Lauren pondered it the next day on the way to visit Grandpa. After all, they'd prayed and Grandpa was going to be okay, despite two brushes with death.

When Lauren reached the room, Grandpa's lady friend stepped out. "I thought you might want to see him a minute."

"Thank you." Lauren smiled as kindly as she could muster, considering she felt entitled to more than a minute. On the heels of that prickly thought came remorse. She should apologize.

"Hey, carrottop." Grandpa looked better today, but sleepy.

"Hey, snake charmer." She rubbed her hand along his.

Grandpa grinned. Knuckles rapped the door. Lauren turned.

"Hiya." Mitch waved from the hall. As he peered in, it seemed to her that his smile brightened when he saw her.

She went to the door so he'd feel greeted. "You weren't in the waiting room when I woke, so I figured you were rounding." Her cheeks tinged, remembering how he'd held her in the stillness and uncertainty until she'd slept. "Thanks for the blanket."

"My pleasure." His gaze lingered before sliding over her shoulder to Lem. "He turned that critical corner."

"I'm so glad. Thank you for the prayers…and everything." He'd been nothing short of a rock last night.

The venom specialist stepped out and let Mitch in. He approached Lem's bedside, shaking his head and grinning. "Some people will do anything to keep from working on tractors."

Mitch's comment made Lem smile. "I did it for attention," Grandpa teased. "Provoked that snake into pert-near killin' me."

"Seriously, they sent the air force after you, Grandpa."

"Those big choppers were for me?" He seemed utterly proud that such a big deal had been made. "I feel like a war hero."

"Whose lack of communication sent an entire elite special operations rescue team plus EMS forces on a wild Grandpa chase."

Smile eradicated, Lem eyed Mitch keenly. "Is she bluffing?"

Mitch shook his head. "Afraid not."

"Mercy sakes, kids. Sorry for the scare I put you and your friends and crew through. No harm meant. Mitch, your boat's in Lady's covered dock. She planned to ask you to oar her out there, but you all scared her away." He faced Lauren. "Especially you."

"I'm sorry." Lauren swiped her forehead. "With all due respect, this search ordeal could have been prevented had you taken your cell phone with you."

Lem scowled. "Now you sound like Lady Arlington."

Okay, maybe Lauren liked this lady after all.

"Grandpa, why do you call her Lady Arlington?"

"That's her name. First name's 'Lady.' Last 'Arlington.'"

"Sounds like royalty."

"She is. Way back in her ancestry. British, I believe. Please pass a message to Lady that I'm all right," Lem said.

"Already took care of it," Mitch said. "She was here when we got here, but you were sawing logs."

Lem scratched his head. "Was I?"

"Yep. Snoring so loud you sucked tiles off the ceiling."

Lem started to look up, then shook his head and blushed.

"Lady said she'll be back to see you after the library fundraiser meeting," Lauren said, feeling bristly again for reasons unknown. She stepped closer to Grandpa's bed than Mitch.

Mitch leaned on the side rail. "Thought she looked familiar. She's the librarian who recently moved here, right?"

"Right. She's also someone I'm growing fairly fond of. You okay with that, carrottop?"

Lauren paused, not knowing what to say. Lady wasn't Grandma, but Grandpa was entitled to live life with who he wanted. "It just shocked me to see you with someone other than Grammy."

"Carrottop, I'll never love another woman like I did her."

"Don't be so sure, Grandpa. Lady seemed to be really shaken up at the thought of you kicking off. You can tell me."

Grandpa bristled. "What I can tell you is that before that slithery varmint intruded, we were just two fishing buddies planning a fundraising event."

"Just buddies? Grandpa, you have matching hats."

"So what? If it becomes more, you two'll be first to know."

Lauren stiffened. There it was again. Grandpa lumping Mitch into the same caliber of importance as her. She cast Mitch a wary look. He watched her carefully. He knew. He sent an empathetic smile her way—but not apologetic. Why would he?

It wasn't his fault she chose Texas over Grandpa. At least he was being sensitive about it.

The next morning, doctors released Lem, and Mitch helped her get him home. "Why so forlorn, carrottop?" Grandpa said.

She decided to be transparent. "Part of my irritation is because being here has made me see how unhappy I am in Texas."

Lem rested a tender hand on her cheek. "You were making do. Making the best of it, like you always did growing up. You gotta quit living life believing there's nothin' better for you."

"You're right. If not for the verbal commitment I made, careers we left, loans and renovations, I could come back."

Grandpa straightened. "You're really considering it?" The

grin that exploded spurred her to do everything possible to move back home. Strange. Mere weeks ago, she'd considered Texas home.

On Sunday Mitch picked them up for church. On the way, Grandpa chewed his cheek, which made him look funny considering how swollen his face still was. "Maybe you can explain the situation to the bank. Surely they'd understand and have mercy."

"Somehow, the terms *mercy* and *banks* don't mix."

Mitch looked as doubtful as Lauren felt, which didn't give her confidence. Until he said, "God can make a way, Lauren."

"Sometimes I forget that God is more powerful than a loan officer." She'd make some crucial phone calls. Talk to her friend. Boy, she dreaded that.

"Bank'll come around. It'll work out."

"Except there's also the matter of renovation contracts," Lauren said.

"She's actually thinkin' of coming back!" Lem exclaimed.

"And selling my house in a grumpy economy." Lauren sighed.

"She's really gonna do it, Mitch!"

"Not if all this doesn't work out, Grandpa. I'm thinking of all my clients waiting for projects."

"Someone else'll do 'em," Lem said, as though it was a done deal.

"Not when they've already paid half up front. And I used that to pay contractors, who are already working."

"Oh, dear!" His excitement waned. He didn't have to say it. But she did. "Seems I've built myself a mountainous mess."

"You catch that?" Mitch asked Lauren after the pastor gave an uplifting message about God moving mountains.

She laughed. "How could I not? You and Grandpa elbowed my ribs the entire message, which seemed ornately fashioned for me."

Mitch nestled her in his arm, warm across her back. "Sweet Lauren, I promise prayer changes things."

She nodded. "I'm beginning to believe again."

She was also beginning to believe her growing attachment to Mitch wasn't going to go away. In fact, it seemed not only here to stay but here to proliferate exponentially by the day.

Dangerous considering his stance on romance.

Tomorrow, he may catch on to her and pull away.

She'd let herself enjoy it, if only for today.

She peered up at Mitch. His eyes riveted to hers with a message that seemed to say, if she were moving back, that changed the game for everyone and everything.

Including them.

He was about to be a goner. One more time of her looking into his eyes like that, and he'd fall to the floor a dead man.

Lauren's phone rang after she changed Lem's bandage once they returned from church. "It's my Texas friend. Pray!"

Mitch and Lem did so as Lauren spoke in subdued tones.

Lauren looked stunned when she reentered. "She was very understanding. Upset, but encouraging."

"Whaddaya mean encouraging?" Lem tried to stand.

Mitch inched him down. He needn't bear weight on the leg.

"I mean, she encouraged me to find a way to stay."

Lem whooped. "Give me the dish!"

"She confessed that she'd always hoped her brother and me would get back together, which was her main reason for bringing me into business with her."

Mitch didn't like the jealous twinges hitting him with that news.

"She assured me she could find someone to take my place, but wanted me to promise to keep in touch with her."

Lem scratched his head. "What about the contractors?"

"She's certain she can handle them, with her brother's help.

He's an attorney. She hadn't wanted to bring him in out of sensitivity to me."

Mitch raised his hands as though he was pausing the air. "Wait. He's an attorney yet drives like an idiot?"

Lem gave Mitch a stern look, which made Lauren grin.

Mitch sat. "What else?"

"That's it for now." Her face lit. "But maybe we're getting our way after all."

The way her face gleamed destroyed his defenses. "So that means there's a chance you'll move to Illinois?"

Why was he so afraid to believe it? Hope for it?

"A big, big chance." Her face beamed like the sun.

Wow. Did this ever change things.

His heart thumped against his chest.

Mitch's phone rang. He eyed the caller's number. Kate— who never called unless it was trauma center–related. "I need to take this. Excuse me." Mitch stepped in Lem's living room and called her back. "Hey, Kate. Everything okay?"

"Yes, but you should come to the center. Mara's waking up. In fact, I need to go. See you in a few." She hung up quickly.

Mitch observed Lauren through the doorway, then called Ian and said in low tones, "Mara's waking. Should we tell Lauren?"

"Problem with that is we have court orders to contact detectives at the first sign of Mara regaining consciousness."

"True." Mitch's mind whirled with what to do.

"Does she know that the family of the boy who died pressed charges?"

Mitch sighed. "Not to my knowledge. We were instructed by attorneys not to speak about the case until depositions."

"Mitch, hate to say it, bro, but this could get ugly."

"Very. Maybe it's best we shield Lauren from the trauma of seeing Mara arrested upon waking?"

"I don't know. Tough call." Ian sounded contemplative.

"She'll feel cheated out of seeing Mara wake." Mitch struggled ethically and emotionally with the right thing to do. "Legally, I'm obligated to inform authorities."

"I don't think Lauren should be present when that goes down." Wisdom and mercy drove Ian's words. Ian was right. But that wouldn't keep Lauren from unloading on Mitch.

"I opt not to tell her yet," Mitch said.

"For what it's worth, I think that's a good call."

"Let's hope you're right." Otherwise the repercussions could shatter Mitch's friendship with Lauren and ruin whatever else was becoming possible between them.

"I'll meet you at the center, Mitch." Ian hung up.

Mitch returned to the kitchen slower than he left. "I need to run to the center for a bit," Mitch said nonchalantly and avoided Lauren's gaze. *Don't ask questions,* he willed.

Lem was used to him leaving suddenly and didn't bat an eye. Lauren, however, had grown acutely hawkeyed.

She rose, as if for once she'd offer to come. Figured. She knew something was off. He chanced a peek on the way out.

Too many questions swirled in her eyes.

He didn't take ten steps before the tortured look on her face began to taunt him. If Mara truly was about to come out of her coma, she'd become incarcerated in an instant.

Lauren was better off not seeing what was about to ensue.

Mitch held to his judgment call and hoped all the way to the center that he'd made the right one. When the prosecutor, attorneys and police were waiting at the trauma center by the time they got there, Mitch felt better about not telling Lauren.

It had been the best thing to do. Right?

He'd find out soon enough.

Soon enough came sooner than Mitch was prepared for. Minutes after the legal team left, Lauren showed up at the center with a tray of sandwiches and suspicion in her vivid green eyes.

She was on to him.

* * *

"Something wrong, Lauren?" Kate put an EKG machine away.

"Mitch is avoiding me like the sharp end of an HIV needle."

"That's odd." She wound cables.

"Yeah, so…about the scrubs you left in my locker."

"Yeah? They fit you nicely."

"Yep. I'm not sure the note does, though."

Kate smiled. "Why not? You think about what I said?"

"I did. I appreciate you encouraging me to be a permanent part of the nursing team here. Your opinion means a lot."

Kate slid sterile kits into cubbies. "Think about the other thing I said?"

"About considering a permanent future with Mitch, too? Yeah, but I think he's still hung up on someone else."

Kate straightened. "Why would you say that?"

"He has some other girl's ring in his glove box."

"You're kidding?" Kate spun and stormed into the hall.

Lauren chased after her. "Kate, wait. Don't hound him."

"Who said anything about hounding? Pounding a big dose of sense into him is more what I had in mind."

Lauren laughed. Then sped. "Wait. You look serious."

"I am. Look, Lauren, I'm not sure why he still has that ring, but I *am* sure she means nothing to him. Not anymore."

Lauren stepped close. "She hurt him?"

"Very badly. More than he knows. The bond between you two has done wonders for him, however."

"Thanks, Kate. That helps. If nothing else, it breaks my stream of bad news lately."

Kate's expression became empathetic. She put her hand on Lauren's arm. "So you know about Mara?"

Alarm screamed through Lauren like an ambulance driving by. Or maybe one really did. Lauren couldn't be sure because her ears rang so loudly with her pulse swooshing in her ears.

She drew a breath. "Actually, I meant bad news from the bank that is holding my money hostage until I pay off a loan that won't let me leave Texas for about ten years. What about Mara?"

Empathy turned to caution on Kate's face. "Oh, wow. Never mind. I'm sorry." Kate made her getaway.

"Kate, please. If there's something I need to know…"

"Mitch will tell you. Because he hasn't, it clearly means you're better off not knowing for now." Kate went for the nearest door.

"Not so fast. Tell me what's going on or I'll step foot out that door and not come back. I mean it. I'll bail for good."

That stopped Kate. She whirled. "Why would you do that?"

"Because if we were *truly* a team, like you and Mitch and Ian claim, I'd already know what was going on with Mara."

Kate's countenance fell but her shoulders rose. She drew in a breath and studied Lauren. "You know what? You're right. But still, due to legalities, Mitch needs to be the one to say it."

"Say what?" Mitch stood at the door with a bag of chips.

Both women eyed each other. "That's my cue." Kate slipped out. And took Mitch's chips with her.

Lauren moistened her lips. "Kate misunderstood a conversation between us and almost let it slip about Mara."

Mitch paled. Came closer. "Did Kate tell you?"

"No. Said she couldn't."

"Good. She was prudent to do so, Lauren. Don't be angry."

"I told her that if we were truly a team, if I was totally trusted and an integral part of your crew as you avidly claim, we wouldn't be having this conversation. Because I'd already be aware of whatever it is that I don't know about Mara."

"It's complicated, Lauren. Come with me."

"What, to the medication room so you can tranquilize me?"

He shook his head. "Conference room. We're having a team meeting about Mara. You're part of that team."

A terrible sense of dread and foreboding gripped Lauren. What was Mitch about to reveal? Could she handle it?

That second, the trauma bell screamed. As loud and disconcerting as questions sirening through her mind.

What devastating piece of Mara's puzzle had they felt the need to keep from Lauren? And why? To protect her? What else had Mitch neglected to tell her?

Had the bond between them been a farce? Lauren wavered between wanting to trust Mitch's intentions and feeling as if everything he said was a lie. If so, all he'd said about her being competent was also a lie. Yet Mitch would never put patients in jeopardy. He took extreme measures to ensure patient safety.

Lauren's feet felt sunk in ten inches of sand as she ran to whatever waited on the other side of those emergency doors. Fear flew back. And doubt, with a vengeance. She forced it aside to focus on providing safe and stellar care.

She'd spent much of her downtime on Lem's computer doing online trauma montages to better her skills. Had it all been in vain?

"This place has been a zoo!" Nita said hours later while scooping up paperwork for the fifteenth patient since midnight.

"Literally." Lauren grabbed another bandage.

Kate came alongside her. "Yeah, what is it with all these animal-related accidents tonight?"

Lauren thought back. Kate was right. "Let's see...we've had a man fall from a horse and fracture his foot and skull."

"A kid bitten by a dog at a park. Not to mention the dog owner's broken nose when the kid's dad bashed him after the bite."

"A man fell off a ladder shooing birds from his gutters," Lauren said.

"A lady freakishly fractures her hip feeding squirrels."

"No, freakish was the kid whose ear swallowed a tree frog."

Kate laughed. "I will never understand how that happened."

"His mom couldn't, either. But I thought she'd die of shock when we told her what his earache was all about." Lauren smiled.

"Freakier is that the frog lived to *ribbit* about it."

"Don't forget the youth leader who choked on a worm."

Kate smirked. "That doesn't count. It was a gummy worm."

"Then how about the attorney kicked by a wild deer who got loose in his office?" Lauren slid his chart in a discharge slot.

Kate's face softened. "Speaking of attorneys, how are you?"

Lauren stopped. "I'm— What about attorneys?"

"Oh, man. Open mouth, insert shoe store. Mitch obviously hasn't had a chance to talk to you about Mara yet?"

Lauren sighed. "Nope. In fact, he's avoiding me again."

"Trust him. Okay? He has your best interests at heart."

"What about Mara's?" Lauren's stomach twisted.

"Helping people is why he became a doctor. No other reason. Know that about him. Believe he has Mara's future at heart."

"Then why do I feel like her only advocate?"

Kate's stance firmed. "She wasn't the only patient that night, Lauren. Understand that many things are out of Mitch's control. Ethically. Morally. Professionally."

"Don't forget legally. You mentioned attorneys."

Kate nodded slowly, confirming Lauren's worst fear for Mara without breaking confidentiality. Someone related to the wreck pursued litigation. Mara had enough on her plate. Lauren couldn't contain the compassion or explain her mercy flowing for Mara, but everything screamed it was God-given.

Things might be out of Mitch's control, but never out of Yours. Despite her mistake, You have Mara's best interests at heart. The nagging knowledge that some consequences stand after forgiveness didn't give Lauren a good feeling. Not at all.

What was Mitch going to tell her about Mara? And when?

The questions dogged her into the night after she retired to the nurses' sleeping room, since she was still on call. Lauren slept in restless snatches. The next morning in the central report room, Lauren, encircled by Ian, Kate and Mitch, surged from the table. "They're putting her in *jail?*"

"Miss Bates, kindly sit," the hospital attorney directed.

Lauren did so. "Excuse me. I'm sorry."

Attorneys nodded. The director scowled at her. Mitch scowled at the director. Apparently the two didn't play well together. Then again, the director didn't get along with anyone.

"She committed a serious crime, Lauren," Mitch said gently.

A lawyer leaned in. "Texting while driving is against the law. She's been charged with vehicular homicide."

"Homicide? She'll go to prison." Lauren's heart thudded.

"Likely." The attorney twisted his pencil on the table.

Lauren could puke. "May I speak to Mitch privately?"

Attorneys nodded. Once outside, Lauren grabbed his lab coat lapels. "Mitch, please. Don't let that happen to Mara. There must be something you can do."

"I can say with all honesty I wish there was. But no."

"Can you see if they'll go for a lesser charge? Involuntary manslaughter?"

"I have nothing to do with it. I haven't spoken to the family since the night I had to inform them their son was killed. With her in and out of consciousness, we can't know if she's remorseful."

"Did you put it like that? That she 'killed' him? Because I can't imagine she meant to."

"I don't remember how I put it. I didn't incriminate her, if that's what you're thinking."

"I don't know what I'm thinking. Look, I understand their side. I do. Mara incriminated herself. But—"

"You're one of the rare few who can see Mara's side, too."

She shrugged. "I guess. I don't know. You're right. Maybe Mara deserves what comes to her." Despite the words, tears streamed.

"Come." Mitch led her down the hall, to Mara's bedside.

"To say goodbye?" Lauren squeaked.

"To say goodbye." Mitch swallowed. Hard.

Lauren took Mara's hand and tried not to cry. *When are they coming for her?* she mouthed. Didn't want to mention aloud that Mara was headed to the jail's sick ward, where she'd be kept until well enough to stand trial.

"Before ten." In other words, within minutes. Lauren bit her lip. Mitch hugged her. "If it's any consolation, I think God's heart for Mara comes through you."

"That means?"

"No idea. Just sounded like the thing to say."

"Maybe it was one of those things you hear from God and speak His mind about without realizing it. You do that often. He operates so naturally through you during codes, triage and trauma care, Mitch. It's beautiful and awe-inspiring to watch."

"That's good to know."

"He's good to know. My comfort and prayer for Mara is that somehow she'll also realize that He is good to know."

She took Mara's hand and prayed exactly that.

Chapter Seventeen

"Lauren, wake up. You have to see this," Mitch said days later.

Lauren looked adorable as she roused herself from sleep in the women's on-call room. Momentary disorientation ebbed with each blink.

Mitch knelt beside her. Kate snored one cot over.

It had been too busy for anyone to leave, and the trauma crew staggered shifts and napped in batches.

Mitch angled his phone screen. Lauren looked into it. Her focus centered on a photo with eerily familiar words scrawled across a medical clipboard. *God is a good person to know. The best.*

Lauren blinked. "Where did that come from? Who wrote it?"

"It came from a chart in Mara's room on her jailhouse hospital bed. She woke up and couldn't talk because her throat was sore from intubation. So she wrote."

"She wrote that?" Lauren sat abruptly, causing Kate to stir.

"Every word, Lauren. I'm not making this up. She penned the *exact* phrase you left her with."

Lauren leaned into his open arms. "She'll be okay."

"I hope this gives you faith for other things."

Lauren nodded. "He hears."

Ian burst through the door. "We got a fallen planker. ETA fifteen minutes. Bilateral leg fractures."

Kate flipped over and up like a pancake, and shoved her feet into shoes before she grew fully awake.

"What's a planker?" the three asked Ian simultaneously.

Ian shifted. "Planking is where people pick odd surfaces to lie facedown and flat on. Then take photos of themselves doing the stunt and post images on social network sites to outdo one another with the coolest funny photo."

Mitch smirked. "I'm scared to ask how you know this, Ian."

He jabbed Mitch, and the two commenced a clipboard joust.

Kate inserted herself like a referee. "What else, Ian?"

"Unfortunately this kid planked on a second-story brick ledge. Eagle Point High School. He fell. Knees first. Onto concrete. Landed hard." They followed Ian to the staff hub.

Kate and Lauren's faces twisted identically. "Ouch."

Ian rapped the desk. "Let's put him in O.R. Three."

Mitch cornered Lauren near the O.R. suites. "So, you scrubbing in with me on this case?"

"Just try and keep me from it."

Kate smiled. "That's what I like to hear."

"No, you like to hear that there's chocolate involved."

Kate laughed. "True. Got any?"

"In my bag at the desk. Leave some for Ian or he might be grumpy."

"Hey, what are you trying to say?" Ian smirked.

"Uh, that you might need a chocoholic intervention?"

"I love the laughter you bring to the team, Lauren," Mitch said as he reached for a sterile hand scrubber.

"Then go with me to the jail to visit Mara sometime, and I'll work with you until the day I leave for Texas."

Mitch paused scrubbing. Wow. She drove a hard bargain. "I'm not sure I can legally do that. She awake?"

"On and off. She'll be devastated when she wakes and gets informed that people died in the accident she was involved in."

"Responsible for."

Lauren's head whipped around. "Have you no mercy?"

Mitch narrowed his eyes. "Not with people who don't pay attention when they drive. That kind of person killed my dad and destroyed my family."

No one moved. Or spoke. Or breathed. All motion ceased.

The only perceptible sound originated through the O.R. door, where vital-sign monitors beeped in anticipation of a patient.

Jaw clenched, Mitch held up scrubbed and dripping hands and backed himself into the operating room with a conflicted scowl on his face. Today was monumentally hard.

He didn't know who he was more irritated with: Lauren for standing up for Mara. Mara for vehicular homicide, which Mitch's dad also died of. Or himself for still being mad about the other two.

Not to mention Lauren had said "until the day I leave for Texas," which indicated intent to return.

Lauren walked in, garbed for surgery. She cast an apologetic glance, same time he did. They acknowledged one another with nods.

"Amazing how you two communicate so well without words. My wife and I never had that." Ian lined his anesthesia tray with syringes and pulled equipment within reach. He eyed Mitch carefully, then Lauren.

Now who was talking without words?

Ian's expression willed Lauren to tread lightly. "It's not that he doesn't have a soft spot for Mara. Today's the anniversary of his dad's wreck."

Mitch wasn't sure he was relieved for Ian's verbal intervention or not. The whole world didn't need to know.

Yet this wasn't the whole world. This was his crew. His closest friends, cohorts, confidants. He'd acted like a jerk to them.

Especially the one he cared about the most. Not that she knew. He sought her out.

Lauren's eyes rimmed with tears. "I'm so sorry, Mitch."

He shrugged. "You didn't know." Obviously he still had festering wounds about circumstances surrounding Dad's death. *Treat that internal ailment ASAP, will You, Lord?*

Trauma techs brought in the youth. He not only looked bruised and bloody, but...

"He looks shocky." Lauren finished Mitch's thought as the crew transferred the patient to the table with a backboard.

"Type and cross him for six units of blood STAT. Give him two now, and I want to see his lab work ASAP," Mitch instructed the circulating nurse.

An orthopedic specialist with whom Mitch had consulted their case-in-progress arrived and stood across from Mitch. The specialist nodded at Lauren. "She new?"

Lauren's nerves rattled as the formidable man sized her up.

"She's my scrub tech." Mitch's answer apparently appeased the intense surgeon. His visual scrutiny stopped instantly, proving his great professional respect of Mitch and his choice in staff. The man would probably hit the roof if he knew surgery wasn't her primary specialty.

But Lauren trusted Mitch, too. If he didn't think her completely capable, she wouldn't be in here. That didn't keep Lauren from hoping like mad that Mitch's judgment was sound.

Doubt crept in. If Mitch had called in a specialist, perhaps Lauren wasn't the best scrub tech for this case?

The specialist's scrub tech entered. After Kate gloved him, he stood opposite Lauren and nodded professional acknowledgment.

"Should I step out?"

"Stay. You'll learn a lot," Mitch answered before Lauren could bail. How did he continue to read her mind and heart?

After Mitch updated them on the patient, the specialist fired up a drill and began piecing bone together with hardware. A burning smell reached her nostrils and made her eyes water, despite surgery goggles. Fine misty powder floated in the air. The smell made Lauren nauseous. She tried not to breathe.

That only worked well for a couple minutes. "Should I go check on other patients?" Lauren asked, feeling suddenly queasier. She didn't like the orthopedic instruments. Or the sounds they made. Particles sprayed the air like sawdust. Lauren leaned in. Was that…? Bone powder. Her queasiness rocketed.

"Soon as we're done here," Mitch answered with his head and hands lowered to the surgical site.

Lauren puffed shallow breaths and begged herself not to gag or pass out. "I—I *really* think I need to step out now."

Mitch eyed her. "You look a little pale. You okay?"

She nodded but couldn't say another word.

When her stomach revolted in a telltale gallop, she knew she was no longer okay. Frowning, she shook her head.

"Go." Mitch nodded to the double doors, which wobbled and turned into four as Lauren stumbled toward them. Or perhaps she wobbled rather than the door. Everything whirled around her.

Don't let me pass out or throw up.

"She's going down!" someone yelled.

Don't…let… Lauren's thought floated off, and so did the surface she stood on. The room tilted. Her stomach sank like a magnet sucked into the floor. She reached out, flailed for anything to hold on to, but air was the only thing within reach.

Besides the pretty floor tiles, which slammed upward.

She had a vague sense of someone swooping in. Breaking her fall. Arms shoved beneath her pits. And so she hung there. Tried to talk but could only blink into Mitch's face, which floated in and out of her vision.

"Get a gurney. Check her blood sugar. We have a nurse on the floor." Mitch's voice. Soothing. Serious. Ordering. Her?

Lauren tried to explain to the voice that there were many nurses on the floor. But her tongue felt like a two-ton anchor.

She slowly blinked eyes open, but saw only an odd ring of green ankles and a blue circle of surgically booted feet around her.

Moments later, Lauren tried to lift her head.

"Whoa. Don't move, Lauren." Mitch's hand rested on her forehead. A poke stung her finger. She looked down. And came fully to, to find herself flat on her back. Nita held a glucose monitor. "Have you eaten today, sweetie?"

She was the nurse on the floor. Literally. On the tile, outside the operating area. Embarrassment and horror hit her. Had she jeopardized the patient by becoming one?

The specialist probably thought she was a first-class idiot with a one-way ticket to Weaklingville.

Speaking of tickets, a Texas-bound flight sounded *real* good right now. She fought a maniacal urge to laugh.

Why did Mitch trust her? Under the guidance of his gentle hands, she sat up slowly. Put her head between her knees, mostly to hide the rush of tears and her blazing red cheeks.

"Lem makes sure she eats," Mitch said. Good thing because Lauren's mouth still felt sutured. "But juice and crackers couldn't hurt," he added.

The team lifted her to a gurney. She hated to trouble them over a stupid fainting episode. Yet they'd scold her if they knew her thoughts. Every patient mattered and somehow, Lauren knew with all her heart, she mattered immensely to them.

Thank You, Lord. Friendship was an unexpected summer blessing.

"Tell me what's going on, Lauren." Mitch's fingers brushed her forehead, so he must not be angry. He certainly didn't sound it, which baffled her. Nita brought juice and crackers and left.

"It's the bone powder. The burning smell didn't help. I think it got to me in there," Lauren said with intense effort and slur.

Mitch chuckled. "That happened to me in residency, if it makes you feel better."

"You passed out?" Lauren blinked, overcome with surprise.

"Whammo!" He smacked his palms together. "Face to the floor." He pointed at his eyebrow to a tiny scar. One she may not have noticed, had he not been so close and pointing it out.

"You had stitches?" That almost made her laugh.

"Only four." He smiled. "But my ego needed a few more."

Now Lauren did laugh. "No doubt." She turned serious and put her hand on Mitch, which seemed to momentarily arrest him. "How's the patient?"

"Better than my scrub nurse at the moment." He grinned.

Then in one athletic motion, he hopped onto the gurney. He used his thigh to brace her back as she sipped the juice. "Don't you dare think a fainting episode is going to excuse you from scrubbing with me." Determination glinted in gorgeous eyes, alongside deep compassion and a killer smile.

"I'm sorry." She dropped her face. Stared at pulp floating in her orange juice.

With the world's most tender motion, Mitch raised her chin. "No need to be sorry. Or embarrassed." His eyes softened as they dragged like silk across her face.

She swallowed. The hall closed in around them. They stilled like two enamored sculptures with gazes tangled.

If anyone walked by, their feelings would be discovered.

In a surprising moment, his fingers slid down her neck and bent her head back in a way that could only position it for a kiss.

Every reason not to marched across her mind and massacred the moment. "I— Mitch, this—" But the safe, sedating look in his eyes killed the protest on her tongue as he responded with a high-caliber hug, and solid muscles squeezed the reasons out.

"I know. No need to be embarrassed about that, either." His voice lowered delectably, as did his chiseled face.

Thrill scuttled through her. Followed by all the reasons this would qualify them for a prescription of Anti-Stupid Pills.

"It can't work. I live in Texas. And you have someone else's stinkin' ring in your glove box," she blurted out before his mouth brushed hers. Heated breaths mingled. Utterly engrossing eyes and luscious, inviting lips hovered millimeters from hers.

Her words must've slapped instant sense into him.

He drew a confounded breath, clenched his jaw and backed slowly away.

And Lauren could breathe again. Think again.

Knock her stupid, stubborn head against the floor again for stopping the ridiculously gorgeous man from kissing her.

Good. Gravy. The near-kiss scorched Lauren's cheeks.

They looked around, startled, as if remembering they were still technically at work. Therefore this near-miss-kiss hadn't been the brightest, most professional idea.

He stood, face rigid. "Don't move until the juice kicks in. I'll have Nita bring more crackers, then I'll drive you home."

"Thanks." Every nerve ending still fizzed.

He lifted her side rail. "I mean it. Don't get up without assistance. You're a fall risk."

The way his eyes bored into hers as he leaned in with his torso, as well as his words and direct stare, Lauren knew he didn't mean "fall risk" merely in the sense that she was likely to pass out again and hit the floor.

He very clearly meant she was a fall risk…for him.

Chapter Eighteen

The second Lauren stepped inside the center the next day, Kate grabbed her and squealed. "Sweet vitals! He almost kissed you!"

"You saw?"

Ian meandered up after Kate. "Saw what?"

Kate clapped. "Mitch almost smooched Lauren yesterday."

Lauren's face heated. She dragged her gaze down the halls. Where was Mitch? What if he heard Kate creating an ordeal? Would he freak out? Avoid her? Ugh.

He hadn't come to breakfast at Grandpa's this morning. Double ugh!

"Finally!" Kate peeled the top off a yogurt with zest. "You two'll get with the program and stop fighting the inevitable."

Ian looked from one woman to the other. He also looked increasingly disturbed. Kate's face glowed as though she was ecstatic at the prospect of Lauren and Mitch being an item.

No question, Ian was not.

Why? Concern infiltrated Lauren. Perhaps chocolate would sweeten Ian up. Remembering the dark chocolate stash Mitch paid for, she scrambled for her satchel. She'd leave Ian chocolate and flee. Mitch approached. She tensed. Swatted Kate, smirking.

How would Mitch react upon seeing her? Caustic like yesterday? Acid curdled up Lauren's throat and burned.

Mitch walked, head bent, eyeing his watch. "I have a meeting with new employees. Be back later." He nodded to Kate, avoided Ian and gave Lauren's shoulder a playful pinch. "Hey."

"Hey." She pressed tangled hands to her fluttering tummy.

As Mitch stepped away, he smiled slowly, expressions revolving like someone stumbling into a state of wonder.

Lauren put a hand to her chest. Relief!

Kate smiled smugly and went to answer a call light. Lauren went to stock rooms. Ian's gaze narrowed at Lauren then Mitch, who paused in the hall, talking with another doctor. Ian obviously fumed about something. What?

He lumbered angrily toward Mitch. An ICU nurse poked her head out of a room. "Dr. Shupe, can you check these vent levels?"

Ian sulked that way. The look on his face said this unchartered conversation was far from over.

Kate joined Lauren stocking rooms and kept humming classic love songs. Lauren swatted her with glove packets. They finished a row of bins and grabbed the next list.

Kate smiled. Pointed behind her, whispering, "Your admirer."

Lauren turned to find Mitch observing her with a tender expression. He walked toward them. When had he returned?

"Lauren, you busy?"

"I was just helping Kate."

"I see that."

Kate snatched the bin from Lauren. "She's done."

Chuckling, Mitch led Lauren from the room. "I saw your employment application in the office." He beamed. "You should put in for a permanent Illinois license...if you plan to stay." The question grew stronger than the gleam in his eyes. *Stay?*

The idea appealed more than he knew. "I found out last night

I get to be here two more months. My Texas friend is doing her best to accommodate me in light of Lem's recovery."

"How is he today?"

"If you'd come for breakfast, you'd see he's doing super."

He nodded but didn't give an explanation as to why he hadn't joined them for breakfast. He had at least phoned Grandpa to say he wouldn't make it. Still, Lauren was curious. Yet not secure enough in their fledgling relationship to ask his where-abouts.

"So how about it, Lauren? Want the job full-time?"

"I guess it couldn't hurt." She nibbled her lip. "As long as you let me transfer to recovery or somewhere less intensive."

Apple in hand, Kate returned and leaned against the wall where they talked. "It's trauma care. Everything's intensive."

"Not like this." Lauren indicated the O.R. suite. "I can do recovery. Also wouldn't mind doing triage."

Muscular arms folded across his broad chest. "I like you better as my scrub nurse."

"But orthopedic surgery is apparently not my thing."

"What if I'd walked away when I hit the floor that day?"

Her laughter faded.

Kate smiled and stepped gingerly away. "He has a point."

Mitch rustled Lauren's hair. Normal at first, then slower, which sent tingles through her scalp. "You've obviously had sufficient surgical experience."

"In school, I worked part-time as a surgery tech. Also in obstetrics, we got cases at night that couldn't wait for morning. They trained the OB crew to scrub in during an emergency."

"You have a knack for it. Regardless, I'd like you on board in any capacity. Think about it, okay?"

She nodded. "I will." Even though a lump of fear the size of Texas sat on her chest.

Did she deserve the trust freely flowing from his eyes?

God, from the time I was little, Grandpa always said You're

The Great Physician. If You'd still entrust the care of patients to me, please help me to know that.

Out of the blue and on the heels of her unspoken prayer, Mitch dialed a number and handed the phone to her.

"Who is it?" Lauren asked. Kate resumed eavesdropping.

Mitch grinned. "Illinois Department of Professional Regulation. Nursing Department."

She shook her head and eyed Kate, who snickered. "When the man wants something, he doesn't waste time."

The caller answered. Lauren explained her situation.

"We'll need to conduct a departmental check. It should be three days."

"For the background check?"

"No, ma'am. For your license to arrive, as long as there are no red flags."

She hung up, feeling like a floatation device. She stared at the phone. "I absolutely cannot believe it."

Mitch sank his teeth into a chocolate square and leaned his hip on the desk. "What'd they say?"

"My Illinois license will be here in three days."

Mitch's grin grew sweeter than any chocolate in existence.

Lauren didn't know what terrified her more. The prospect of doing nursing full-time again. Or the giddy way her insides crooned when Mitch looked her way.

She stood on three precipices that could go very badly. Or very well. Hopefully her streak of hardship was over. Being able to work as a nurse without making a single mistake. To move to Illinois near Lem, like she'd always dreamed of. Growing a relationship with a dashing doctor.

Any one of the three going wrong would break her heart. Hard to hope for all to work out well when her life hadn't been without heartache since age ten. Lem had been the one bright spot.

"Chocolate for your thoughts?" Mitch brandished her candy.

She smiled. "Things seem too good to be true. Not sure I remember what it feels like to hope and have it come true."

"Thankfully we know Someone in the business of restoring hope." Mitch's gaze tracked Kate, who was leaning their way. "She's nosier than a plastic surgeon's office agenda."

"Ya think?" Lauren laughed.

"Although she did bring up a good point to me yesterday. Said she hoped you'd end up working here with us permanently."

"How'd your meetings go?" Lauren hedged.

"Excellent. We headed off a serious staffing shortage. I put out a community call for employees and have interviews lined up for weeks. We'll soon have two more trauma teams in force."

Which meant he was moving on, with or without her longterm. Mitch was the kind of man who would. That made her feel glad and sad at the same time.

Glad for the community. Sad for her? "I'm a nut job," Lauren announced decidedly.

Mitch laughed. "You trying to convince me I wouldn't want you working here with me?"

"I'm trying to convince both of us." She groaned when call lights went off. "Shall I answer that? Or make the doctor?"

He smiled. "Either way. You let me know."

She headed toward the light. "Since it's a nurse's job, I'll cut you a break." She aimed her finger at him. "But know without a doubt I'd be far too much trouble for you."

That stopped him in his tracks. She went on to the room.

"May I trouble you for an extra pillow?" the mother, at the side of her son—the recovering planker—asked Lauren.

"It's no trouble." Lauren turned to get it and rammed face first into something hard—Mitch's chest. She looked up, up, up. He grinned down and raised well-built arms. A pillow dangled from each hand. He must've followed her into the doorway and heard the mother's request.

What kind of doctor delighted in answering call lights?

"Thanks," Lauren muttered and snatched both pillows from him, then helped the mother plump them around herself.

"Thank you, Nurse Lauren. You certainly knew your calling."

Her words stopped Lauren. She felt Mitch's stare, and probably his knowing smirk, on her frame from the door.

"Uh, thanks." If the woman only knew… Lauren entered the hall, not surprised to see Mitch still outside the door.

"You, trouble?" He draped an arm around her. "Maybe so, *Nurse Lauren,* but I'm quite convinced you're worth it."

Two hours later, he met her at the time clock. "Shift over?"

"Yes. But if you need something—"

"No." Mitch ushered her outside. "I need to set something straight, and it would be unprofessional to do so on duty."

Beyond curious, she followed. He led her to a cozy lakeside bench canopied in a flower-woven trellis beside the parking lot.

Before Lauren could blink, Mitch bent and thoroughly kissed every last question out of her mind.

For the next few electrifying minutes, his mouth took exquisite care with hers. Intent. Gentle. Delicate. Deliberate.

As he broke contact, deep feelings surged between them. His fervent eyes softened as he dipped his face in earnest once more, with delectable pressure and the promise of devotion.

Every slumbered nerve, every hope, every emotion—awakened.

Every fear, every reservation, every doubt—demolished.

The world dwindled to just him and her and the ardent kiss between them.

A startling sound pulled Lauren back to earth. Still in the bliss that was Mitch's arms, she turned.

Ian stood, scowling, one fist clutching a bag of fast-food, the other clenched into a fist. He stood seething at the end of the employee parking area.

"Yikes. Big mistake," Mitch muttered and moved toward Ian. What? Did he mean the kiss?

Or something with Ian?

Mitch approached Ian intently, but Ian shook his glaring head and stalked off until he disappeared inside the building.

Mitch came back, braced Lauren's shoulders and bent his mouth close to her ear. "In case there's any question, I meant every single second of that kiss. My only regret is I didn't do it sooner."

With that, Mitch pulled her in for a caring follow-up that more than adequately proved he meant it.

"Speaking of trouble, here it comes in spades," Kate said to Lauren and Mitch at the break table the next day.

Everyone turned.

Ian tanked toward them like an irate military interrogator. "What's the scoop, Lauren?"

He turned his wrath next on Mitch. "You're my best friend. I shouldn't be the last to know."

No question Ian was still miffed. He hadn't answered Mitch's calls yesterday or this morning.

Lauren looked to Nita for help.

"Shall I translate for all of you then?" Nita stood. "Mitch and Lauren care deeply about one another, but each of them has been too scared, scarred or stubborn to admit it. In fact, they are probably falling flat-faced in love as we speak."

Everyone's mouths fell open. Including Mitch and Lauren's.

Kate's eyes widened. "Wow. This is better than a TV drama."

"Lauren?" Ian pressed.

"I seriously have no idea what that means."

Mitch did. But didn't want to say it the first time with an audience. He studied Ian. Pangs of regret hit that he hadn't mentioned his feelings for Lauren. But the truth was, he only recently came to terms with admitting his feelings to himself.

He'd prayed for permission yesterday and gotten a green light while Lauren went to the jail to visit Mara.

"So it's not true about you and Mitch?" Ian's jaw clicked.

"I, er, I'm not sure what's going on there." Lauren seemed more bewildered by the minute. She nervously wrung her hands.

Kate passed Mitch looks as if he'd better do something fast. Ian was out of control. And completely out of character.

"Making out on hospital property meant nothing?" Ian said.

That did it. Mitch's anger boiled against Ian over his badgering Lauren. Ian needed to pick on someone his own size. Besides, he and Lauren were far from making out yesterday.

"Ian, can I talk to you privately?" Mitch rose formidably.

Ian's jaw clenched. He fell into wordless step with Mitch.

"Peace offering." Mitch shoved Ian a bouquet of Lauren's dark chocolate once they were down the hall.

Ian didn't crack a smile, however, and instead hulked, hurt and humorless, ahead of Mitch into the physicians' lounge.

"Why didn't you tell me you and Lauren are dating?" Ian's tone seared into Mitch like flaming shrapnel.

"We're *not* dating, bro."

Ian's head tilted. "You're…"

"No. She's a respectable girl and I told you, I'm doing things right this time around. We haven't technically been on a date." He needed to remedy that ASAP.

As soon as he fixed this rift with Ian.

"You said if you ever fall in love again, you'll do things differently. You saying you're in love with her?"

"No, man. I, maybe. I don't know. All I know is that, where you're concerned, I'm sorry. This is coming out all wrong. I didn't want to talk to you about it because, well, I thought that would be insensitive since you're…" Mitch's hand tilted.

Ian straightened. "What? Headed to Divorceville, and you're headed to Blissville?"

Ian's voice had softened somewhere in the middle.

Mitch looked up, glad to see Ian half smiling now.

"She's why you've been dissing me." Ian laughed with the self-revelation, bringing Mitch great relief.

"Ian, you're my best bud. Like a brother. The last thing I want right now is to bring more pain and suffering upon you. So, while my intentions of being cautious were good, I might have waited too long to tell you." And too long to make a move with courting Lauren.

"Might have? Best buds don't keep things from each other."

Mitch dropped his chin to his chest, knowing that.

"Yeah, I'm hurting but I'm not so weak of a guy that I can't celebrate with my best friend when his heart revives and his life turns around from shards and shrapnel to songs and sunshine." Ian snatched the chocolate. "So what's the scoop?"

"We like each other. A *lot*. The attraction is out of this world. I want a future with her."

"But?"

"You know me well. But she lives in Texas and she's strapped to a whopper of a building loan, among other things."

"But otherwise she'd consider moving here?"

"Yeah. She'd love to."

"That'd be good for Lem, too. He seems to have a lot more vitality with her around these parts. You, as well. In fact, you look so smitten you border on goofy." Ian shook his head and smirked.

Mitch loved how Lem had adopted his entire team. Kate, Nita and Ian had begun to call him Gramps, which tickled Lem pink.

"I thought you'd ask me if I've been popping Stupid Pills." Mitch laughed but dipped his head.

Ian clamped a hand over Mitch's shoulder and turned ten shades of serious. "Nah, man. I'm happy for you...*if* you can find a way to make this work. And *if* you're over the betrayal Sheila caused you."

Ian, not always the realist. Just these days.

"You *are* over her and your breakup. Right?" Ian scratched the five o'clock stubble along his jaw.

"Her? Yes. The breakup? I'm getting there." But the words felt like razors across his tongue. And by the concern taking Ian's face hostage, he found the words lacking certainty, too.

"Maybe I was more in love with the idea of being in love than with Sheila, which wasn't fair to her."

"Bro, if you still have that tendency…"

"The potential for Lauren's heart to break is there." Mitch's heart felt as if it dropped into his stomach. Was he in any kind of position emotionally to pursue a low-risk relationship with Lauren?

The question put a sick feeling inside because Mitch didn't honestly know the answer with full certainty. Was he ready?

Not according to the doubt creeping up in Ian's eyes. Because Ian knew him better than anyone. Better than he knew himself, at times. In fact, Ian's head tilted in a telltale way. "You don't still have the ring?" Ian had a surgical way with questions.

Mitch didn't answer.

Ian got nose to nose. "Mitch? You still have it? Because dude, if you do, that's *not* cool. Lauren could get hurt if you don't have it all back together emotionally after your breakup."

"Lauren isn't a rebound fling, if that's what you mean."

"I know that. You and Sheila had drifted apart, thanks to the distance. My concern is Texas is a whole lot farther from Illinois than Sheila's unit was from ours when you two imploded as a couple." Ian turned to go. "Keep that in mind."

"Trust me, I am."

Doubt assailed Mitch. Was it merely infatuation? Was he simply caught up in the excitement and newness of attraction?

Or, like Nita said, was it love on their horizon?

He could easily fall for Lauren. Felt as if he was already in the beginning stages of caring that deeply for her. Part of it was that he did deeply know and care about her from years and years of Lem's gazillion colorful stories.

Lord, don't let Ian be right. Don't let this love be wrong.

But while Mitch could think that, he couldn't bring himself to pray it with meaning. That wasn't the right way to pray.

He dipped his head where he was. "God, please. Don't let me act foolishly. I don't want to hurt Lauren or Lem."

But an acute knowing sank teeth into Mitch that whatever was going to happen, happiness or hurt, was already in progress.

Mitch fled the break room and paced a barren, under-construction hallway.

Was their relationship prognosis good or grave?

Regardless, it was already in motion. *No reversing it.*

The gravity of that thrust Mitch to one knee right there in the trauma center's section of a deserted construction hall.

Fist to his bent forehead, he focused on God. "Fitting, huh? I'm under construction in places, too. I know You're on it. Thank You. I'm here to ask for Your excavating services, too. See, there's this mountain that I can't move alone. I could really use a hand. And a little guidance, too. I'm moving forward. So if I'm headed in the wrong direction, I know You can drag me out of cornfield-high blindness and set me on the right path."

Chapter Nineteen

The situation with Lauren, and Ian's admonishment, made for a rough week. For days, grace eluded. Though home from battle, Mitch still felt very much at war. With himself and his past. He wavered between caution and hope for a future with Lauren. All the while, fending off pitchforks of uncertainty and guilt over Ian's words of wisdom. The rift between himself and Ian would work itself out. For now, Mitch's growing desire to spend more meaningful time with Lauren won out over any reticence.

At the next shift change, Mitch met Lauren at the time clock as she punched out her card reader. He pulled her aside. "Look, I know things are up in the air, but I'd like to take you to dinner and treat you to a movie."

At her stunned look, he grinned and added, "Lem approves this message."

With all the political campaigning on TV lately, that made her laugh. "I imagine he does." She shifted her handbag and peered shyly at Mitch. "I prefer plays, but I'd gladly go to the movies with you, too." Her eyes grew vulnerable. "In fact, I'd follow you to the moon if I could."

He grinned. "Next time the local car-rental place runs a special on rocket rentals, I'll take you there. As long as there are no lunar geese orbiting around."

Lauren's beaming expression rivaled the fullest of moons. It stayed on her face all the way to the mall, where they browsed shops and bought Lem a stuffed snake for a gag gift.

Later, on the way out of the mall after shopping, the movie and dinner, Lauren took Mitch's hand when he reached. A rocket ride could not compete with the rush and out-of-this-world thrill of being close to her. Stars winked approval overhead as they stepped from the mall curb to the lot where Mitch had parked. He squeezed her hand as she stepped over a patch of loose gravel in the median. She held tight, and all sorts of emotions stirred inside Mitch.

His heart felt as big as the movie screen.

He caressed Lauren's hand and walked slower to draw out the moment.

"Even the flowers seem to smile when we pass," she whispered into the softness of moonlight. What was it about the luminescent glow that made a moment so conducive to a kiss?

Mitch smiled, too. He'd never been happier to have parked at the edge of the lot. Good way to exercise. And take every opportunistic second to court a woman who deserved it.

Her answering smile could light the galaxy, as if the stars whispered Mitch's secrets and his heart's thoughts to her soul and mind. "I know," she said, drawing a breath as long and deep as the Mississippi River. "I could get used to this. Everything seems to come to life and become magic and animated when two people start to fall in love."

Her words stunned them both, and made them pause in their steps.

Her vulnerable look. The silver hue that moonlight and streetlights cast around the edges of her glistening eyes. Her hair, red like hearts.

Exquisite.

He tightened his grip on her hand. And his past loosened its hold on his heart. A little. At least, for now.

He captured her nervously flitting gaze. "Lauren, if love

is what's breathing magic in the air between us, I hope the magic stretches this special moment into the longest, most lingering Forever."

Today was the day.

Mitch had courted Lauren for a month, which was all it took to make him want to seek Lem's blessing for a permanent future with her. Mitch ascended Lem's steps early to ensure she wasn't awake.

Lem met him outside. "I've never seen you so serious. What's more important than another hour's sleep?"

"Lauren," Mitch said as they sat on the gliding rocker. Mitch looked Lem in the eye. "She's important to me."

"I gathered that. She's sweet on you, too."

"I'd like to take our relationship more seriously. The kind of serious that I hope will lead to marriage."

Lem's grin exploded. "If you're asking my permission, all I got to say is what took you so long?"

Mitch chuckled. "So I have your blessing?"

"Indeed! Nothing would make me happier." Lem frowned. "Wait, if things progress, you'd rope her into moving here, right? You wouldn't skip off to Texas on me, would ya?" Lem's countenance fell. He grew genuinely upset at the prospect.

Mitch put a steadying hand on him. The man really did not want to be alone. "You have my word, Lem. I'll get her here." Lem still looked distraught so Mitch added, "I promise."

Lem's quivering limbs relaxed. "When you gonna ask her?"

"Soon. I'll let you know. First, I need to be sure she feels the same."

"Whoop!" Lem leaped like a man half his age.

Joy detonated in Mitch because if Lem was this happy about them, he'd turn inside out when the time came to say vows. And Mitch had every intention of doing so. He rose. "Let's boot her out of bed."

"I'm awake." Lauren stumbled out, looking half asleep and

half annoyed. "What's all this carrying on right by my window?"

Uh-oh. "How much did you hear?" Mitch approached.

"A bunch of whooping and hollering." She woke fully and tugged her robe tight.

"We're going to hit the lake on jet skis today."

She smiled with still-sleepy eyes. "You keep saying that, but every time we plan it, trauma tsunamis roll in."

"Precisely why we're starting early. Ready?" Mitch was anxious to get going.

She looked down. "Right. People go wave-running in pajamas."

Mitch laughed, properly chagrined. "Let's eat on the way."

"Are your feet on fire? Give me ten minutes."

"Five. Your makeup will just wash off in the water."

"Who said I'm putting on makeup just for you?"

Mitch smirked. "You always do."

"You're suffering a terrible case of confusion." Cheeks adorably flamed, Lauren bolted into the house. Mitch followed.

She doused water on her face. "I should hold your head under. You embarrass the daylights out of me."

"I love to see you blush."

"And I hate to blush more than almost anything."

"See? We're made for each other."

Lauren smiled and met his gaze in the mirror.

"By the way, today's another group date. But next time we go out, it'll be just you and me again."

She drew a breath. "And my nerves."

He smiled. "What would you have to be nervous about?"

She shrugged. "Oh, I don't know. That whole getting my heart stomped on thing."

He moved close. "I'd never hurt you, Lauren."

She held up a finger. "You'd never *mean* to hurt me."

Mitch didn't have a rebuttal for that because in truth, no one entered a dating relationship intending to hurt or be hurt.

Lauren rustled around a tiny zippered bag and fished out a tube. "Waterproof mascara to the rescue! Something's better than nothing, right?"

He smiled at her. Next she raised gloss and ran it across her lips. "I, uh, should go sit with Lem while you get ready," Mitch stammered.

She continued the face-paint ritual. "Is he going with us?"

"Not today, he said. I invited." Mitch went to sit with Lem.

Four minutes later Lauren emerged in a pair of pink sporty shorts and a trendy rhinestone-scrolled T-shirt.

"Impressive. I only see you move that fast in emergencies."

"This *is* an emergency." She patted Mitch's cheek in passing to put her satchel in his truck. "I forgot to pack a swimsuit."

"No stores'll be open this early, carrottop," Lem said.

Her shoulders slumped. "That's right. I forgot this is the country. That makes me really miss city living."

A bad feeling hit Mitch. "Kate'll be there. See if she has one you can borrow," he suggested as he opened the car door for Lauren.

Mitch felt Lauren's eyes meld to him as he watched traffic and maneuvered accordingly.

At a red light, he extended his cell to her. "Call Kate."

"You're bossy."

"Nope. Just pining to see you in a swimsuit." He laughed.

She socked his arm. Hard. He deserved it. But laughing with her and seeing her face flush that adorable red was worth it. "You're beautiful when you blush. It becomes you," he said tenderly.

"I'm not sure about this," Lauren said to Kate a little later as she viewed herself in the hallway mirror of Mitch's lakeside home. Nita napped on his couch, ice water at her side.

"It looks fine," Mitch assured.

Kate nodded. "It's very modest. But if Mitch strokes with you wearing that, you're running his code and not me."

They shared a laugh on the walk to Mitch's dock to meet Ian. He stared across the lake beneath hands shielding the sun.

Mitch approached. "What's so interesting?"

"I think that's the army medic who helped us that first crazy day at the center." Ian indicated a man and woman skiing in playful circles on matching wave runners out in the middle of the lake.

Mitch squinted. Sure enough, the man resembled Caleb. "Let's invite them to hang with us today."

"First we have to service your other wave runner. It needs oil. Also, your grill needs propane before we can cook."

"Plus I need to talk to Lauren about how I feel. Not leave her in the dark like I left you."

Ian chuckled. "Hey, I apologize for my outburst last month. Being negative and instilling doubt. I was tired and feeling sorry for myself instead of happy for you. Just had an off day. Don't take anything I said seriously. I was way wrong."

"I don't know, Ian. Maybe not on everything. We'll see."

"What do you mean?" Ian moved close. "Everything's all right with you two, huh?"

"It's going better than I ever dreamed it could." He cleared his throat. "I—" Mitch coughed into his hand "—think I love her."

Ian's forehead inclined, and his eyebrows disappeared beneath his ball cap. "There's no *think* to it. You either do or you don't."

Mitch straightened. "I do. Really, *really* do."

"Whoa. Wow. That was fast. She know?"

"Not yet."

"When you gonna talk to her?"

"Today sometime."

"You know how trauma goes. Better get the time while the getting's good. Never know when cases will roll in and the current crew might call us in." He took keys and burger tongs from Mitch. "I'll man the jet ski and the grill. You go man your future with the girl."

"Thanks, Ian. I appreciate your support. Especially in light of…everything you're going through."

Ian scraped the charred grate. "Hey, what are friends for?"

"Getting gook off my grill." He indicated Ian's motions.

Ian laughed. "You'd do the same for me on all counts. Not that the tables will ever turn. I got off to a rocky start. You two'll be great together. You have God on your side."

"So do you, Ian."

His motions slowed, and he peered up at Mitch with an expression of such absolute anguish, Mitch didn't know what to do. "I don't know anymore, man." Ian struggled to snap out of it, then nudged Mitch. "Go. Get your girl before I knock you down."

He left Ian, now laughing. Or trying to. *God, let him know You haven't abandoned him. That his life still harbors good things.*

Vest applied, Mitch approached the table where the ladies talked leisurely. "Hey, beautiful, will you have this ride with me?" He extended her life vest like a romantic invitation.

She stood like a blooming rose. "Thought you'd never ask."

Mitch helped her on the jet ski, then fired up its engine. "I think Caleb's on the lake. We'll invite him over in a bit."

"Good idea!" Her hands came around his shoulders as he sat. *Oh, yeah.* He could stay like this all day. But, alas, the lady wanted to ride. Mitch revved it, and Lauren squealed in his ear.

"Ow," he said, then laughed. But he enjoyed her giggles as he sped to full throttle, veering sharp left. She responded by holding him tighter and laughing hysterically. So he cut as far to the right as possible without dumping them in the water.

She scooted suction-cup close, held on for dear life and laughed like crazy. He loved the carefree, uninhibited sounds.

"Little detour." Mitch took a scenic route to his dock. "Having fun?"

"Yes, but I thought you were inviting Caleb?"

"I'm waiting for Ian. He went to get propane for the grill and juice for the other jet ski." Mitch assisted her onto the dock. "Also, I need to talk to you. I'm going to be direct and share my feelings. Hints aren't getting across."

"The kiss got across." She giggled.

"Well, yes, but that was probably impulsive."

"You regret it?"

"Absolutely not. I crave it." He stayed his gaze on her eyes and not her lips. Kissing would get nothing else accomplished. "I'm trying to tell you how I feel and where I see this going. And by that, I mean all the way to the altar."

"Wow. Did not expect that." She smiled, but sadness overtook it. "My life is in Texas. There's a lot you don't know, lots to consider."

He bent his forehead to hers. "So let's phone the bank Monday during business hours. For now, I'd love an answer."

"Depends on the question."

He laughed. "You somehow have me wanting to propose at this point, but for now, I'll settle for you admitting your feelings."

"I'm only here for the summer."

He leaned back. "Seriously, Lauren. Summer's all you got?"

She sighed. "Mitch, I care for you. A lot."

He grinned smugly. "Lem says you love me."

"I never told him that!"

"He says you don't have to." He turned superserious. "If you love me, I'd like to hear it from you."

She dipped her head and murmured into his shoulder—something that sounded like three magic words.

"What?" he asked.

She tipped up her face and flashed eyes no longer embarrassed. "I said I love you, too."

His eyebrow arched. "How much? Past Texas?"

"We'll see."

"Not the answer I was looking for." Still, he didn't want to push too much and end up pushing her away. "Let's see if Caleb's around. He must live on the lake."

"Have you thought about asking him to work for you if he's going to be around?" Jet ski started, they rode away from the dock.

"I like how you think." Mitch rounded the bend, glad to see Caleb and the girl still frolicking in the waves. Only now they rode one jet ski together. The pair turned at their approach.

"Having trouble?" Mitch indicated the ski, dead by the dock.

"Hey, Doc Wellington, sir!" Caleb heartily saluted Mitch.

He smiled and waved Caleb's hand down.

Caleb indicated the limping ski and grinned sheepishly. "I ran it out of fuel. This is my sister Bri."

"Hi," Bri said shyly.

"This is Lauren." Mitch grinned. "My nurse and girlfriend."

Caleb laughed. "That's convenient."

Everyone chuckled. Lauren's face beamed through her blush. He wound fingers through hers. She clasped back and smiled.

"We're having a cookout. I have an extra jet ski and fuel. You two are welcome to join us," Mitch offered.

"Really?" Caleb turned to his sister. "Want to?"

Bri eyed Mitch and Lauren tentatively.

"It's no imposition," Mitch assured.

"We'd love for you to come," Lauren added.

"This is the decorated military surgeon who founded the trauma center," Caleb explained when Bri remained leery.

Decorated? Word must travel fast, is all Mitch could figure.

"Oh, cool!" Her face lit then fell. "I wish your center had been here sooner." She eyed her brother with intricate care.

Caleb hugged her shoulders before facing Mitch. "Our mom just had a heart attack. She's on a transplant list but doesn't have much time. Dad is gone. So I'm on military medical leave and Bri is renovating the lodge our mom owned."

Lauren's face showed compassion, probably because the siblings faced losing both parents, as she and Mitch had.

"I know that lodge. It's been closed awhile," Mitch said.

"Mom's health declined. She couldn't take care of it," Caleb said. "Bri wants to reopen it so she relocated here."

"Lauren's also relocating," Mitch said. But when Lauren stared down and didn't speak, another caution railed Mitch.

Wait. She'd mentioned there being things he didn't know.

Days had been hectic. He'd been so busy with the center, hiring and other agendas, plus courting her, he hadn't taken much care to ask how the Texas red tape was rolling.

What new piece of information was he apparently missing?

Yet the bigger question: Was the problem reconcilable?

Or insurmountable?

Chapter Twenty

How could she tell him?

Lauren couldn't. Not without crying. The assessment she'd had on the building was far less than she owed. Also, her ex was using legal leverage to bind her to her agreement against his sister's wishes.

Mitch motioned Caleb. "I'll take you to get some gas for your downed ski while the ladies get acquainted."

At his retreat, emotions tossed over Lauren like waves. Aggravation over her unwise financial choices. Dismay at Mitch's unrealistic expectations of her to simply pull herself up by her bootstraps and ditch her obligations. It wasn't that easy.

It also wasn't the time to angst over it.

Lauren set aside her own struggles and focused on Bri. "I'm so sorry about your recent loss and struggle."

Bri fiddled with her swim vest. "Every day I look into the brave eyes of my mother and search for what to say." She peered up, as if Lauren were the life vest and Bri sinking. "What do you say to someone who knows their only chance to live means someone else must die?"

Lauren spontaneously crossed the dock and pulled Bri in. "You say everything you never have and everything you'll wish you had once they're gone. I never had that chance." Lauren choked up. "God can help."

Bri leaned on Lauren's shoulder. "I hope."

"I know."

Bri swiped tears from one cheek while Lauren tended the other. "Caleb and I recently started attending church back home. Now we have to find another church here."

"I've started back recently, too. You could visit mine. Refuge Community lives up to its name."

Lauren calling Grandpa's church hers revealed how much her heart had detached from Texas.

"I'd like that." Bri craned her neck toward something behind Lauren. "They're turning around," Bri said of the guys.

Lauren noticed. And by the imminent look on Mitch's militant face, there could only be one reason.

"We have a trauma page." Lauren surprised herself by including herself in the team. Truly, she finally felt like it.

Bri faced Lauren as the men approached. "I'd like to know you better, since you're moving here. Could we do a rain check?"

Lauren gulped. What if she couldn't move here? She got the feeling Bri was so shy, it took a lot for her to reach out. Which meant she needed friends. "Sure," Lauren said. "I'd like that."

Mitch waved Lauren over. "Air trauma fifteen out. Coming?"

"Of course. Can we redo the picnic tomorrow at nine?"

"Great plan." Mitch faced Bri and Caleb. "You guys game?"

"Long as Mom's having a good day, we'll be here," Caleb said. Bri waved as Mitch and Lauren headed to the trauma center.

"Caleb appeared disappointed not to be part of the trauma page," Mitch said to Lauren as they prepped for the helicopter.

"I noticed," Lauren said, unable to say much else.

Bri's excitement over thinking Lauren was definitely moving here was increasingly disconcerting. If Bri was disappointed, Mitch would feel terrible for presuming. Besides that, what was he doing to try to make this work?

Mitch going around telling people she was moving here didn't solve the real problems keeping her from doing so. He had no idea how binding her contracts were, and how vindictive her ex could be. Lauren fought frustration at the entire situation, but shoved it mentally aside and readied for what they faced. "What's the trauma?"

"Hang gliding accident. A power line got the better end."

"Ouch. When you said air trauma, I assumed that just meant the patient was arriving via helicopter." Adrenaline surged in Lauren, yet not the stark fear she'd been experiencing.

Moments later at the trauma center, a flurry of activity erupted as two gurneys crashed through the doors. "She struck a young male bystander on the way down," the helicopter pilot explained.

His crewmate nodded. "We didn't know until we reached her. She got hit with lethal voltage. He has a nasty head laceration."

"I see that." Mitch checked the man, conscious but shell-shocked. He said to Lauren, "Get him a CT STAT."

Lauren nodded and rushed the gurney to the imaging area, holding pressure on the young man's head as she went.

"Ma'am, where'd he say I am going?"

"To get a CAT scan." Lauren adjusted his lines.

"Whew. Not the morgue."

She laughed. "No. Today's not your day."

"A scat can you say?" The man rubbed his nose drowsily.

Scat? Lauren looked down. Had his words slurred before? "No. Cat. Scan. Of your head."

"I'm pretty sure I don't have any cats in there." He tried to smile past the wince of pain.

Lauren laughed. "We're about to find out."

"What hit me?" he asked as she rolled him into the room.

"A hang glider."

"A person?" He tried to sit up.

Lauren guided him back down, a real feat since he was built like a bodybuilder. "Yes."

The man strained upward again. Why? "Sir, stay put for me, okay? You're hurt." And becoming combative.

Which could mean a slew of bad medical things.

"What about the other guy? He gonna make it?" he asked.

"She. We'll do everything we can for her."

"Whoa. A girl knocked me down? Wow, I feel even worse now. Probably not half as bad as her. I'm sure I fared better than she."

Lauren had thought that too at first, but now she wasn't so sure. "Sir, are you feeling all right?"

"Depends. You got night crawlers?"

"Tell me where you are."

"Eagle Point Bait Shop."

"Are you kidding me?" Lauren asked because the man had been a jokester. He'd also been more alert before. Not now. His blue T-shirt emblem arrested her.

Eagle Point Sheriff's Department?

Ice went through her veins. A sheriff's deputy would know what a CAT scan was.

A horrible feeling hit Lauren that he'd been misdiagnosed at the triage level. She pushed the gurney faster.

This patient was far from stable.

"You have the best fishing lures here. Little pricey, though."

"Sir, you're at the trauma center. Don't you remember?"

"Trauma? Now you're kidding me." They reached the room.

"Afraid not." She upped his oxygen. The imaging tech walked in. "His color does not look good," Lauren said. "Get a bag."

The tech's eyes bugged. The patient's eyes rolled until all Lauren could see was white. His eyelids and fists violently clenched. His broad chest heaved and he frothed.

"He's seizing." She watched his chest a full minute after the seizure ended. "He's also not breathing. Bring a CPR cart now."

While Lauren yanked the emergency cord and started re-suscitation, the tech ran for a medication cart.

Another tech ran into the room. "I'm new. What do I do?"

Lauren pointed to the loudspeaker phone. "If I can't stabilize him, I'll signal you. Call the operator, who will page the code overhead."

"What's happening?" The tech snapped close to the phone.

Lauren watched the man for ominous signs.

"I fear he's crashing."

"She's crashing." Mitch observed the hang-gliding patient. "Might wanna trach her, Ian." Mitch indicated the woman's numbers, which fell to lethal levels.

Ian performed the procedure.

"Thank goodness," Kate said as the woman stabilized.

The overhead speaker crackled. "Code blue, imaging! Code blue, imaging, room four. STAT."

Kate gasped. "That's where Lauren headed."

Mitch's heart fell to his toes. "With the other patient." Mitch and Kate sprinted to imaging, leaving Ian to attend the electrical burn patient.

Lauren ripped open a package as they entered. "He stopped breathing after a seizure. I resuscitated. He's still unstable."

"Repeat the meds and up the oxygen."

"Done."

Ian joined them. "The burn patient is stabilizing."

Over the next few minutes Mitch and Ian rattled off order after order. Lauren performed each instantly without error.

If Mitch had any doubt in Lauren's ability to perform under fire, it dissipated now. She acted swiftly and confidently.

As he told her the first day...in her element.

"Normal," Lauren said of the man's levels thirty grueling minutes later. Litter covered the floor.

Mitch stepped over various tubing and thrown plastic bags,

which had held equipment they'd opened to save the man's life. "Well done, everyone." Mitch faced Lauren. "Especially you."

Lauren sighed. "He's not out of the woods yet, is he?"

"He will be after we get him into O.R.," Mitch assured.

Lauren observed the man's head wound. "It didn't look that bad from the outside."

"As we all know, looks can be deceiving," Ian said.

They thought the hang glider was the least stable of the two. Not so.

"In trauma care, things can turn on a dime. You held up fantastic, Lauren, and once again, your quick actions and keen assessment skills saved a life."

She didn't appear to know how to respond. She drew in a brave breath and faced him and Ian. "To surgery with him we go?"

Mitch smiled. "To surgery we go."

"How's the female?" Lauren asked after surgery.

"Come see."

Moments later, Lauren stood over the stabilized girl whose glider crashed into a power line pole, causing electrical burns.

"She's so young. And so badly scarred." Lauren looked closer. She paled. "Mitch, she's also the mayor's daughter."

Mitch peered past facial burns, and recognition came. "You're right. I remember her from the ribbon-cutting day. Anyone called him or other next of kin?"

"Doubtful," Ian said. "She didn't have ID on her. The sheriff called minutes ago and is on his way. He found her license and other items a few hundred yards from her crash site. He also asked to visit the injured deputy she fell on."

"I'll go meet him and phone her dad."

Ian rubbed his neck. "We need consent to transfer her to a burn facility once she stabilizes in a day or so."

"Yeah, she'll need restorative surgery that we're not equipped to perform here." Mitch peered at Lauren quizzically.

"I'm good. Go," Lauren said before he could ask.

He smiled.

The sheriff met Mitch in the lobby. "Found her cell phone. Thankfully she had *ICE* logged by her dad's number in her contact list so we knew who to call first. He's on his way."

Mitch knew ICE was a universal acronym for laypeople and first responders that meant *In Case of Emergency—call.* "Good."

The sheriff adjusted his hat. "How's my deputy?"

"Better. He was worse than it first appeared. It's that golden hour in trauma. Anything can happen. Lauren caught and quickly reversed it."

"Speaking of Lauren, is she here and able to talk?" The sheriff scratched his temple and looked tense.

"I can relieve her so she can be. Everything okay?" Mitch asked in case he needed to cushion Lauren for bad news.

"You know the young girl she visits over at the jail?"

"Mara? The teen who texted and caused the fatal crash a few weeks ago?" Mitch's heart clenched.

"About that…we have new developments. In fact, you all ought to hear the update. It concerns your team and my force."

"Is Mara okay?"

"Much better. Thanks mostly to Lauren. You know she alerted us to Mara's suicidal ideologies, right?"

"No. Didn't realize that. When?" Mitch became aware that he hadn't known a lot of things.

They still needed to talk about Texas and whatever adverse developments were going on there.

"Week before last. Lauren expressed grave concern over Mara, who woke up and went into extreme emotional duress upon finding out the boy had perished. She confessed to Lauren she wanted to die. Lauren talked her into getting help from a counselor."

"Is she?" Deep concern for Mara penetrated Mitch.

"Yes. We set it up. She's drastically improved, thanks to counseling and Lauren. She'll want to hear what I have to say."

Mitch gathered the team and shared the sheriff's missive. He walked next to Lauren to infuse strength by osmosis.

Her face expressed the query in everyone's mind: *What* was going on with Mara?

And what did it have to do with the sheriff's department plus them?

Two steps from the conference room, the sheriff's radio toned. He plucked it off his belt and stepped outside.

A minute later he returned, bearing an apologetic expression. "I'm afraid I need to reschedule, folks. I've got a domestic dispute to deal with, then I'm off duty."

"No problem. How about tomorrow morning, here in the conference room?" Mitch asked while watching Lauren slip out.

"Sounds good." The sheriff gave a backward wave upon exiting.

"I wonder what that's all about." Ian leaned casually.

"Me, too," Mitch said. "We'll know tomorrow." In the meantime, where had Lauren gone?

And why was she avoiding him?

Chapter Twenty-One

The team clustered into a private conference room the next day when the sheriff arrived.

Mitch caught Lauren. "You and I really need to talk."

"Let's hear the sheriff out first, okay?"

"Okay, but let's carve out time, preferably today."

She looked as if she really dreaded it.

Which meant whatever she had to say probably wasn't good.

He nodded reluctantly and gathered his remaining crew.

The sheriff motioned stragglers to seats. "Folks, the main thing I need to say is that the family of the boy killed the night he and Mara wrecked dropped all charges."

Mitch straightened. "Why the change of heart?"

"They obtained their son's phone records. Messages culled from that fateful night revealed Mara used his phone to text."

"Why would that make them drop charges?" Lauren asked.

"According to texts, their son was intoxicated to the point of becoming unresponsive. He'd called Mara for a ride because she wasn't, as he put it, 'a party girl.'"

Everyone listened intently.

The sheriff flipped open a report. "Evidence proves she picked him up from a party and was driving him home. Somewhere along the path, though, she diverted to the trauma center.

At some point frantically attempted to reach his folks through his phone. Those texts were sent the second she crashed."

No one moved. The air even felt as if it stopped breathing.

The sheriff looked up. "I think the summation of the accident is that Mara was a young girl scared for her friend's life, and therefore not thinking clearly."

All eyes mopped floor and walls with his words.

Ian straightened first. "She wrecked trying to help him?"

"Yes, but fact is, she texted illegally while driving and knows that's what ultimately caused the wreck and took him out. Here's the wrench. According to your toxicology reports, his blood alcohol level could have also contributed to his death."

That perked everyone up. The sheriff stood. "Despite that, Mara convinced herself she's at fault. Made up her mind to take her own life as recompense."

Mitch watched Lauren carefully.

The sheriff cleared his throat. "Mara wrote a suicide note saying she can't forgive herself and doesn't expect others to, especially not his family. Said she wished she'd died in his place and would do anything to bring him back to his family."

Lauren began to tear up. He folded the letter.

Lauren stared at it. Myriad emotions crossed her face.

The sheriff steepled his hands. "Mara planned to overdose on pain meds she got from the infirmary nurse."

Mitch knew by Lauren's fallen face that she thought the nurse was probably devastated. Rightfully? He didn't know anymore. People had choices and found ways regardless. Yet that didn't ease the horror and the heartbreak for family and friends left wishing they could have seen it coming and stopped it. Mitch faced the sheriff. "How'd you find out before she went through with it?"

The sheriff looked Lauren in the eye. His gaze generated immense respect. "Your nurse here called out of the blue. Said she had a strong feeling we should check on Mara. We did.

Found her stuffing the note and pills behind a drain. She tearfully confessed to Lauren when she came in, as mentioned prior. I felt it would be helpful for Lauren to learn the contents of Mara's note."

Lauren licked her lips. "May I see her?"

"Certainly." The sheriff seemed glad she would. "I'm off duty several days, so next week's better."

"Can we go, too?" Mitch and Ian asked in contrite unison, causing Lauren's mouth to gape.

"Me, too," Kate said. "Visiting Mara is long overdue."

"That would be great." The sheriff stood to leave.

"Is she still in a lot of trouble?" Lauren asked.

"My force is at fault for the medication incident. We're in far worse trouble than Mara at this point. She'll likely be charged with a misdemeanor. At the most, involuntary manslaughter, which I doubt the judge will hand over considering the circumstances."

"When would be the best time to come?" Ian asked.

"Tell you what—Mara could use the fresh air. I'll get clearance to bring her here to see you folks all at once instead of you having to go to the jail one by one. Less paperwork, too."

"Sounds good," Mitch said. "But bring her to the beach docks. Returning to the center might be too traumatic for her."

After the sheriff left, a helicopter arrived for the burn patient. Surrounded by family, including Eagle Point's mayor, Mitch loaded her for transfer to a burn rehabilitation facility.

Several sheriff's deputies visited their downed cohort in ICU, whose condition had improved.

With so many visitors in and out, Mitch's crew took turns sleeping in call rooms. Lauren avoided Mitch but made one phone call after another. Which reminded him. Today was Tuesday.

He found Lauren. "Hey, sorry. I totally blitzed. I promised to call your ex's superiors with you Monday."

"It wouldn't have mattered." She drew a breath. "They're

not budging. I've been getting legal opinions on the contracts, but things aren't looking good. The bank isn't budging."

"That means?"

"I may not be budging, either. I may be stuck in Texas."

"There must be something we can do."

Her eyebrows slashed. "Really, Mitch? *We?*" She shook her head and stalked off. What on earth was she mad at him for?

Ian jabbed his back. "Dude, you better find out what's wrong. She looks pretty ticked."

Unwilling to let this go, Mitch went after her. "Lauren, about us—"

She whirled with eyes flaming, like her hair. "Is there an us, Mitch? Because you seem to let Texas stand in our way."

Mitch took Lauren's hands. Strength entered his eyes. "Hear me out."

She nodded and forced herself to be quiet.

"Long-distance relationships rarely work. Ian was torn up yesterday. He got word his divorce is going through early. I've never seen him so distraught. I don't want you or me to have that kind of heartache."

"You were in the military long enough to see at least one marriage survive deployment separation. Am I wrong?"

"No. Most marriages did. But we can only be together here. In Illinois. I promised Lem. I can't go back on that."

Great. Bring on the guilt. On the other hand, Grandpa was the one who had taught her financial integrity. "I'll do my best. But I can't control the bank." An odd tension sat between them now.

"Say your heart, Lauren. Why are you angry with me?"

"I'm frustrated because you don't seem to want to budge, yet expect me to. The problems escalate the more I pray."

"So keep praying. I will, too. And we'll pray until something happens."

"Have you considered that maybe we aren't meant to be?"

"No. I refuse to consider that."

"God speaks through circumstances at times, doesn't He?"

"What about Lem?"

"He survived without me this long. I can visit more often."

"What about us?"

"If you're not willing to budge, there is no us."

"Lauren, I opened a trauma center. The community depends on it. I can't pack up and leave all that, or even take it with me. I'm not being selfish. I'm being practical."

She simmered down and thought about that. It made sense.

He massaged her clenched fists until they relaxed. "Please believe me when I say I want to make this work. You can always move your seamstress shop and do that here or anywhere."

He was right, but still, he didn't get it. "Mitch, by not budging, I meant on your stance that long-distance relationships never work."

"They never work for me. I've tried."

"You don't seem to want to try very hard this time."

He grew quiet. Contemplative. The way he did in surgeries that stumped him. Cases with the poorest prognoses.

Lauren felt a sudden weight of despair concerning Mitch that she hadn't experienced before. She placed a hand on his heart and said softly, "Maybe Sheila took the fight out of you, Mitch. For that, I'm sadder than you'll ever know."

He pulled in her hand and held her close to his heart. "I want this to work. I really do."

"Me, too. But I can't snap my fingers and make my legally binding loan go away. Morally, I can't walk away."

He let out a resigned breath. "I know. You're right."

"About what? The loan?"

"Probably all of it." He released her in what felt sickeningly like a symbolic gesture and, worse, put several feet of distance between them.

Her throat knotted. Chest tightened. Heart pounded. "But?"

"But what?" He looked at her as though she were a stranger.

I'm losing him.

Just as they'd watched fatally wounded patients go down the tubes, she hovered over their relationship the same way now. Watching it fade before their eyes, even as they tried in utter futility to save it. Helpless to help something hopeless, and unequipped to save something too far gone.

They saved many, many lives, but some were too wounded.

Was it like that for them? His heart? Their relationship?

Was this salvageable? She searched for any spark of hope in Mitch's eyes. Nothing. Like a flat line on an EKG screen of a patient already gone. No breath. No beat. No blip of hope.

Mitch stared at the floor now. The way he did after they called time of death in every code that ended unsuccessfully.

Then, like an unexpected spike, he peered up, looking nearly as distressed as she felt right now. "You're upset."

"Of course I am. And you're aloof every time I mention Texas. What if I can't move, Mitch?"

He turned his face and didn't respond. Not one word.

"Mitch?" Insides quivering, she stepped toward him.

A muscle rippled along his jaw, and still no comment.

"Are you saying the distance is still a definite deal breaker?" He didn't answer, which spoke volumes.

A tense week later, Mitch paced halls waiting for word of Mara's arrival. She'd decided to meet at the center to thank everyone who'd taken care of her and saved her life.

Ian accosted Mitch before everyone arrived. "I need to say this. It's off subject, but I have to get it off my chest."

"Okay, shoot." Mitch knew today was hard on Ian. His divorce loomed.

He looked Mitch straight in the eye and said militantly, "My marriage is DOA as of this time tomorrow. And you're going to lag like a coward and let Lauren walk away over something as trivial as one thousand miles?"

Mitch froze, riveted by Ian's words. He sighed. "Fine. Hold down the fort. I'll be right back." He headed to the chapel downstairs. *Lord, if there's a way, something I'm not seeing or haven't thought of, I'm consulting with You. Show me.*

A seed of a solution came to Mitch. Vague at first, then clear. Mitch smiled. He knew what he had to do.

That was fast. Thank You.

When Mitch got back upstairs, Kate huddled next to Lauren. Their friendship had bloomed in a beautiful way. Ian stood at the window, watching Nita wheel Mara toward the center.

"She's still in casts from the wreck," Kate said softly.

"Keep in mind her wounds go deeper than the physical," Lauren urged. "So let's be as caring and merciful as possible."

"You were right from the outset, Lauren. I'm curious," Ian said. His voice went raw, his face more so. "We've had other texting patients in since Mara. Yet you never took up their cause the way you did hers. Any reason why?"

"Not sure. I just felt she didn't have a voice."

Full-force remorse hit Mitch. "So you became her voice. Gave her the benefit of the doubt when no one else would."

Lauren nodded. "People are supposed to be innocent until proven guilty. But when victims come in mangled, we sometimes want to think of those who logically appear responsible as guilty until proven innocent." Ian and Mitch nodded.

Kate nodded, too, then leaned on Lauren. "Mara's going to be okay physically. You should keep reaching out to her emotionally."

"Definitely." Ian repositioned as Nita settled Mara in the private conference room where they could see in but Mara couldn't see out.

The sheriff joined them in the hall. "Update. She's headed to a psychological care facility where she'll receive extensive counseling. She'll be under suicide watch 24/7."

Lauren gravitated toward the glass behind which Mara sat. "Hopefully once she's better, she'll come back and see us."

"She has conscientious potential to help multitudes of others learn from her mistake," Mitch offered.

The sheriff faced Lauren. "You keep pep talking her, and I guarantee she'll do something great. She plans to be a counselor specializing in suicide prevention. Meanwhile, she wants to tell her story at schools. We're helping her make a 'BFFs don't let BFFs text-N-drive' video, using images from her wreck with permission from the families involved. No one wants others to endure this."

"Who came up with these ideas?" Lauren asked the sheriff.

"Mara," he said. "One by one after each of your visits."

Tangible relief flooded Lauren's face. She pressed knuckles to her mouth, closed her eyes and smiled. Tears broke through.

Ian motioned. "Guys, come. Mara's nervous and waiting."

Ian, Mitch, Kate, Lauren and the sheriff stepped into the room. Mara turned. Apprehension filled her face until her eyes lit on Lauren, whose smile wiped all fear away. "Hi."

Lauren bent close. "Your fan club's here. You're not alone in the world, okay? We want you to live. A lot of people will be very sad if you don't. You made a mistake, but your life is still worth something."

A tear streaked Mara's face. Ian gently brushed knuckles across it. "Hang in there for us, okay, kiddo? Lauren's right. Things might look bleak now, but I promise life'll get better."

Mitch faced Lauren and knew she hoped the same as he did. That Ian would believe his own words and be okay.

"God will see to it," Lauren added, to Ian's admonition. "And, if you stick around, so will we."

Kate knelt on Mara's other side. "You're kinda like family to us now, ya know? You were here so long."

"We might even name one of the ambulance stalls after you." Mitch chuckled. "Mara's Place."

A shy smile overcame Mara's trembling mouth. Her chin quivered with emotion as she squeezed their hands hard enough that they knew she'd be okay. "Thanks, all of you." Mara roved grateful eyes over each person, then paused on Lauren. She smiled and reached out for a hug. "Especially you. Don't ever stop being a nurse or someone who helps people. You're good at it."

Once the sheriff helped Mara into the car, she turned and, through the window, latched on to Lauren's gaze.

Lauren waved until her wrist ached. The patrol car pulled away. Mara's face and hands pressed to the glass as if she could draw strength through the clear pane. Mara's now-hopeful eyes held Lauren's until the car passed Mitch's dad's cross at the roadside and taillights shrank out of sight.

Overcome with emotion, Lauren slipped from the entrance to flee. Mitch held her up against him in a doubt-crushing hug. "She'll be okay, Lauren." He kissed the top of her head and squeezed her again. Firmly. "And so will we. Okay?"

She nodded but couldn't speak. She hugged back, with all her might, choosing to believe in Mitch's goodness—and in God's.

"I didn't mean to make it seem like my love's conditional." Heartfelt sincerity deepened his voice and filled her with reassurance that melted fear.

"I'm glad. More than I can articulate." She gave him another hug, then looked up as Ian approached.

He squeezed her shoulder. "Hang in there, Bates."

"Boy, did I fall apart back there. I could barely comprehend the sheriff's report. She's just a patient."

Ian shook his head. "No. She's a troubled young girl who couldn't bear the weight of what she'd done. She's a person who made a huge mistake that made her sorry enough to want to die. I'm a cynical doctor who should've shown her more compassion."

Seeing Ian's face all pinched up made Lauren laugh. "You were compassionate. You just didn't want anyone to know. I saw your moist cheeks at her ICU window when she became comatose."

"It was sweat." Ian grinned sheepishly.

"From your tear ducts? Then you'd better see a specialist because something's askew with your eyes."

Ian chuckled.

Lauren patted his cheek. "Ian, God won't abandon you like your wife did."

His smile faded. She hoped he'd listen. Really listen.

Lauren faced the man she loved. "And Mitch, God won't abandon this center. So don't worry about money."

Mitch jangled his keys. "What makes you think I'm worried about that?"

"You're borrowing money to help with the trauma center or something. A bank officer kept calling for you in the middle of all those codes last shift."

Mitch stared at her for three seconds, then burst out laughing. "You're under the influence of a few minor misunderstandings. But trust me, tomorrow everything will be made clear."

Chapter Twenty-Two

"Don't dislocate your neck, Shupe," Mitch said to Ian the next day when Bri passed by to greet Lauren, setting up for the rescheduled picnic.

Ian's head whipped around. "What's that supposed to mean, Wellington?" Ian moved forcefully into Mitch's personal space.

"You practically got whiplash when Bri came down those steps." Mitch stood his ground. And tried not to grin.

"I'm not divorced yet, Mitch."

Mitch sobered. "Sorry, man. When's it final?"

"Two o'clock today." Ian twisted the band on his finger. Mitch knew he refused to take it off until papers were inked.

"Speaking of rings, I ditched Sheila's."

"What do you mean *ditched*? Thing cost you an arm and a couple legs."

"Sold it to a high-end jeweler. I paid off Lauren's half of the building loan with it, plus used a CD I cashed in."

"She know yet?"

"No."

"The proposal still a go for today?"

"Definitely."

"How's this gonna go down?" Ian asked.

"I'm having an ambulance pull up with a *Marry Me* message on a gurney, instead of a patient. I have another crew covering

us today so my proposal doesn't get squashed by real traumas."
A horrible feeling hit Mitch. "Man, I'm sorry. I didn't realize
your divorce was going through today."

Ian's chin rose. "No sweat. I'm happy for you, man."

A flashing ambulance came down the road.

Mitch smacked Ian. "It's time." His pulse hammered.

But he hadn't considered something.

What if she said no?

A siren pulled Lauren's attention from slicing brownies for
dessert today. "Oh, dear, we have trouble, guys." She jumped
up and bolted toward the trauma center.

But strangely, everyone lagged.

She darted looks over her shoulder. Rarely was she first to
the ambulance stall.

Everyone must be tired today.

Lauren approached the paramedic who rushed out of the
cab to meet her. "Lauren Bates?"

She skidded to a halt. "Yes?"

"This patient specifically requested you." The paramedic
clasped the ambulance door handle and yanked it open.

Her face tilted in. "What? There's no one in here."

The paramedic grinned but pulled out the gurney anyway.

He stepped back and up stepped Mitch, still the most gorgeous creature to ever own two legs.

Only now, he also owned her heart.

And there, in the center of the gurney, sat a bright pink
stethoscope curved into the shape of a heart.

She turned to find Lem and everyone staring at her with
excitement and anticipation that could only mean one thing.

"Mitch?" Lauren searched his to-die-for eyes. "What's going
on?"

He nodded toward the stethoscope and grinned. "Read it."

She scooped the stethoscope, sheathed in a soft, washable
fabric dotted with tiny green tractors.

Just like the one at Lem's that she loved to drive.

Tears sprang to her eyes at Mitch's thoughtfulness.

She turned the stethoscope over and over, then looked at the bell. "A Littmann!" she breathed. "And not a cheap one."

She looked closer. He'd engraved her full name in it.

Lauren Esther Bates, RN

Below that was a Bible verse, the same one engraved on the building: "The Lord turn his face toward you and give you peace. Numbers 6:26."

Then below it, the words *Marry Me?*

Lauren sucked in so much air, she almost aspirated. "Oh!"

Mitch drew close. "Only a stupid man would let you get away. I'd like to think I'm a little smarter than that."

He dropped to one knee.

She gasped.

He took her hands in his and turned as serious as a stroke. "Lauren Esther Bates, you're worth every mile, even a million if I have to walk it. Texas or not, will you marry me?"

She rose on tiptoes like a giggling schoolgirl. "Oh, yes! Yes! Yes! Wait. One question. You don't still have that item of my greatest ire in your glove box, do you?"

Ian snickered.

Mitch grinned. "Come see."

He'd already gone to that glove box, gotten rid of the ring for good and had ripped up Sheila's Dear John letter.

Lauren pulled out a sheet of paper, which held Mitch's handwriting. The beginnings of what looked like a romantic poem. "What's this?"

"My end of our wedding vows."

She smiled. "You took out the letter and ring and replaced it with this, for me?"

"For me, too. For us. Also this." He pulled out an envelope.

She opened it. "The note to my half of the building? This says it's paid off!"

Mitch smiled.

"Mitch Wellington, did you?"

He put his fingers to her mouth, then his lips.

She leaned back. "When did you do all this? Why? How?"

"The details aren't important. All you need to know is you can securely, legally, morally and ethically leave Texas in the dust. I also got your ex to back off completely."

"How on earth?"

"A call to the D.A., who has a particular interest in protecting speed limits…and enforcing justice on those who disregard public safety."

Her smile erupted. "How did you manage all this?"

"Consulted with The Great Physician. Everything fell into place. Ian knew the D.A. We thought of a fellow war vet with a health-care-management degree looking for a place to open a clinic. He loves Texas. Said your building location's ideal." Mitch handed her a card. "Have your Realtor give him a call."

"I don't have a Realtor."

"You do now. Took care of that, too. You'll have a substantial amount left. And your business partner said she'd better be invited to the wedding, or you're in big trouble."

"Of course! She's not upset about the building?"

"Hardly. She's relieved to be rid of the contractors."

Lem's teeth clacked as he laughed. "Who were horrible and perpetually delayed the timeline."

Lauren shook her head.

"You can open a seamstress shop here if you like."

"I'd rather sew from our home and stand next to you in surgery. Is that full-time permanent position still open?"

Mitch grinned. "Until you start having babies. One of us will have to keep them out of Lem's cornfields."

She laughed. "But where's my ring?"

"Lem said you always played pretend with your grandma's engagement ring, passed down to your mother."

"I'd be honored to use it!"

Lem swiped tears. "Nothing would make me happier. Except a passel of great-grandbabies wreaking havoc in my cornfields."

Mitch grinned at Lauren. "We could oblige."

Lem chuckled, dug in his overall pocket and brandished the heirloom ring.

Mitch slipped it onto Lauren's trembling finger.

She held it to sunlight, then to her heart. "I hoped and it came true," she breathed. Then hugged Mitch so hard she punted air from his chest. "I love you."

"I love you, too, my favorite nurse and future wife. To heaven and back."

"To heaven and back." Lauren laughed. "But thankfully not to Texas."

* * * * *

Dear Reader,

During the writing of this book, I not only lost my grand-mother, my husband was involved in a tragic head-on collision that killed the other driver, whose car skidded into my husband's lane on an icy curve. The accident happened just down the road from our home. I heard several ambulances and had the thought to call my husband. When he answered severely shaken and out of breath, he said, "It was me, but I'm okay." I couldn't comprehend at first what he meant. Being the nurse that I am, I rushed to the scene to realize that the precise moment I was speaking to my husband on the phone, another young wife was losing hers.

My children have their daddy, but that day, other little ones lost theirs. This same family lost their home and all possessions to a house fire two months before. I don't understand why tragedy comes in relentless waves at times, but I trust in God's goodness in bad times as well as good. Please keep the Watson family in your prayers. If you are overwhelmed by hardship, I would love to pray for you. Feel free to write me at my publisher: Love Inspired Books, 233 Broadway, Suite 1001, New York, NY 10279. Or email me at cheryl@cherylwyatt.com.

I'm active on Facebook. If you'd like to connect and keep up with book news, "Like" my author page at https://www.facebook.com/CherylWyattAuthor. I give away goodies at intervals there. I also provide book updates and extras to my newsletter subscribers. If you'd like to be a part of the community of readers I love so much, visit my Web site at www.cherylwyatt.com and sign up for my newsletter. We'd love to get to know you!

If you're an aspiring writer, visit a fifteen-author mentoring community at www.seekerville.net. Also, joining www.acfw.com is a helpful thing to do as well as frequent the writing articles and community at www.harlequin.com

The Lord turn His face toward you and give you peace!

Blessings,

Cheryl Wyatt

Questions for Discussion

1. Grandpa Lem was afraid of turning seventy because his father and grandfather died in their seventieth year. Could you understand his fear? Why do you think Lem's outlook on aging and health improved after Lauren came to visit?

2. Why do you think Mitch kept the rejected engagement ring in his glove box?

3. Lauren learned that we will often have opposition when we try to pursue our dreams. Have you experienced this? If so, how? Likewise, what dreams have you realized?

4. Lauren's dream of becoming a nurse was inspired by a traumatic event in her childhood. What people or events in your own life influenced your career or other life choice/s?

5. Mitch also lost his parents in a traumatic way. His dad's death inspired his choice of location for the trauma center. Have you experienced a traumatic event in your life that inspired you to reach out to others or your community in some way?

6. Mitch struggled with opening his heart to Lauren when he saw his best friend going through a painful divorce. Have you had a difficult time seeing someone you love experience difficulty or disappointment?

7. What person/s and/or event/s in the book do you think most helped Mitch turn the corner as far as being willing to plan a future with Lauren despite the possibility of her having to return to Texas?

8. Can you understand Lauren's fear of hoping for good things in her future? Have you experienced loss that made it hard to hope? Please discuss.

9. Between Mitch and Lauren, who do you think compromised the most to make the relationship work? In what ways do you feel they met in the middle?

10. In what ways do you think Lauren's life would have turned out differently had she lived with Lem full-time after the death of her parents?

11. Do you think Mitch's life would have been drastically different had he not experienced the loss of his father and mother? If so, how? Do you think the trauma center still would have been opened?

12. At what point in the book could you begin to sympathize with Mara? If this were a real teen, do you think her telling her story to other teens would prevent them from texting while driving?

13. Mitch and Lauren grew close as a result of getting to know one another through Lem's stories. Is there someone in your life who you got to know through a story before meeting them in person? Please discuss.

REQUEST YOUR FREE BOOKS!

2 FREE INSPIRATIONAL NOVELS
PLUS 2
FREE
MYSTERY GIFTS

Love Inspired

YES! Please send me 2 FREE Love Inspired® novels and my 2 FREE mystery gifts (gifts are worth about $10). After receiving them, if I don't wish to receive any more books, I can return the shipping statement marked "cancel." If I don't cancel, I will receive 6 brand-new novels every month and be billed just $4.49 per book in the U.S. or $4.99 per book in Canada. That's a saving of at least 22% off the cover price. It's quite a bargain! Shipping and handling is just 50¢ per book in the U.S. and 75¢ per book in Canada.* I understand that accepting the 2 free books and gifts places me under no obligation to buy anything. I can always return a shipment and cancel at any time. Even if I never buy another book, the two free books and gifts are mine to keep forever.

105/305 IDN FEGR

Name _____ (PLEASE PRINT)

Address _____ Apt. #

City _____ State/Prov. _____ Zip/Postal Code

Signature (if under 18, a parent or guardian must sign)

Mail to the **Reader Service:**
IN U.S.A.: P.O. Box 1867, Buffalo, NY 14240-1867
IN CANADA: P.O. Box 609, Fort Erie, Ontario L2A 5X3

Not valid for current subscribers to Love Inspired books.

**Are you a subscriber to Love Inspired books
and want to receive the larger-print edition?
Call 1-800-873-8635 or visit www.ReaderService.com.**

* Terms and prices subject to change without notice. Prices do not include applicable taxes. Sales tax applicable in N.Y. Canadian residents will be charged applicable taxes. Offer not valid in Quebec. This offer is limited to one order per household. All orders subject to credit approval. Credit or debit balances in a customer's account(s) may be offset by any other outstanding balance owed by or to the customer. Please allow 4 to 6 weeks for delivery. Offer available while quantities last.

Your Privacy—The Reader Service is committed to protecting your privacy. Our Privacy Policy is available online at www.ReaderService.com or upon request from the Reader Service.

We make a portion of our mailing list available to reputable third parties that offer products we believe may interest you. If you prefer that we not exchange your name with third parties, or if you wish to clarify or modify your communication preferences, please visit us at www.ReaderService.com/consumerchoice or write to us at Reader Service Preference Service, P.O. Box 9062, Buffalo, NY 14269. Include your complete name and address.

LIREG11B

Love Inspired®

— TEXAS TWINS —

Follow the adventures of two sets of twins who are torn apart by family secrets and learn to find their way home.

Her Surprise Sister by Marta Perry
July 2012

Mirror Image Bride by Barbara McMahon
August 2012

Carbon Copy Cowboy by Arlene James
September 2012

Look-Alike Lawman by Glynna Kaye
October 2012

The Soldier's Newfound Family
by Kathryn Springer
November 2012

Reunited for the Holidays
by Jillian Hart
December 2012

**Available wherever
books are sold.**

www.LoveInspiredBooks.com

LICONT0812

When a baby is left on the doorstep of an Amish house, Sheriff Nick Bradley comes face-to-face with his past.

Read on for a preview of A HOME FOR HANNAH by Patricia Davids.

The farmhouse door swung open before Sheriff Nick Bradley could knock. A woman with fiery auburn hair and green eyes stood glaring at him. "There has been a mistake. We don't need you here."

The shock of seeing Miriam Kauffman standing in front of him took him aback. He struggled to hide his surprise. It had been eight years since he'd laid eyes on her. A lifetime ago.

"Good morning to you, too, Miriam."

After all this time, she wasn't any better at hiding her opinion of him. She looked ready to spit nails. Proof that she hadn't forgiven him.

"Miriam, don't be rude," her mother chided. Miriam reluctantly stepped aside. He entered the house.

His cousin Amber sat at the table. "Hi, Nick. Thanks for coming. We do need your help."

Ada Kauffman sat across from her. The room was bathed in soft light from two kerosene lanterns hanging from hooks on the ceiling.

He glanced at the three women facing him. Ada Kauffman was Amish, from the top of her white prayer bonnet to the tips of her bare toes poking out from beneath her plain dress. Her daughter, Miriam, had never joined the church, choosing to leave before she was baptized. Her arms were crossed over her chest.

Amber served the Amish and non-Amish people of Hope Springs, Ohio, as a nurse midwife. Exactly what was she doing here?

He said, "Okay, I'm here. What's so sensitive that I had to come instead of sending one of my perfectly competent deputies?"

"This is why we called you." Amber gestured toward the basket. He took a step closer and saw a baby swaddled in the folds of a quilt.

"You called me here to see a new baby? Congratulations to whomever."

"Exactly," Miriam said.

He looked at her closely. "What am I missing?"

Amber said, "It's more about what we are missing."

"And that is?" he demanded.

Ada said, "A mother to go with this baby."

He shook his head. "You've lost me."

Miriam rolled her eyes. "I'm not surprised."

Her mother scowled at her, but said, "Someone left this baby on my porch."

*Will Nick and Miriam get past their differences
to help little Hannah?*

*Pick up A HOME FOR HANNAH by Patricia Davids,
available August 2012 from Love Inspired Books.*